Elegantly Wasted

Second Edition Published in the United States by:

MIKE'S PRESS

a brand of v22 Design LLC

Copyright © 2022. All Rights Reserved.
Library of Congress

Soft Cover Print ISBN 978-0-9853396-3-0
ebook   ISBN 978-0-9853396-4-7

Second Edition Edited by:
Hallin Burgan

First Edition Edited by:
Jennifer Elaine Pulsipher-Smith

Cover Design:
Erin DeMoss

For Amie and Amanda

el·e·gance

noun 1. the quality of being graceful and stylish in appearance or manner; style.

a woman with grace and elegance.

CARA VESCIO

ELEGANTLY WASTED

Chapter One

All the events of my life boiled down to a single choice. It's often the story with such things; you made a decision and it had permanent consequences. It warped your life forever. It only took a few seconds. I made these types of choices for other people all the time, but it had never affected me this directly before. What if I was wrong? What if I made the wrong choice?

I didn't know how I got to the breaking point, but I was there — and oddly, I was smiling.

The awkward grin was plastered on my face for two reasons.

First, my grandmother had died, and her funeral was about to commence.

Second, I was going insane.

Somewhere in there, my brain and my body weren't exactly on the same page. I felt like if I blinked, shifted my weight or made any small attempt to move, I would start screaming at the top of my lungs. So, I sat in a church pew near the back of St. Francis Xavier Catholic Church, afraid to move.

I tried to keep up with the speed of my thoughts, the effort leaving me with a dull pounding in my brain. I was used to the headache by now, but my newly found due-north moral compass was annoying the shit out of me. What if God really existed and he was pissed that I was sitting in his church? Fire, brimstone, smite... all that crap might be on my horizon. Consequences never scared me before. I didn't understand it, and my anger grew by the minute.

"Frankie," I felt an elbow jab in my side. "Stop grinning like a goddamn psycho."

My face remained in its twisted grin.

"Kat, you can't just say goddamn in church," I whispered. "You're going to hell."

"Frankie, you and I are both ending up there, and you know it."

My smile spread to Kat, and we both stifled laughter —no laughing at funerals. I pursed my lips together for a quick recovery. I started to relax, despite my odd predicament: that damn choice that I had to make before the funeral was over....

My name is Francesca Fairholm. Everyone calls me Frankie. I am demented. I am a little lost. I am a bit of a sociopath. There's an edgy term for what I do. So, I hate saying it, yet it appeases my inner demons. Let's just say I solve other people's problems and have plenty of money in my bank account to never depend on my wretched family.

The funeral I attended was not the best of circumstances, but that didn't stop me from being happy about it. The woman in the coffin had been horrible, and don't you dare feel sorry for her. If I dissected my life entirely, I would say she was the main reason I was this fucked up in the first place. She was the reason my entire family was nuts.

Joan Rosemary Fairholm lay dead in a shiny platinum casket just up the aisle from me. On all sides, I was surrounded by a horde of money-hungry family members, ready and waiting for their part of the Fairholm fortune. I kept my distance. Truthfully, they disgusted me. I couldn't remember any instance when I enjoyed being around them, and they all played their small parts in this Shakespearean tragedy unfolding in my head.

Our family's own Lady Macbeth, my Grandmother, died of a stroke a few days prior. I had felt nothing when my mother's words floated through my cell phone.

Her obituary should have said something like: "Joan was born in Aberdeen, Scotland, in 1918. She was a North Sea oil heiress, two-time widow and one-time divorcee. She moved to Phoenix, Arizona, after she had killed off her first two husbands and then proceeded to raise a family with her third victim. She is survived by her four daughters, and five grandchildren. She didn't love any of them, but loved to see them bicker amongst themselves—usually over her acceptance. She loved money, power and Corgis. She hated accountability."

"You're not going to do it," Kat whispered to me, interrupting my thoughts. "You're better than that."

My dear Katharine. My rock. My sanity. Kat was one of my cousins. The other had yet to show up, which was totally not her style.

"Where is Addi?" I ignored her, mainly out of guilt. "She's supposed to be here."

"Late," was all Katharine said. Kat wasn't too happy with me at the moment. She knew what was going through my mind. She knew what I was contemplating. Kat had to know how conflicted I was, but she showed no signs of giving a shit, which also fed my anger.

My mother, Marlene, sat on the opposite side of the church in the front, where family was supposed to sit. Next to her were her three sisters—the trifecta from hell. Aunt Audrey was the youngest. She was Kat's mom, the eyes and ears of everything in the family, yet she was usually too drunk to be taken seriously. Next came Aunt Bette, Addi's mom, the forensic pathologist with a minimal sense of humor and fondness of cats. Then there was eldest, Greta. I didn't like talking about Greta.

My mother turned her head toward me in that moment. She gave one of those mother looks, like I was the main annoyance in this sea of jerk-offs. She was probably even happier than I was at this point, but that still didn't mean I could whisper, smile or laugh during this ceremony. She had very little tolerance for rudeness... even if she hated her now-dead mother.

Dead. The word kept running through my mind, taunting me. Even as I sat and gazed upon her coffin, it wasn't registering. I half-expected my dear grandmother to leap out of the coffin and scream that we were all disinherited for believing she could die.

This family wasn't virtuous. We weren't cookie-cutting, home-making, smiling, happy people. Those people were delusional. The Fairholms were emotional black holes, alcoholics and at least two of us were cold-blooded killers. I glanced at the empty space next to me.

My nerves were grinding like the rusted gears of a neglected table saw. Where the fuck was Addi? I was beginning to lose my cool. Katharine could only do so much to ease my mind in this potentially catastrophic situation.

I cast my gaze back to my mother. She would have been so disappointed if she knew how I had really turned out. She tried so hard to raise a good kid. I wasn't good. I was clearly the opposite of good, as I contemplated death, murder and a serious absence of love for my own grandmother under the gaze of a loaded Catholic arsenal of holy shit.

I wanted to take a huge, deep breath to calm myself down, but I would have just choked on the acrid smell of Mothball No. 5 that was wafting over from all the little old ladies in front of me. My headache wasn't letting up.

I still had time to make my choice. Despite what Kat wanted to believe, I was undecided. There was too much to consider. She couldn't make the decision for me, as much as I was sure she wanted to. It was all up to me—and time was running out.

Elegantly Wasted

Chapter Two

I wasn't always a killer. I wasn't an angelic kid, but I was a happy kid if I didn't have to deal with family. I was inquisitive. I skipped first grade and was reading at college levels by the time I was in eighth grade. This caused some personality issues that still plague me today. For one, I didn't know when to close my mouth. I had no filter. This would piss my grandmother off to no end. Second, I didn't really have friends. Kids my age liked me just fine, but I couldn't stand them. I knew how to chase off would-be friends in no time; I was condescending and mean to them. Most kids had no tolerance for that bullshit.

It went something like... adorable cherubic girl with golden ringlets in a brand-new designer cutesy, frilly, throw-up-in-my-mouth pink dress would come up to me and give me an over-enthusiastic "Hello, want to play house?" introduction, and I would respond with "Go fuck yourself, Blondie."

"Your child is an anti-social bully," my Aunt Bette would tell her younger sister. "You should keep an eye on her, Marlene. Kids like that can grow up to be a problem."

Anti-social bully. A problem. That was me. Bette was a fucking oracle.

Bette loved to sit back in the wings and just throw out ideas every once in a while. She would only talk to my mother. She refused to talk to anyone else she shared DNA with. Bette would always be up my mother's ass when she was between husbands. The woman didn't like anyone, yet she didn't want to be alone. It was a weird sort of pairing: like Patsy and Edina from Absolutely Fabulous, only more manic-depressive.

Bette had been right though. I wish my mother had taken her more seriously. My sociopathic behavior wore her down. She gave up trying to control me by the time I was in high school.

The guy I called my father left her when I was 8, when he found out that I wasn't really his kid, rather the fruits of a torrid affair between my mother and some guy I never met. I certainly never saw my father much after that, except for the occasional ski trip or Disneyland outing. Once he remarried, he tried harder, but I think that was more his next wife's idea.

During my influential years, my mother had very little help raising me, even when Bette was around. My aunt had her own nutball kid to deal with.

When I was young, I tried, and failed, to conform to my family's insatiable ways. I tried to love money and treat it like my best friend. I tried to act snotty and materialistic to the point of self-suffocation by the mountains of Prada purses and Neiman Marcus bags in my closet. I tried to act normal by my grandmother's standards, but the more I tried, the more I got angry, and the evil thoughts crept into my head. There were too many jumbled thoughts to form any cohesive action; although at one of my grandmother's garden parties I did imagine rigging the lights to electrocute everyone while they ate their farm fresh Osetra Amur Caviar.

Already teetering on the lowest limb of the family tree, I finally broke the branch clean off on the eve of my high school graduation. I woke up one day and realized I hated my grandmother. I hated everything she stood for. I hated her voice; I hated her tightly curled hair; I hated anything she said. That hatred trickled off into her double, her oldest child, my Aunt Greta.

Greta Siriso-Fairholm (hey, you better say it all when addressing her) was the person who held the saw that helped that branch break. Bette called her God-Awful Greta. She was a prized piece of work in this gallery of assholes, that was for sure. Her story was tragic, but I couldn't ever find it in me to feel sorry for her.

In the '60s, she married a very wealthy Italian lawyer named Anthony Siriso. They had twin boys, Alexander "Lex" and Nero. I wasn't close to them because they had disappeared from the family when they were twenty-one—right after their father shot his face off in his study, and I was lucky enough to find his body. I was nine years old. I didn't need the added trauma.

I was both fascinated and devastated by Uncle Anthony's death: fascinated because I was a morbid little shit, devastated because it wasn't someone on TV —it was my uncle, the one person in the family who I genuinely liked. Go fucking figure.

One week my uncle was pinching my ear and calling me "Beelzebub," and the next I was looking at his motionless body in a casket, asking Lex if he thought getting shot hurt or if it was just over too fast to feel anything. (How much blood was there? Did you see his body?)

Uncle Anthony always liked me a lot—but not in a cliché uncle late-night sneaky way. None of my other uncles gave a shit about anyone but themselves, but Anthony was different. He was nice. He was genuine in my young and naive eyes. I couldn't figure out for the life of me how he managed to fall in love with someone like Greta.

Everyone in the family took his death hard—except for Greta. She seemed detached, irritated, even. She fascinated me the most about the situation. She didn't cry. She sat there draped in black with her equally rigid mother at her side. It infuriated me. I couldn't feel much myself, but I understood then that something was wrong with me. I refused to think the same was wrong with Greta. I had to say something. I was notorious for saying things to Greta that would make her fly off the handle, and her husband's funeral was no exception.

Again, I was nine. I was supposed to be a good little girl. Yet whenever Greta and Joan got together to alienate the entire family, I was right there to call them out on their behavior.

"Why don't you cry?" I finally asked her, after the service was finished.

She gave me her usual glare of contempt. "Mind your own business, little girl."

"Why should I? Your husband is dead. You should be sad about it. What is wrong with you?"

My mother came up quickly and pulled me away from Greta by the arm. I'll never forget the look on her face, though. It was pure hatred. The woman loathed me and my pushy, inquisitive, no-filter persona.

"Keep your daughter away from me, Marlene," she said through clenched teeth.

Anthony had a sizable estate, which he left to his boys. According to the family gossip, there was no mention of Greta in his will. I didn't know what had been going on between husband and wife, but you don't just leave everything to your kids unless you don't care about your significant other's well being. Salt in an open wound—husband offed himself and left you nothing. Greta had no choice but to resent her kids for it. It seemed easy for her. Addi theorized that Greta had affairs with various people and was secretly bi-sexual, due to the fact that she spent all her time with her "friends" Veronica and Tricia. Addi insisted that they had secret lives and that led Anthony to become depressed and bitter toward his wife.

"She's got a KD Lang poster hanging up in her closet," Addi told Kat while I pretended to read on my grandmother's couch. "And did you see Veronica at the Wake? She was giggling in Greta's ear and touching the middle of her back. That's hardly appropriate."

"If she wasn't so hypocritical, I'd love it," Kat commented.

Veronica also had a lawyer husband, this one less-than-ethical, who had magically allowed Greta to lock up all of Anthony's assets into her own accounts by convincing a judge that Anthony had been having extramarital affairs, which therefore released the conditions of their prenuptial agreement.

The twins reacted the way I'd imagine most people would. They left town. No one had seen nor heard from them since.

A couple years later, Veronica and her husband died in a car accident in Switzerland, and Greta lived up to the reputation of the actress she was named after. She was outwardly devastated, crying at the drop of a hat, cowering in corners if someone noticed. There was something performative about it. Greta got her attention by pretending she didn't want it.

I didn't see her much until my later teen years. She spent her time in a reflective funk, as Kat's mom, Audrey, would call it. Greta paid me no mind, she focused on philanthropy to appear benevolent, and it was nice being seemingly off her radar while I dealt with teen hormones.

On the eve of my high school graduation, Joan threw me a lavish party and invited a hundred people I didn't give two shits about—all of them trying to climb over each other just to move up the prestigious social ladder of good old Phoenix.

Joan had to make the statement that I was graduating and going to an Ivy League college that she picked out. People showed up to wallow in Joan's lifestyle more than anything else. I certainly didn't have any friends—by choice, might I add. It was safer for people my age if I wasn't at sleepovers, contemplating smothering them with pillows. I wasn't a kid anymore. Now, I was fairly certain I was capable of killing someone. The thought crossed my mind a time or two. I had the discretion to stay far away from regular social situations. I didn't interject myself into family affairs.. I smiled and nodded when Joan shoved the applications for Dartmouth into my face, and I hadn't said one word to Greta in quite some time. I was doing well, as far as my family thought. The only people who saw my obligatory eye rolls and behind-the-back sneers were Addi and Kat.

I walked upstairs to be alone for a few moments when Greta came around the corner, ice clinking in her glass of vodka. This wouldn't go well. Our interactions in public were nothing compared to the ones in private.

Greta looked a lot older than she was due to her smoking habit, which also contributed to her smelling like a dirty ashtray all the time. She had these piercing grey eyes that would have been pretty if not for the permanent scowl on her face and her condescending stare. She was much like her mother and wore extravagant jewelry to show her social status. Rings, large diamond earrings, a brooch or three... they seemed to weigh her down.

"Baa, Baa, Black Sheep," she slurred in a mock-singing voice. The long, golden points of her largest sapphire brooch twinkled in the false light and made my eye twitch.

She poked me in the shoulder. "Actually made honors? I didn't even think you'd make it out of grade school with your attitude."

I hated three things at that moment: one, Greta; two, being poked; three, being referred to as Black Sheep. I was well aware that I was the odd one out in this family, and I didn't need this dried up old hag to mock me for it.

Greta hated the idea of me. *Oh no! Francesca thinks on her own and forms intelligent opinions! Stop her!* Little did she know my thoughts often consisted of burning down the mansion with her trapped inside.

I tried to sidestep Greta, but she grabbed my shoulder and dug in her claws, making me flinch.

I locked eyes with her. "Why are you always such a nasty bitch? Does it cause you physical pain to be nice? I'd even settle for tolerable."

"Excuse me?" Her face melted slightly.

"Here let me help you out," I continued, clearing my throat to speak in an over-embellished Greta voice. "Well met, Francesca. Congratulations on your accomplishments in high school. I am happy to hear that you made honors. Hard work pays off, you know. I hear you'll be venturing to Dartmouth in the spring, where the rest of us Fairholm Fillies went to find husbands to support us and our lavish, yet slightly insignificant, lifestyles. Best of luck to you and your new ventures."

"You disgust me," she seethed, pushing me away from her, yet not letting go.

"You disgust me," I countered. "So it appears we are at an impasse."

"You think you're so special," Greta chuckled. "You'd be going nowhere if it weren't for Joan paying your way through college. You're nothing but an insolent bastard child."

She over-enunciated the word "bastard" as if she was having a mouth orgasm.

I reached out and yanked at the big sapphire brooch. It came off easily, and I brought it down hard into the arm that was holding onto me. She screamed and backed up quickly to the wall. I advanced and began to stab her repeatedly with the harsh, golden edges of the massive eyesore. I sliced her neck open and giggled, escalating into a full laugh as her eyes widened and her blood began to spray out in all directions, covering my face. Yes... it was hysterical to me... stabbing the shit out of Aunt Greta.

But no, Greta was still leering at me, shifting her vodka glass slowly so the clinking ice made just enough sound to put my nerves on edge.

I swallowed hard, willing my rising anger to go away, but it kept bubbling up, making me fantasize awful things.

"Your grandmother is paying your way," she repeated, as if she forgot exactly what she was saying. "So you remember your place in this family. The bottom."

What. A. Cunt.

I couldn't stop the rage. I could only take so much. My face got hot and I lost what little control I had over my disposition. I restrained my hands from grabbing her neck.

I could've choked her right there and pushed her down the stairs. People would've thought she tripped over her drunken feet. I could've ran back around to the kitchen stairs and snuck back into the living room, and no one would be the wiser. Much cleaner than stabbing her to death with her own jewelry, right?

Do it, Frankie. She's a fucking bitch.

"No wonder your husband killed himself," I whispered. "No wonder your kids hate you."

She brought her face closer to mine. Her breath mixed with my anger and made me feel dizzy, but I fought through it so I didn't lose my ground.

"Shut your mouth, you piece of shit," she growled.

This is where I should have head-butted her and shoved her ass backwards down the stairs, but something stopped me. To this day, I'm not sure what it was. Perhaps an ounce of humanity reminded me that Greta wasn't worth it. Still, I had to get out of this situation before I hurt her.

"Let go of me before I snap your neck, you fucking cunt." My voice was barely my own.

I wish I could have framed the look on Greta's perfectly tragic face at that moment. It was the first time I had seen her look scared; I relished it.

"If you ever touch me again, I'll kill you," I told her.

I pushed her out of the way and proceeded to descend the stairs and storm into the dining room buffet, where Kat was stuffing her face with cheese. She looked over at me and alarm crossed her face.

"Are you okay?" she asked me, still trying to swallow the cheese.

I opened my mouth to answer, but I couldn't. I was swimming in a sea of red, there was a loud buzzing in my ears, my throat began to swell shut. Something was wrong with me. I had never felt such a wave of fury.

I started backing away and blinked hard, trying to clear the anger. I shook my head at Kat, who put down her plate and rushed over to me.

I phased everything out, turned and kept walking until I got to the huge double doors of Joan Fairholm's fancy Scottsdale mansion.

In the distance I could hear Greta shrieking to my mother about me. Fantastic.

"Marlene!" she shouted, most likely making everyone look at her. "You will not believe what your daughter just said to me!"

Get me the fuck out of here.

I pushed Greta down the stairs over and over in my head. I pictured myself clapping gleefully as the dumb bitch flew head over heels, her vodka spilling out in circles around her. I could have done it. Why didn't I do it? I wasn't a good person. I didn't have some inner core that wanted to help people and be nice. I wanted to hurt people—all the time.

Tears started to pool in my eyes. I blinked to clear them.

I threw the doors open with a loud bang. "Make an entrance, make an exit," was a well-known Fairholm credo. I didn't care who looked or questioned. Fuck them all.

Out in the warm desert air, I took in a deep breath. The smell of my grandmother's lemon trees began to overwrite Greta's acrid breath still stuck in my nostrils.

Holy shit, I thought to myself. I actually was about to kill my own aunt. I wanted to hear her fragile bones break. I clenched my hands until they stopped shaking.

What is wrong with me?

This anger was new to me. Greta had never pushed me to the edge of violence before. Usually we jabbed back and forth and then rolled our eyes and went on our merry ways.

Sure, I had imagined myself killing her plenty of times, but I had never felt my hands come so close to actually doing it. I'd never said those threatening words out loud to anyone. The low buzzing was tearing into my skull. I let out a shaky breath and placed my hands on the hood of my 1967 Mustang—a gift from my father. He had it refurbished in black with cherry red interior, the only proof he knew a little bit about me.

To my right, shadows began to shift, and I thought I heard footsteps.

I quickly climbed into my car before anyone had the chance to stop me. I revved the engine and drove off, away from my bitter and impudent family.

It was a lengthy drive back to my house. Time for me to blast music and try to push all the growing darkness back. My mother and I lived in the historic district of central Phoenix near Encanto Park. I pulled into the driveway and sat for a moment, trying to welcome the silence.

I loved silence. It was empty and cold, a welcoming feeling.

I loved awkward silences. Most people hate them, but to me they were like welcomed sighs of relief. Above that, I think I loved how awkward it made people feel. I'd sit there and smile, watching their eyes shift while their idiot brains searched for something to say. I was thrilled when people didn't have anything to say to me. It meant I didn't have to come up with some bullshit answer to keep the conversation going.

My anger was dissipating. The buzzing had stopped, leaving a dull headache in its wake.

I sighed as if I had just won a lengthy battle, and looked over at my dark house. A new feeling rose up—sadness. There I was, seventeen years old, about to start my life. No friends, no family. I might as well make the most of my night and sit at home watching Empire Records.

Happy graduation, Frankie.

Elegantly Wasted

Chapter Three

The phone rang as I unlocked the door. I fumbled for the light and grabbed the phone on the fifth ring, knowing who it would be. "What?"

"Did you really call Greta a cunt?" Katharine's voice was hushed. I could hear Addison laughing in the background.

I paused. That was the question? Not "Hey, Frankie, did you threaten to kill Greta?" That seemed like a more pressing matter. Did Greta even mention that I threatened her life?

"No, I called her a *fucking* cunt," I muttered, looking around. The house was really cold, despite the ninety-degree early summer night. My mother must have left the AC blasting.

"Yeah, she did," Katharine said to Addison, which made her laugh harder.

"That's all she said? That I called her a cunt?" I breathed hard into the phone.

"Oh yeah—she was pissed. Your mom couldn't calm her down. Grandma had to take them into another room."

"Let me guess," I grabbed a knife from my mother's wooden block and clutched the handle as if it were a security blanket. "Joan is reading her the riot act about how rude I am and that I lack Fairholm distinction."

"I think the words she used were 'uncouth and insolent.'" Katharine chuckled. "You know, the usual."

Swell, I thought. *What's new?*

"What did she say to you?" Katharine pressed.

My grip tightened on the phone and the knife made a loud clang as I dropped it onto the counter. "That I wasn't going to amount to anything. That I was a bastard child piece of shit or whatever."

"Fuck her," Kat spat. "She's a drunken idiot, not to mention a total hypocrite. She wouldn't have amounted to much of anything herself if she hadn't landed her rich husband. Grandma didn't speak to her for ten years after her freshman year at college, when she found out Anthony was half Sicilian. I don't even think Grandma went to their wedding."

"I never knew that," I muttered, my eyes focusing on an envelope on my kitchen counter. The name Francesca was typed neatly across the front.

"You're not a bastard, Frankie. You belong in this family just as much as anyone else," Kat said. Her voice was sympathetic, but I was too distracted by the envelope to really absorb the familial feelings.

"I'll call you back later." I hung up before Kat responded.

The envelope hadn't been there when I left earlier. My first thought was that it was from my mother, but it wasn't her taste—too plain. I grabbed it and ripped it open.

There was another, smaller envelope inside, along with a packet that had the American Airlines logo plastered on it and a letter.

The letter was printed on black paper. *Creepy*, was my first thought. There was a graphite-colored circular logo with what looked like a black hieroglyphic of a man bowing to another man, next to the word Osiris.

How very Egyptian. I frowned at the letter.

Francesca,

Life is full of choices. Time to make your first big one. Go to the airport and get on the flight indicated on the ticket. Tell no one where you're going. You'll need your passport, some clothes, and a few personal items. Once you arrive at your destination, we will let you know more.

Or you can go to Dartmouth and become exactly what your family wants you to be. The choice is yours. However, should you choose our path—the choice is permanent.

The letter wasn't signed.

What the hell. I fumbled with the airline ticket to see where it would send me: Pisa, Italy. *The fuck? Permanently?* That was a serious commitment. The flight departed at midnight. Three hours away.

The phone rang again, making me jump. I grabbed it quickly.

"Yes?"

"Francesca Beatrice Fairholm." My mom's voice was riddled with anger. "Honestly, why can't you behave at a single function, let alone a party that your grandmother went through a lot of trouble to put together?"

I suppressed a laugh. *Because you're all a bunch of self-centered elitist jerkoffs whom I can't stand. Yes, the proper use of whom... see, I fucking pay attention in this family.*

"I don't know, Mom," I answered. "Guess I've never been one for parties."

"You owe Greta an apology."

"I owe her shit," I spat. "She insulted me and you in one sentence. She got exactly what she deserved. If you won't stand up to her, I will."

My mom was quiet for a moment. "She said she congratulated you, and you responded with 'don't speak to me, you cunt.' I hardly think that's appropriate."

"First off," I said, laughing, "she's a lying sack of shit. She came up to me, drunk, slurring a fabulous rendition of 'Baa, Baa, Black Sheep' and then she started going on about how I'm an ignorant moron who wouldn't be going anywhere if not for my rich grandmother. I responded accordingly with 'no wonder your husband killed himself.' So there."

"Frankie," my mom was almost pleading now, "you can't talk to her like that. Just walk away if she confronts you."

"She cornered me!" I felt the anger returning. "For once in your life, Mom, have my fucking back!"

She let out a frustrated breath. She knew I was in the right. She just wouldn't admit it.

"Just please come back and at least apologize to your grandmother for storming out."

No. Fuck you.

"Who delivered this letter on the counter?" I asked suddenly.

"What? I have no idea what you're talking about." She was getting irritated. "Get back here now."

"I can't," I responded, clutching the letter. "I have to get out of this town. Goodbye, Mom."

My poor, self-loathing mother once had spunk. I could tell from the photos she kept hidden in the back of her closet. She was an adventurer. She had taste and even some of my dry wit when she wasn't depressed. She traveled with Bette when they were young. She had her whole life in front of her. Then she got married.

I was a bastard child. Greta was right about that.

The way I remember it—or how it was told to me through my aunt Audrey's drunken ramblings—my mother married early at nineteen in her first year in college. Mistake. She wanted so much to experience life, and she thought that if she got away from her mother that would happen. But in the sixties it was difficult for women to break free from much of anything. She dropped out of what would have been a successful career as a lawyer to marry Daniel McGregor.

Business man, workaholic, and ex-mortician turned limousine/hearse distributor and drug king pin: he moved her back to Phoenix, exactly where she didn't want to be.

Daniel was a provider, but not a comfort for my mother. She needed comfort and love more than money at that point in her life; she found comfort and love in one of my father's business partners and the son of one of the biggest morticians in Phoenix.

What's funny about the situation is that the mortuary business in 1970s Phoenix was a large drug trafficking highway—one that was never unearthed by the Feds. Some guy owned the mortuaries and the coffins that held the drugs; Daniel McGregor ran the transportation that moved the drugs, and my uncle Anthony's connections owned and operated the now-extinct Terminal One at Sky Harbor Airport, allowing the drugs into the country.

Drugs would come in by plane from South America or Mexico and avoid search... they would go into the coffins in the limos and that was it. Not one side of the family was ever legit.

Somewhere in there, my mom fell for one of the lackies. Daniel wasn't there, but plenty of money was there to keep her busy. One day,I was born although

Daniel and Marlene hadn't had sex in over three years. Awkward.

Daniel spent a large part of his time in denial, and since a lot of his nights were spent in a drunken stupor of scotch, my mother actually convinced him that they had sex and he got her pregnant. As I continued to get older, Daniel started to notice that I looked nothing like him.

The bombshell dropped in early November on my eighth birthday. I wasn't really Daniel's kid; I was someone else's. I don't remember much about it, but it was really ugly as I walked in on a group of people trying to calm my father down, trying to keep him from physically hurting my mother. The room consisted of Bette, Anthony, Daniel, my mother and two people I had never seen before: another woman and man off to the side, but I couldn't focus on him due to the poor lighting in the room. Anthony had to keep Daniel back as he struggled and shouted.

"How could you both do this to me?"

Everything stopped when I entered. I stood there, perfectly dressed in a white and black striped party dress with a big red bow in my hair: my three signature colors to this day.

When everyone turned to see me in the doorway, Daniel turned and snatched me up quickly, fleeing the house. He took me all the way to Disneyland for two weeks and bought me a new wardrobe. I was oblivious to what was going on and happy as a pig in shit, missing school.

My mother had a breakdown in my absence. Bette brought out the big guns, gave my mother sedatives and tried her very best to explain to me why she wasn't coherent for the next few months.

Not only did Daniel find out my mother was cheating, but he had to deal with the fact that I wasn't really his kid. That kind of stuff destroys men's souls. No one knew Audrey had spilled the tea. No one knew that I knew the entire story, or that I remembered the important details. I still don't know if she meant to tell me.

My grandmother was horrified that Marlene would do such a thing, tarnishing the family name. She declared that no one would speak of it, and we were all to act as though my father was Daniel McGregor—a rule Greta could never follow whenever she saw me.

So, to recap, I was born into this world a love child, I was brought home from the hospital in a limousine that was bought with Argentinian drug money... and the father listed on my birth certificate didn't know I wasn't his until I was a young kid.

My mother regained some of who she was once she divorced Daniel, but of course if you're attracted to one asshole, you're attracted to them all. She had married a plastic surgeon when I was in sixth grade. I didn't think much of the guy. He loved himself way too much, and thankfully he didn't have time to pay much attention to me.

His major drawback was that he was sick—weak heart. My mom opted to nurse him through his medical issues because she could inherit his small fortune and amazing health insurance.

Like I said, my mom wasn't the most virtuous of people. She was loving and nice... and a little narcissistic.

He died a few years later. His heart gave out and his will hadn't been updated. He left everything to his ex-wife. Karma would say that my mom deserved it, but I always thought differently because no one had honestly taught her to take care of herself. She was just doing what she thought she had to do to survive, all while removing herself from her controlling mother as much as possible.

The alcoholic gene took over soon after that. She shut down, and I spent a large part of my high school years trying to clean up after her. She had evened out somewhat by my senior year, but it would still be a big blow to her world, with me suddenly gone. But I knew I would have to leave eventually anyway.

She would understand at some point. She had to.

I picked up the phone and called a taxi service. They said they'd be there in fifteen minutes.

I took the letter upstairs to my room and closed the door. It had just occurred to me that someone had been in the house. Not that it was Fort Knox, but it was still unnerving. I opened the slim envelope in my quaint, little stalker package and pulled out ten crisp hundred-dollar bills and a passport for an "Alice Stewart" with my photo. *Mother fuck.*

Two scenarios crossed my mind at that point. One, it was some sort of weird joke—a lavish gift from my family... a European vacation. Or two, I was going to follow the instructions and end up dead in a river before sunrise with no trail to my whereabouts.

I grabbed my Prada duffel bag, a birthday present from Kat, the Queen of Taste. I pulled the first articles of clothing I saw from my drawer and threw them into my bag. I was just crazy enough to do this. Whoever this was, they caught me on a good night. I was fueled for something more and this seemed like exactly that. Alice followed the white rabbit. I followed the hieroglyphics.

Fifteen minutes later, I hoped for option one as I left the keys to my Mustang on the counter and locked the door behind me.

Twenty hours later I remembered that my family didn't have a sense of humor, and I started to wonder exactly how cold the Arno River was this time of year.

Elegantly Wasted

Chapter Four

I turned my head slightly toward the clacking of heels on the stone floor of the cold church.

Addison Fairholm knelt quickly at the edge of the pew, and instead of the usual father-son-holy-spirit motion, she raised her middle finger toward the coffin and brushed herself quickly into a sitting position beside me.

"Nice of you to show up." Kat said, her eyes hidden under big Gucci sunglasses. She liked to pretend she was more important than she was, and that meant wearing sunglasses inside. Either that, or the bright light pulsing through the miles of stained glass was way too much for her massive hangover. Then again, I was pretty sure she was still drunk.

"I was trying to pick out the right outfit for this grand finale," Addi whispered harshly.

"Stop encouraging her, Addison, this is serious." Kat drew her glasses down a bit and glared at her cousin with bloodshot eyes.

"She's a big girl; she can make her own decisions," Addi spat back.

"You honestly don't think this is ethical, do you?"

In the middle, I sat as they talked about me like I wasn't there. *Typical.*

They started more arguing in hushed tones. Luckily no one under the age of one-hundred-and-two was sitting near us and could overhear.

"You're a real piece of work," Kat went on, slurring her words ever so slightly, making my eye twitch. "I'm not going to be a part of this, regardless of what either of you think."

"Why is this such a big deal? And why are you using words like 'ethical,' you hypocritical bitch?" Addi leaned over me slightly. I awkwardly leaned back, signaling my lack of comfort with closeness.

"Eat shit, Addi. You know how fragile Frankie is, and you're pushing her to do something that's flat-out wrong. You're using her. Don't think you're virtuous just because you've saved children in third world countries. You're still a bad person."

"Ouch." Addi yawned.

Blah, blah, blah, I thought. These two would go at it all day if they could.

It wasn't so long ago that I was alone in my "top secret profession." Then one day, they fell into it with me.

That was my fault. I wasn't the most elegant killer. I slipped up once, I didn't read between the lines, and it ended up with me here—both of them arguing over my head, calling me "fragile"—the strongest bitch in the family. Excuse me, but I've killed an ambassador from Iceland with a syringe, what have you two done?

Sometimes I wish I could go back to the days when I just didn't know them as well... back to the days I up and left town on a neatly-typed dare.

"And what's with this sudden conscience of right and wrong?" Addi snorted. "You were doing so much better. Now you're back to square one."

Addi had an interesting story. She only had a few notable kills to her name. Kat, on the other hand, refused to take a life. She had other jobs... but was involved nonetheless.

"Maybe it's time I left the company," Kat snapped back. "I shouldn't have joined in the first place."

Son of a bitch.

I was irritated to say the least, and the two harpies on either side of me weren't helping. I could feel the anger rising. I could feel that void of emotion creeping up, getting me ready for the choices I made in life, allowing me to do the things I did without too many conflicting thoughts.

"I'm doing it," I spoke up softly.

They both closed their mouths and focused their eyes on me.

"So shut the fuck up." I kept my stare forward.

It was time for the funeral to start.

Elegantly Wasted

Chapter Five

I was eighteen when I became a contract killer. My company calls us Strikers.

It didn't happen overnight. It took a year and change of initial training and another year or so shadowing an established hit man. You know, less than a doctorate, but more than a liberal arts degree.

Even after all that time, I wasn't too sure I was cut out for the life of a murderous profiteer. I did know one thing though, I liked what I did. I was born to kill people.

I never went to Dartmouth. I hear it caused a shit storm of drama back in Phoenix, but I disappeared, so what could they do? My mother wanted answers, yet she didn't have enough backbone to find me.

On paper it said I attended the Florence University of Arts and got a degree in photography... superheroes need secret identities to hide the good deeds they do. In reality I was given an SLR camera after my training and told to Google "Photography."

Those were technicalities.

What really happened was that night, after I received the letter, I jumped on a midnight plane to Europe on a whim with a fake passport. I had a stupid sense of adventure that didn't calculate that I didn't fucking speak Italian. What was I doing? What was I thinking?

I stood in the middle of Galileo Galilei Airport in Tuscany, thinking all of these things over and over, when a man in a black suit approached me. He nodded to me and grabbed my bag.

"Ms. Fairholm," he started. "Please follow me."

Something struck me as odd at that moment. I wasn't scared. I should have been. For some reason I had been focused on my venture, and I hadn't processed that this was the dumbest thing a white girl had ever done. Looking back now, I could have been sex trafficked, killed for sport or subjected to a plethora of other scenarios. Not one of them involved joining an elite company of trained killers. I guess I was lucky.

I just followed the man until he held open a car door for me. It was a black car with really tinted windows — perfect for kidnapping stupid American women.

"If you're taking me somewhere to dismember me, I'll be very upset." I pointed my finger at the driver.

He smiled at me with crooked teeth. *Oh, this is just perfect.*

I got in, and the man closed the door after me. Once he was in himself, he raised the middle partition that separated the front from the back of the car. I guess he just didn't want to talk to me.

The air conditioning turned on and blew into my face. I backed up, irritated with the gesture.

The car took off into the winding streets of Pisa. It was my third time in the country. Or was it second? Wait, maybe I had never been. Where was I anyway? I squinted through the glass. Things looked different. They looked shiny... and fuzzy... and pretty... everything began to spin.

Goddamn it.

I blacked out.

Billie Holiday woke me up. My head was wading through a thick haze as a slow and creepy rendition of 'Bless the Child' wafted through the air.

I could hardly move. As my head regained focus, I realized I was tied to a chair. My neck was killing me, and my mouth was dry.

I lifted my head slowly.

There was a bright light shining in my face, blacking out whatever lay beyond.

I could hear someone moving around. They were tapping something, metal on metal. It was unnerving to say the least.

I started to panic. I jerked against the duct tape that held me to the unforgiving metal chair. Nothing budged. I was fucked.

Footsteps.

I struggled harder against the tape, twisting my wrists a little too far as I squinted at the light, trying desperately to see what lay beyond.

"Hey!" I cried out with more fear than I wanted to convey. "Let me go!"

Something flew through the light toward me, and I screamed as I was drenched in water—very cold water.

My whole body froze in shock, and I started to breathe even faster, to the point of hyperventilating.

"What the fuck," I said, spitting water out of my mouth. Dry mouth problem solved.

Billie Holiday's voice faded, and Patti Page's 'How Much is that Doggie in the Window' started. I was officially creeped the fuck out. It was like the music was playing from a very old record player and was warping and skipping. My nerves were screaming.

The footsteps circled around me slowly, methodically even.

Shivering from the cold, I had no choice but to just sit there and whimper as the unknown person circled and looked at me. This was beyond insane. *What the fuck did I get myself into?*

I squinted into the light and could see two more silhouettes. From their size I made an educated guess that they were men.

"Hello?" I found my voice. "Hey assholes! What the fuck? This is illegal, you know. Let me go!"

"She's ready," one man said to the other.

"I told you so," was the response.

Oh, swell. This was going great. Wonderful idea, Frankie—really.

I could hear the men talking in hushed tones as they walked away from me. A door opened and closed; it sounded heavy, like a dungeon door. Seriously, where the fuck was I—the Sixteenth Century?

The music shut off, thank God. But now the silence was even more unsettling, and I was still wet and freezing.

"I'll sue your asses if I catch pneumonia!" I yelled into the darkness, trying hard to make my voice sound as steady as possible. Maybe if I put up a cool exterior, it would work out for me.. I could hope.

The bright light turned off, and I could finally see my surroundings.

Cozy, if you're Ed Gein.

This place was a total dungeon—rock walls, metal doors, weak lighting hanging from the walls.

The door opened again, and a man walked in. His dark skin blended in with the even-darker rock walls. He was older—in his forties—with a serious face. I had a twinge of recognition, but I knew I didn't know him… he just had one of those faces… pleasant. It made me relax a little.

He smiled at me and started to rip off the duct tape.

"Hello, Francesca," he said. "Pleased to meet you."

"Fuck off," I spat, hoping he wasn't a murderer. "Tell me what's going on? This all seems highly unnecessary. This was a nice Fred Siegel shirt you just ruined."

I was free, and I sat up quickly. He held out his hand and I jumped away from it as if it were a spider.

"My name is Judah Cohen," he said, noting my uneasiness. "I'm sorry for the dramatics, but given the nature of our company, you'll understand."

I took his hand hesitantly and shook it.

"Nature of your company? What company? Where am I?"

The smile never left his face. "Osiris, Ms. Fairholm. You're in one of our many training facilities. You've been asked to join an elite group of contract killers."

I threw him an incredulous look. "Ahh, what?"

His smile became riddled with mild frustration. "Contract," he enunciated. "Killers. I'm here to train you to be a weapon."

Odd that this scenario didn't enter my mind at all. *Silly me.*

"Look," I did my best to straighten myself out to my full and unimpressive five-foot-three. "I don't know what drugs you're giving out down here in Buffalo Bill's basement, but I know a felony when I see one. Kidnapping is a felony."

"You got on the plane, Ms. Fairholm," Judah responded. "So obviously you were prepared for a worst-case scenario."

"Yeah but I didn't think…"

"That you could be tagged as a potential assassin right out of high school? I know." He rolled his eyes. "But you're here, and that's my offer. So take it or leave it."

"Awesome, Mr. Rogers," I frowned. "And if I say no?"

He smiled. "I can't guarantee a safe return to the United States, but the letter specifically said make a choice. You could have stayed home."

The man had a point.

He gestured across the room. "Walk through that door and your life will change."

"Hey, I know this movie!" I laughed. "Keanu Reeves takes the red pill. You must be Morpheus."

There is no spoon, motherfucker.

"Right this way, Ms. Fairholm."

Elegantly Wasted

Chapter Six

For about the next year, I had no concept of time. I didn't know where I was and was more or less a willing prisoner. Most of my questions went unanswered, and I was fairly certain I was watched every moment of my day. It took me that long to grow accustomed to my surroundings, which were dismal.

There were no windows, the walls were rock and cement, the floor was a hard-plastic mesh and everything was always cold. All of these factors led me to believe I was underground. I probably could have asked Judah, but the less I talked to him, the more pleasant he seemed.

Time wasn't a concept for me and I had no idea how much passed before I got to venture outside of the large missile silo I called home.

My mother eventually forgave me for disappearing. At least, I think she did. I was allowed to call her once I regained consciousness. She had to understand that I wanted to forge my own path. She cried a little, but I told her that I needed to get away and a person of her sketchy history could certainly understand that.

"You have the spirit I always tried to obtain," she told me.

I have more than that. I have spirit, sharp wit, unrelenting cynicism, and to top it all off, I was just issued a suitcase of weapons.

"Tell Addi and Kat that I miss them and will get a hold of them when I can," I said. "Everything will be fine, Mom."

I meant it. As weird as my situation was, I felt safe.

Judah was my teacher for the year I was stuck in the dungeon. He was the one who asked me the big question.

"Do you want to work for Osiris?"

Well let's look at the other option. Don't want to work for Osiris? Francesca Fairholm died in a tragic car accident in England. Poor thing was just about to start college, too. They needed her dental records for identification.

Fuck yes, I want to work for Osiris.

Who was Osiris? Dumb question. Why me? Another dumb question.

The less I knew, the better.

I learned the intricacies of contract killing from Judah, who sat across from me in a small room with a one-way mirror and stale air.

"We seek out people who fit our company's profile," Judah told me. "People we can use before they become a problem."

"A problem?" I frowned. *Where had I heard that one before?*

Judah smiled. "You're a killer."

I paled.

"I haven't killed anyone," I spat.

"You will." He smirked and stepped closer to me.

I felt the color drain from my face. I honestly tried to keep a hard front up when having our psychotic little "sessions," but this guy was a whack job.

"You want to." His eyes bore into mine. "Say it."

He stopped when his face was an inch from mine. A familiar scent hit my nostrils—tobacco and peppermint.

Most of the men in my life had carried this air around them... pipe or cigar smokers who tried to hide it from people by chewing copious amounts of gum.

At that intense moment I relaxed a bit, holding my ground a bit longer.

"No," I whispered.

Part of me wanted to let go and give Judah what he wanted to hear. The other part was terrified of the words escaping my lips. There was a finality about it—there was indeed no more running from who I was.

"Say it," he repeated.

I bit my lip.

"Say you want to kill someone. Say you want to watch their eyes as you take the life from their body."

My head started to pound painfully and I began to shake—from aggravation and the fact that this guy was an inch from my face, smelling like my dad, my uncles and any one of the numerous men my mom had dated over the years.

"Say you want to hear a person's neck break, or you want to see how much blood would come out of them if you stabbed them. Tell me how you love the crimson color and would gladly paint the walls with it."

Suddenly the pain subsided, my shoulders relaxed and I narrowed my eyes at him.

"Yeah, I want to do those things."

"Say the words," Judah pushed.

"I want to kill someone," I said. I didn't want to hesitate any longer. *Why continue running from who I really am?*

He smiled. "Of course you do. You're angry, a friendless loner, an imaginative sociopath who thinks about taking life."

Oh good, now he's trying to make me insecure about it.

I mean I was an edgy teenager. I didn't have friends, but that was by choice. Girls wanted to be my friends, but I was afraid their petty teenage problems would make me stab them in the face. Didn't that mean I at least had self-control?

Sure I wanted to bash my talkative step-mother, Diane, over the head. I liked silence! And who could really fault me for wanting to kill Greta?

"We want what's best for you. That means making you into a weapon for a more commercial use... rather than letting you run free with your deadly thoughts, killing innocent people. Which, don't be fooled, would happen eventually."

Ouch. It's tough confronting the fact that you're fucked up in the head.

After that, I started to like our sessions more.

Judah Cohen was amazing. He knew me. I didn't have to hide a thing. He was my teacher, philosopher and psychologist. He was also the first person I was ever sexually attracted to, but I attributed that to my fucked-up daddy issues and nothing more.

He was a bit geeky, but sophisticated, and he knew a lot about killing. He reminded me of James Bond—only Judah was black and from the Bronx. He was also Jewish, and although he left me to my religious preferences, I did see him keeping his food kosher, and I would occasionally hear the faint melodies of Neil Diamond coming from his office. If Joan Fairholm's racist ass knew I was learning life lessons from a black

Jew listening to "Girl, You'll Be a Woman Soon," she would be furious.

Judah didn't take my bullshit. If I opened my big, fat mouth, he closed it by punching me in the stomach. I didn't let it break me. I learned to respect him, but I'd be damned if he took an inch of my personality. I liked myself too much.

The more difficult side of my time with Judah was the loneliness. He wasn't there to be a friend or a family member. I had never been so secluded, so out-of-touch, and so away from simple things I took for granted: sunlight, donuts, soda, my mom. As much as I disliked her at times, she was a constant presence and a familiar warmth to whatever emptiness was pushing at me. Without her around, the emptiness weighed much more. Maybe that was a lesson, too.

I did notice myself change though—there was no stopping it. Aside from the dark circles under my eyes and the sickeningly pale shade my skin became, I became hyper-aware of my purpose. I thought less and less of my mother, Kat, and Addi, and more about Osiris and what Judah expected from me. The subtle, cult-like shift didn't go unnoticed. I just knew I'd be better off on my current path.

Judah was a trainer, and he was training me to be a predator. He brought out my dark side, introduced us and then molded us into one functioning creature. There was a smoothness about my transition that made me wonder if I was ever really the sweet girl my mother had tried to raise me to be. My training felt more like the answer to a long-lost question in my head. What was I good at? This.

There was one major thing left. I actually had to kill someone. I could face any amount of truth Judah threw at me, but until I was actually a killer, I couldn't call myself one. I could only fantasize so far.

47

After months of intense physical, mental and emotional training, Judah took me out of the complex and into the nearest city—which was Florence. I was trying hard to hide my excitement, because in the back of my mind I knew this was it. He was going to pick someone for me to kill.

The thrill of being in civilization again, and being thrown into such a vastly beautiful place, overpowered me. Take all of those anxieties, pent-up frustrations, and I was a time bomb. I tried my best to look unimpressed and keep myself in check.

"What are we doing here?" I asked him as we checked into a hotel.

"We are people watching," he responded.

"Well, I look like I'm terminally ill, so people will actually be watching me," I was irritated. Instead of listening to my complaints, Judah drew back the curtains in my hotel room and pushed me onto the balcony into the sunlight and told me to stand still for thirty minutes.

Judah then prepped me as though he was a stage mother. Little black dress, high heels, hair done up, makeup on.

He handed me a knife and told me to put it in my small clutch, then proceeded to talk down to me for hours. It was infuriating. He would stop, for no reason, and talk to someone while I stood there like an idiot. He dragged me around the city like a dog on a leash. I must have looked ridiculous, but figuring out a system for walking in stilettos kept my mind from wandering.

"Stop slouching," he'd say. "Pick up your feet and stop scowling at me. You're a refined lady—I know you know how to behave. Your grandmother saw you to finishing school herself. Act like a fucking adult."

This made me straighten up, but inside I was still pouting. Refined lady... with a concealed weapon in her purse.

Judah pointed to a large hill with makeshift steps that led up to nothing that I could see.

"You're kidding, right?"

He started walking up. I was starting to get furious. Forget the fact that I hated high heels—I hated steep inclines and stairs more... combine these and I was in hell.

"You could have at least let me wear a track suit and tennis shoes if we were doing some sort of endurance training, Morpheus," I called out after him. The heels were killing me. I never had to wear them until now. I hated them immediately.

There were a few people making their way up the stairs, all of them looked at me questionably since I was the nicest-dressed athlete on the track. About a half-mile later, I reached the top of the stairs to see Judah making his way toward a church at the top of yet another hill. If he was honestly dragging me to church, I would kill him. End of training.

I wasn't tired, I was pissed. Run me all over town if you must, but asking me to negotiate cobblestone in heels for hours on end was really pushing my breaking point for some reason.

The next set of stairs was actual stone and led, quite specifically, to a monastery where I could hear a soft melodious singing wafting on the breeze. I collapsed onto the hard stone of the low wall that surrounded the area, disregarding the crumbling cemetery that lay beyond. I kicked the heels off of my rapidly swelling feet and sighed in relief. I adjusted the ruffles in my black dress and dangled my bare feet off the edge of the stone wall. I watched Judah walk to the door and greet an angry-looking priest.

The priest handed Judah a piece of paper. As Judah looked down at it, the man looked over at me. He looked me up and down, and I felt a wave of nervousness. I knew that look anywhere—a look my grandmother had thrown me countless times during my young life: judgment. Religious people gave me the creeps, which was fine, because I suppose in my new line of work I would creep them out just as much.

But why was Judah meeting up with a priest on a hilltop in Florence? It was a question that would undoubtedly go unanswered: it was none of my business. I did note that the priest didn't make any sort of gesture toward letting Judah inside. Did he know who we were and what we did?

The little exchange was over quickly, and Judah snapped at me to follow him back down the hill. I couldn't bear to put the heels back on, so I did my best to walk across the terrain in my stockings.

The sun was settling into the surrounding Tuscan countryside and, as irritated as I was, I couldn't help but love the view.

"So, you had to drag me up to the highest church in the city to talk to a priest? What is it? Your yearly confession?"

"That was a monk," Judah replied, as if I gave a shit. "You should learn the difference around here."

I lifted the heels above me and threw them at his head. He effortlessly caught them, turned and strode up to me. "You're not a child," he spat. "Act like the weapon you are or I'll dump your body in the next trash can I see." He handed me back my shoes.

I remained silent as we made our way back into town.

Judah finally sat me down at a cafe and started to sound like Mr. Miyagi as he talked about surveying not only the people around me, but the environment as well. Smells, feelings, using my senses to grasp varying situations that would mean life and death.

"Hone your predator instincts," he would say.

"Her," he said, pointing to an elderly woman sitting across the room with a pug at her feet. "Tell me about her."

He watched me intently as I gave a light sigh and turned my gaze to the woman.

"She's American," I said. "Her voice carried over here a bit ago with a Boston accent. She's wearing a wig, which means she's either a cancer survivor or just has bad genes. I'm guessing she doesn't have family due to the fact that she's alone, with a dog, in Florence in the middle of April. A widow, perhaps?"

Judah nodded. "What else?"

I tilted my nose upward.

"She's wearing a lower-end shitty perfume, but a five-carat diamond ring on her middle finger... which leads me to believe she's richer than shit and eccentric, since she's also reading the finance pages of the New York Times... from last year."

Judah gave me a smile. "She's a widow from Boston. No children. She moved here because a psychic told her to."

"Oh, so she's like Lady Winchester," I chuckled.

"How about him?" Judah nodded toward a man who was just sitting down with another man whose back was to me.

I frowned. There was definitely something off about him. He wasn't dressed especially well, he had bad skin and he ordered alcohol. It was as if I could sense that he was dangerous—a criminal of some sort, dirty and crass.

"I don't like him," I said. The man sensed that he was being watched, and our eyes locked briefly. He gave me a creepy smile that made me turn away quickly. "At all."

"What don't you like about him?" Judah asked.

"He's a creep," I said. "He doesn't take care of himself, he smokes, his socks don't match, and he's drinking a vodka tonic."

"Oh yes, I forgot about you and people who dress in the dark and drink vodka tonics." He rolled his eyes.

"He's bad news." I shrugged.

"What makes you say that?"

"His eyes," I said. "Look, can we go? The sun is setting, storm clouds are moving in and I'm getting cold."

Judah studied me for a moment. I could tell he wanted me to elaborate, but he decided against it and gestured for the check.

"Two more stops and then we can retire for the night," Judah said.

Wonderful. I resumed my spot walking slightly behind him, assuming people thought I was some sort of mail-order bride.

Judah stopped at a bakery and bought bread, meringue cookies and cheese. He then threw the paper bag containing the items into my hands. It was around then that I let one of those sighs out—Addi called them "Frankie sighs" because they were a special drawn-out tone of all the aggravation I was feeling. Usually the exhaling of air kept me from running off at the mouth—or in this case, choking the shit out of Judah.

I grew weary and frustrated as the day turned into night. I followed Judah into a long dark alleyway. "I enjoy the fresh air; trust me, it's better than inhaling mold and stale, recycled air all day. However, I can't say this is exactly enlightening. First off, fuck you for making me hike up a shit ton of stairs. You're just running errands, and you've asked me to profile a senile old lady and a scummy guido."

He ignored me, which just aggravated me even more.

"Can't I at least wear flats if you're going to drag me all over this city?" I asked. "I mean, I'm cold, it's drizzling, I can't even feel my big toes and I'm pretty sure numbness in my feet means I have circulatory issues."

I stopped short as Judah came across a man exiting a narrow doorway. It was the same seedy guy from the cafe. Judah moved like water, grabbing the man by the shoulder, moving behind him and swiftly snapping his neck.

I gasped loudly and dropped the groceries as the man fell to the ground in a heap. I backed up quickly, wondering if I should stay to help or run the other way.

"Drug dealer," Judah muttered. "No one will miss him."

Judah bent down and rifled through his clothes, taking out two large packs of white powder and emptying the contents onto the wet cobblestone ground.

He stood back up and looked over at me and my gaping mouth.

"Oh, I'm sorry." He laughed sarcastically. "You were saying?"

"What the fuck?" I shook my head in disbelief.

"You noticed it," Judah said. "You knew he wasn't right. So why didn't you elaborate?"

My mouth opened and closed a few times. His actions made sense, but my brain wasn't allowing me to keep my cool.

He smirked.

"Holy shit!"

"Am I to believe that you didn't know this was coming?"

"Fucking warn me before you kill someone!"

It had just occurred to me that I had never seen a dead body, let alone seen anyone kill someone outside of a movie. My eyes transfixed on the dead guy.

He looked like a drunk guy in an alley, only his neck was at an angle that no neck should be. I must have been staring, because Judah cleared his throat.

"Paolo, dove sei andato?" A voice sounded from inside the building.

Judah stepped quickly to the side of the entryway and drew his gun.

Not knowing how to react, I naturally froze as another man came out into the alleyway and glared at me.

He waved his hand and began to shout Italian at me before he focused on the dead man to this left.

That's when Judah swung his gun down onto the man's head, hard. He fell to the ground in a heap next to his friend.

At least, I assumed they were friends. *Drug dealers had friends, right?*

The drizzling turned to a steady rainfall, and I was shivering as I watched Judah relieve this man of his drug stash as well.

He looked up at me. "Well?"

"Well what?" I managed.

He straightened himself out. "Finish him off."

My breath caught in my throat. I backed up a step, as if that would help better my situation.

"Judah…" I started, "I can't—"

Sink or swim, Frankie.

"I gave you that knife for a reason. We can't shoot him and draw attention to ourselves."

"But," I stammered. "We'll be caught, right? I can't stab a guy in the middle of Florence and get away with it!"

"We don't exist here," Judah said, his voice menacing. "Now do what I fucking ask or pay the consequences."

I swallowed hard and brushed my wet hair from my face.

Judah watched my every move as I reached down and freed the knife from my purse.

With shaky hands, I walked over to the unconscious man and knelt down close to him.

"Breathe," Judah reminded me. "Follow through."

One. Two. Three. I felt my arms rise as if I had no control over them. Time seemed to slow down, as did the falling rain. I could hear the sounds of a distant city, smell the wet cobblestone mixed with the street garbage that was discarded in the alley. I took a short breath.

I aimed for his heart.

Elegantly Wasted

Chapter Seven

It felt good. I won't lie.

I watched the man's face as it twitched and he stopped breathing.

It wasn't such a big deal. I thought it would feel different, more intense or something. Instead it was just a sort of blankness. It was over fast, and I found myself just staring at his relaxed face.

I don't recall how long I stood there, pressing a knife into his chest, but Judah had to gently lift me off the guy and pry the knife from my fingers.

"Very good," was all he said.

He wrapped the knife in a handkerchief and placed it inside his blazer.

He led me back to the hotel and made sure I was responsive.

"More tomorrow," he said, leaving me alone.

These types of "sessions" happened every month. The monks commissioned Osiris to take down a rather large drug ring that had risen up over the years. *Go figure*. Religion was just about as shady as anything else in my opinion. Judah decided to confide in me a bit more and told me that the monks were actually their own assassin ring called Adficio.

The Adficio were old and operated on strict religious guidelines. Even these days, bishops and cardinals still needed to be silenced, apparently. Osiris worked hard to make friends in the killer-for-hire arena and did small tasks for the Adficio that fell outside religious jurisdiction. It was a win/win really... I could handle these tasks as a developing agent, and the monks didn't have to anger God any more than they already had.

So, this became my life, learning the skills of a professional killer. I was refined, perfected and most likely even brainwashed a bit. Judah was like the Crazy Girl Whisperer.

I was also taught a regular curriculum of college-level courses: international affairs, languages, history— the list went on. My favorite part was that I didn't have to see or hear from family... although I missed my mom and found myself worrying about her.

Osiris had a structure. It had departments and hierarchies just like any company.

At the very top of the chain were unknown investors, followed by unknown owners. What I did know about the "upper division" was that the guy in charge was always watching. Judah said he was great at keeping tabs on all of his employees, and he handpicked all of them.

Under them was a chain of secretive military connections, and then came the actual agents.

We have Strikers. That's me. I was going to be a field agent, a hit man. Strikers are the most expendable agents, but the highest paid. We work alone, with the exception of texted instructions, and if the job is high profile enough, we have an extra set of eyes in the form of the Wingback. The Wingback is someone I would never see, but know is there. They are information collectors, scouts, and archivists. There were a lot of Wingbacks within Osiris and they had divisions that handled different jobs. They found the new talent, pushed papers and documented everything, but their most important job was casing targets prior to hits. They trolled hangouts, investigated behavior patterns, discerned the target's likes and dislikes, their habits—anything of use to a Striker.

This information is also sent to a Sweeper if something goes wrong. Sweepers clean up hits-gone-wrong or stage evidence to point a murder toward an accident. A Sweeper is an older Striker—someone who had been around longer and had proven his or her worth in the field. Osiris doesn't have many Sweepers—Judah told me there were two—so chances were I'd (hopefully) never run into one... if a Striker botched a job enough, a Sweeper would also kill them.

Rounding up the group are Stoppers. Stoppers are medical agents. They are placed around the world and called on whenever an Osiris agent needs any medical aid, from infected paper cuts to surgery. If I ever needed help, I'd have to send out a distress text, and a Stopper would contact me and give me my agent number and the safe phrase that I chose in my early days of training. That phrase granted them my full trust for the duration of my medical treatment.

Osiris was a well-oiled machine. It had flaws like anything else, but I was impressed nonetheless. Even my identity was changed, in case I was caught. I was still Francesca, but my fingerprints and dental records pointed to someone named Alice Stewart. My family never had to know I was a murderer.

I got comfortable in my surroundings and adjusted to my disjointed life. It was nice to be myself for the first time in eighteen or so years. I could have stayed forever.

"You're leaving tomorrow." Judah walked into the library where I had been reading.

I glanced up from a book, my only small escape. "Just like that, Morpheus?"

He smiled at me. "My job is done. You're moving on to shadowing."

I had known it was coming. I would leave the training facility, travel back to the States and live with another faithful Osiris employee for two years.

"You'll get a little of your life back. Rejoin the real world. Time for you to be more social."

A social killer. *Nice.* I considered pointing out the Osiris "gag and bag" philosophy was a little off path if they wanted us to be social as well. In my year underground, I hadn't spoken to anyone but Judah. Their only other people were a maid who didn't speak or make eye contact, and the cook, Alberto, who kept to the kitchen and thought he was Luciano Pavarotti.

I wasn't ready to leave the complex. It sounded crazy, but I felt safe in this structure of restraint. I could be myself, a privilege I'd never been awarded much before, at least not without a lot of push back.

"Pack light," Judah interrupted my thoughts.

That was funny. I didn't have much. I wore a pretty boring uniform consisting of a black tank top and grey pants day in and out. I had the essentials—pajamas and underwear. I had kept the few dresses that Judah had given me on our outings. I wondered if I should pack the guns that had been issued.

"You will receive all of your artillery in a few weeks," Judah said, seeming to read my mind. "You report to your trainer in Long Beach. He'll take over from there."

"He will?" I scrunched my face. *Another man to deal with. Jesus, am I the only woman on staff who doesn't do manual labor?*

"Don't disappoint me, Francesca."

Elegantly Wasted

Chapter Eight

Spark Dawson didn't look like a killer. That was a trademark for Osiris. None of us really looked like anything special.

I was short and a bit on the curvy side. My long chestnut hair frizzed in the humidity. I might have had more fashion sense thanks to my upbringing, but I still tripped in my Louboutin's.

Spark looked like a beach bum. He was husky, around five-foot-nine, with bright blue eyes and brown hair that was shaggy, but not long. His attire consisted of a Quicksilver shirt, cargo shorts, and gray Vans with bright red laces—no socks.

He opened the door of his home in the Belmont Shore area of Long Beach and gave me the once-over.

He smiled, and I tensed a bit. He was cute. "Ooh, a looker, thank God. I was starting to think they didn't like me!"

Wonderful, he was a pig. How this guy managed to be a trained killer, I still boggle over today. I was pretty sure that contract killing really took away from his sit-on-the-beach-and-drink-beer time.

He grabbed my bag from me and motioned me into the house. It was minimal and very clean. At least he wasn't a slob. He led me to my room and threw my bag on the bed. I had been up for thirty hours, so the bed looked amazing to me.

"I'm Spark." He turned to me and grabbed a piece of paper that had been sitting on the dresser. "You're Agent twenty-two. And we're going to be working closely for about a year, so I hope you're not an alpha bitch."

"You can call me Frankie." I smiled at him. "I'm an omega bitch."

That made him smile as he looked down at the paper.

"Do you have family anywhere nearby?"

"Phoenix," I responded.

"Arizona... how tragic." He seemed to be enjoying himself. "You ever want to contact them?"

"Not really."

He shook his head as he looked back up at me. "Good to hear."

He didn't elaborate from that point on. He just shrugged and left me in the room. The second phase of my training had begun, apparently. I unzipped my bag and pulled out the book I had yet to finish.

He came back a moment later. "Hey! I lead, you follow, got it?"

Oh, silly me. I rolled my eyes, let the book drop and then tried to make my footsteps display my irritation as I walked after him.

He led me to the garage and closed the door behind me, then reached down and lifted up a large metal hatch in the floor. "Ladies first."

I dropped down the hatch and motion lights sensed my presence. I gaped at the amount of guns he had stored down there. It was like a doomsday prepper's bomb shelter.

"Have a seat," he said, motioning to a tall working table with three metal stools.

I did as I was told, and he started to buzz around the large bunker. I shifted my eyes around the area, trying in vain to get comfortable in the unforgiving seat. The harsh fluorescent lights did their best to give me a headache.

"What's the best weapon for a low-visibility, high-distance shot?"

"What?" I wasn't prepared for a pop quiz.

"I'll start slower," he put two large rifles on the table. "These are what we call guns."

I frowned at him as I reached out and picked up the sniper on my right, which was heavier than previous ones I had trained on. I examined it quickly. "This rifle has an infrared high-powered scope with thermal reading. That's your best bet."

"Oh, you do listen."

I smiled sweetly. "Sorry, Lebowski. I don't speak fluent asshole, so you might have to repeat a thing or two."

He smirked back at me.

He was testing me, sizing me up. He wanted to see if I was a push over.

I must have passed the test, because a moment later a large buzzer echoed into the room and he jetted back up to the house to welcome the "pizza dude."

The metal hatch crashed shut and I remained seated at the table, staring intently at the sniper rifles in silence. I hadn't quite grasped everything until that moment.

I wanted to move, but couldn't. I had grown accustomed to dark bunkers. The salty, sweet air and the massive ball of light outside worried me a little… as did my scruffy new partner. What was I supposed to do from here? You'd think I'd have picked up a phone to call my mother the moment I got back to the States, but that didn't happen.

What was I supposed to say to her? She'd just want to see me, and I couldn't handle that at the moment, nor was I allowed.

"Hey," Spark's loud voice sounded from an intercom on the wall, jolting me out of my thoughts. "You gonna come upstairs and eat or sit down there and stare at the wall for rest of the night like a prisoner?"

I let out my trademark sigh.

That was my introduction to Spark Dawson and the start to the next one year and two months of my life... plus five days, not that I was counting.

Spark wasn't his real name. I asked what his real name was once, and he responded with, "Whatever you want it to be, darlin.'"

He started calling me Frankenstein, because I was the clumsiest hitter he'd seen. Not to say I was clumsy in general—I really wasn't. I looked both ways before I crossed a damn street; I paid attention to open pot holes and shaky ladders.

I was a creature of extraordinary grace, until I tried to climb walls or sneak around a darkened house like James Bond.

I really hated heights and high heels. Combine those two with gravity and I became a hazard. Two weeks in Spark's care and I had acquired a bruised tailbone and a concussion, and broke my most comfortable pair of heels. On top of all that, Spark would just point and laugh.

There was a flip side to that coin though.

Slinking around rooftops and stairs? Sure, I was a bull in a china shop. With a gun though, I was like a symphonic prodigy.

Even early on, Spark was impressed with my accuracy.

There was something unusually steady about my hands as soon as I held a gun in them. I had always had steady hands, even as a child. I crushed anyone when playing Operation—Cavity Sam's big stupid red nose never lit up for me.

I suppose I could have gone down the surgeon road like my cousin, Addi, but I don't think saving lives was in the cards for me. The hand I was dealt was that of a killer—Judah showed me that much.

Life went on. I gathered enough emotional energy to call my mother, a call that went surprisingly smooth. I told her I met a guy. I left out the part where he wasn't my boyfriend, and the part where I wanted to beat him to death with his own arms. She seemed thrilled and worried at the same time.

Spark's favorite movie was the Last Dragon, and he played video games way too much. He quoted Call of Duty on a regular basis and made me play a slew of first-person shooters, stating that, while it probably wouldn't help hone any real firearm skill, it couldn't hurt.

The Osiris rules were straightforward :

1. Don't get killed, it's expensive to replace you.

2. Always cover your tracks.

3. Follow the instructions of the hit. Do not deviate.

4. If you get injured, you must seek out an Osiris Stopper for treatment. Do not try to treat your own injuries.

5. Don't kill anyone else but your mark, unless they are a direct threat to you.

6. Keep your cover.

7. If someone discovers who you are, kill them.

8. Don't return to your home base until the hit is finished.

9. Be precise, be knowing, be dauntless.

10. Do not get emotionally attached to a hit, and never socialize with a mark in public.

I thought the last one was too specific, almost like that exact situation had happened before.

Hits were issued to our smartphones by a text from out of the country, untraceable according to Spark—something boring about government hookups. The text had a link to a temporary webpage with as much hit information allowed. We booked airfare, got to our destination hotel where a big envelope always waited from Parker Larabee: Investment Bankers. It outlined our business trip: travel itinerary, times of meetings, location of meetings, helpful information, and a check-out time.

Meetings were usually parties or places where the hit socialized. Check-out time was the suggested time of execution if it wasn't specified in the original texted link. Wingbacks made sure there were items to help us out with our hit if we needed it, and there was a code to text if we got in any trouble.

I had a fake passport, ID, business visa—you name it. My alias was Alice Stewart.

My first real kill was a woman in Paris, France. By real, I mean not gutter trash in an Italian alley.

She had been a rising politician and embezzler. Someone didn't like her. I wasn't too much into details.

I just did my job. I shot her in her hotel room from the rooftop of the Hotel Regina.

I was a mix of nervous and excited. I felt a connection with the sniper rifles in Spark's bunker. I felt them calling to me. I wanted so badly to use one. It was like a kid's first day at Disneyland. I chose my position on the cold stone roof with Spark watching over my shoulder. All that mattered was my hand on the trigger and the woman in my scope.

I could feel my heart thud in my chest. It was as if time slowed down. Everything came down to this. Was I as cold-hearted as I thought I was? Would I be able to follow through? In all my preparations, I never gave a second thought to the fact I might choke when the moment came, but my beating heart now threw me the possibility.

I wasn't all that inhuman. I had remorse, at least I think I did. I would never kill an animal. *Most serial killers tortured small animals during childhood, right?* I wasn't a total monster.

Emilia D'Aubigne looked beautiful through my sniper scope. She was a woman who cared deeply about how she looked. She was ever so graceful, wearing only a silk robe. Her hair was still done up to perfection from that night's festivities.

I could feel Spark's eyes boring through the back of my head... or perhaps it was his rifle scope ready to take Emilia out if I missed. My hands weren't shaking, but my pounding heart rate felt like it was jolting my arms, making the barrel jump.

I used a Remington M24 Bolt Action Rifle, firing the .300 Winchester Magnum Round... nothing fancy. It got the job done, and Spark didn't even have to say a word. One shot and Emilia wasn't beautiful anymore. I could almost feel the bullet piercing her as she jolted back and blood sprayed out of her head, painting the wall behind her. She disappeared from the window.

The patterns her blood splashes made gave me mixed feelings. They held their own beauty, like a work of art. The splatters triggered a sliver of remorse, yet I reminded myself that everyone dies. There was a calm that followed, quieting my mind.

Spark said that was the trademark of a killer. It was as if my path was finally set in stone. This was it. I'd always be a killer.

My skills came easier while the marks seemed to get harder. I often argued with Spark over who got the kill shot.

"You're like a druggie," he said, rolling his eyes, "just waiting for that next fix."

I realized he was right. I was a nervous creature until I had a mark. The rush of my very own kill pushed me forward and kept me centered.

Time went on. Spark yelled at me less. There was a hit every two weeks or so and everything else was downtime. My bank account was under my alias, and it was starting to look fantastic. I earned my own wealth and wouldn't need my succubus of a grandmother to threaten me with disownment ever again..

Spark quizzed me on my attention to detail. He challenged my approach to hits and he taught me a great deal about soft spots—where people died the least painfully. I didn't tell him I wasn't all that concerned with a mark's comfort. Sometimes I got the feeling I made him uncomfortable with my lack of sympathy. That was one thing Spark always had over me—he cared a little bit.

Our business relationship was an odd one. We had to trust each other even though we didn't get along.

We fought... a lot. He called me stupid and I called him a shithead. His lack of patience would get on my nerves, and I wondered what sadistic bastard actually made him a trainer. That old married couple shit was classic. It was like I had to put up with this ass-clown, and I didn't even get the tension release of sex.

Not that I thought about screwing him... very often. It crossed my mind a few times because I was only human (for the most part), and my only sexual experience to date was with a vibrator my own mother had bought me for my sixteenth birthday.

Faults aside, I liked watching Spark work. He was interesting to say the least. His favorite method of killing was something called the Set Cocktail.

Set was a drug developed by Osiris. The god of death developed the god of violence. I wasn't sure how deep my company was into the government, but my guess was pretty darn in there. This was some scary shit. It made me question how much influence Osiris had over the world.

One teaspoon was lethal. It stopped a heart in five seconds, caked itself onto the major arteries and calcified, never leaving a trace of suggested foul play.

"Goes down smooth," Spark would say. He always thought he was so damn funny.

Spark would stalk a hit. That was part of the protocol. We had to observe the hit first. We couldn't approach them until we were ready to strike. Then Spark would act like he knew them for a moment, make them feel at ease, then make his move.

Depending on the specified time of execution (which varied, but was specific in our orders), he would inject the five cubic centimeters of Set into the person's neck. Spark made me do it from time to time, but usually as the person slept, because I was still working on my "social prowess," as he called it.

"Unfortunately, killing is one of those things that gets easier the more you do it," he'd say. "That's from Metal Gear Solid."

As the year stretched on, Spark and I talked a lot more and started fighting less. He was pretty deep. He loved philosophy and psychology. He knew how fucked up he was, yet he laughed about it—usually while cleaning his array of guns. He told me how he used to be considerate of human life and had never touched a weapon... then his little sister was brutally raped and murdered by his step-father. The demon moved in after that. In return, Spark cut off the guy's genitals, hung him upside down and bled him out slowly. He was sixteen at the time. He told me the story as if he had trouble remembering the details. I didn't blame him.

He joined Osiris then, the youngest recruit ever. He had been in the business for nine years and had only needed a few months of shadowing, outdoing me in the prodigy department by a long shot. He never talked about it boastfully. He seemed sad he had been damaged so young.

He didn't have any family anymore. He didn't elaborate, but I noticed he never mentioned a father and that he aimed his anger at his mother.

"Realistically, my sister's death was her fault," he told me. "She was so desperate for companionship she invited a monster into our home. She always made bad choices."

He never said more than that. He was pained, but he used his occupation to distract him. It was refreshing to know that he was like me—damaged. Damaged people make the best killers. Hell, they make the only killers. You have to be fucked up in the head to take another person's life. It's a cardinal sin. Sure, I'd never be president of the PTA, but I'd kill the president of Exxon without batting an eyelash.

"What about your family?"

I blinked in surprise at his question. We were sitting on his back porch, listening to jazz and drinking, which had become a favorite downtime. Southern California was beginning to spoil me. I had allowed myself to relax into my environment, taking in the cool ocean breezes and soft music. Leave it to Spark to snap me back into tense mode.

"What about them?" I frowned.

"Well, they must have fucked you up somehow to get you here," he chuckled.

Funny. I never viewed them as any sort of reason I was in this line of work until that moment.

"Well, there was certainly no raping of sisters." I took a drink from my glass. "I just don't like them. My grandmother and aunt can't stand me. My mom is a self-loathing alcoholic. I don't fit in."

"Let me get this straight, your grandma's a bitch, and your mom is an alcoholic, and you're mad you don't fit in?" He didn't seem impressed. "You never snapped and beat your aunt with furniture or something?

"It was more than not fitting in," I responded, trying to keep my voice steady. "My mother cheated on my father. Turns out I wasn't even his. I was some other guy's kid—someone I'll never meet. I was a bastard child and the Fairholms aren't people who sympathize with things like that."

"Lots of people cheat," he pointed out.

I felt anger rise in my throat. This guy didn't know a fucking thing about my family, so it was pissing me off that he was trying to minimize all my issues.

"Yeah, those people aren't the Fairholms. They have a reputation to uphold. Funny thing is, I'm not the biggest embarrassment to the family... Addison is a manic-depressive, Kat's first husband was gay and my uncle killed himself. But since they can't control me or my insight, I'm the villain."

"You're definitely the villainous type." Spark gave a short laugh. "The hidden, evil bastard of the Fairholm Family!"

"Shut up." I rolled my eyes.

"No, really," he said, and sat up straighter. "I've read Judah's files on you. Those people are all idiots. I'm sure there's a bigger explanation for why they are such assholes. You just have to find, you know, the big secret."

I shrugged, despite the rising hurt feelings. "I don't dig around for answers I don't want. I'm not like a single person in the Fairholm family. I can only assume I'm like my father and I'll never know him."

Spark gave me a strange look, but said nothing.

"But all is good," I continued quickly. "I got picked up by this company. They saved me. I had been moments away from murdering someone when I got that ridiculous letter."

"Yeah..." He suddenly seemed distracted. "Osiris has a good profile list for efficient killers. I'm glad they picked you up."

I looked over at him and our eyes locked.

"Osiris just seems like a place for lost children," I said, and suddenly felt sad, though I wasn't quite sure why. "No one wanted me around, so I had to leave home and join a company of killers to feel wanted."

"That's not true," he said quickly. "Your mother loves you. And it sounds like your cousins do, too. People care about you, Frankie."

"Sometimes I'm not so sure. I mean I've been gone for years. I wasn't there for Katharine's divorce. I wasn't there to help my mom through her depression. I wasn't there—"

"Who cares? None of those things were your responsibility." His tone was hard.

"You know you're the only person that I've ever really talked to? How sad is that? I can't even talk to my own family about my inner demons."

"Well they'd probably keep you chained in the basement." He winked. "Frankenstein."

"God, I hate you," I said.

"I hate you back." He smiled.

Elegantly Wasted

Chapter Nine

During my last week shadowing Spark, my perception of him permanently changed. We were on a job in Prague. It had gone a little sour due to the fact that we were balancing on a high ledge of a rooftop and it had rained earlier that day. I had the target in my scope, when whimsical me lost my footing and botched the shot.

"Completely worthless," Spark swore. Luckily the target was stupid and he came to the window to investigate. Spark took the shot easily.

"Oh, go fuck yourself," I snapped. "I slipped on this wet ass roof! It's been drizzling for days, for fuck's sake! Why are we even out here, Han Solo? Why didn't we Set his ass?"

"I should deny your last evaluation and have you shipped to another trainer for a few months. You'll get killed on your own," he lifted the sniper strap over his head to secure the gun to his body and did his best to storm off the roof in a manly fashion. Never mind I had almost fallen nine stories to my death, and never mind the hit was still dead.

Later that night, I was letting my angry tears fall as I took a shower. At least that way they mixed in with the water. I didn't cry a lot, but when I did it was purely selfish.

I was angry and I felt foolish. Maybe Spark was right, I wasn't good at this. I had lost count of how many times he had angrily called me idiot, worthless or dumb shit in the past two years, but that night hurt. Maybe it was because I should have known better. Maybe it was because prior to that night's hit, I'd really thought I was ready. I didn't want to disappoint this company… or Spark.

I hated disappointment in any form. It crept up and reminded me of how I couldn't escape being someone's big letdown. Here I was at the end of a few years' worth of training and I would probably get killed at the starting gate. I thought I was so slick.

Judah had told me that a real killer never gets cocky —that they don't have much emotion at all. Tonight, that wasn't me.

I stopped crying and exited the shower, walking out of the lavish hotel bathroom. The spectacular view of the city skyline was all the light I needed. I caught a glimpse of my naked body in the large mirror near the bed. I wasn't half bad, really. My wet hair draped down my back and stuck to my arms. My boobs (or tits, as my mom called them) were a little too big for my body, *oh woe is me*. I was about to reach for my robe, when movement caught the corner of my eye.

My newly-tuned reflexes allowed me to react quickly and grab the handgun on the dresser, pointing it in the direction of my would-be attacker. I'm sure my short, naked frame looked anything but elegant in that moment.

Spark got up from the chair in the corner and stepped into the dim light. My heart was beating fast, and I narrowed my eyes at him.

"You really are an asshole. Aren't you done with surprise attacks? Or are you trying to teach me one last lesson?"

He didn't say anything, but he approached me quickly, never breaking eye contact. He had done this to me before to keep me on my toes, attacking me in the dark, but it was usually when I entered a hotel room, never when I was naked after a shower. I half expected him to start trying to beat the shit out of me like his usual lessons. I contemplated shooting him, but he was too quick for me.

He grabbed the gun from my hand and aimed it at me for a brief second before tossing it out of the way. In one swift movement he had backed me up to the wall. He grabbed my head.

He kissed me, hard, as if he were punishing me. My damp hair became tangled in his hands and my head began to spin. This was the first time I had been kissed, and I mean really kissed—not just me sitting behind the high school with the burnouts trying to see exactly how human I could act.

I was not expecting Spark to kiss me with such intensity, yet it was exactly what I yearned for since my first glimpse of his bright blue eyes.

He released one hand and began to search the rest of my body, snapping me back to reality.

It had to be some kind of test. Everything was a test. Perhaps some extension of weird rule number ten. If it was, it felt great.

My mind couldn't be silenced. This was a business of smoke and mirrors... we were manipulative, dangerous liars... and we got paid to not give a shit. I needed to pass this test. I needed to gain back control, but how?

Spark lowered me to the bed, just close enough to the nightstand where I had carelessly discarded my wet shirt and belt with utility knife attached.

He shed his shirt and pants quickly. He was muscular, but had a slight belly he attributed to Snickers and beer. He towered over my petite frame. I could feel his excitement pressing through his boxer briefs.

It was then I tried arguing with myself. It wasn't a test, he just wanted me after months of sexual tension. I deserved this moment. I deserved to feel wanted.

His lips moved to my neck and I turned my head to the belt. He kept moving down toward my breast. Using the distraction, I reached over, snatched the belt and pulled it hard. The buckle struck Spark on the side of the head, making him lift up enough so I could get a foot up to his chest and kick him backward, off the bed, to the floor.

He let out a weak murmur as I flung the belt back, grabbing the knife.

In a flash, I was on top of him, pressing the blade to his throat. I leaned in close, breathing hard.

Spark regarded the knife, then fixed his gaze on me. "My safe phrase is pickles and ice cream."

I blinked, willing the ridiculous situation to make some sense.

"Get fucked," I spat.

"I'm trying," came the dry reply.

I leaned into him, letting the blade cut him a little. He swallowed.

"Frankie." His tone softened.

Spark slowly reached a hand up to caress my face. The gesture was so welcoming that it overwhelmed me. I closed my eyes and dropped the knife.

Spark lifted himself up and pulled me to his bare chest. It felt safe. I opened my eyes, finding myself gazing into his. I kissed him.

He had me back on the bed in an instant. In another quick movement, he was naked and kissing me all over. When he finally thrust himself inside me, I let out a weak cry of surprise and pain. He pulled his face back slightly to look at me so he could watch my reactions. His face twisted into a playful smirk as he continued.

I was a virgin. I don't think that topic came up in any of our conversations, and I didn't think it wise to bring up in the heat of the moment.

Whatever pain I felt subsided and was replaced with increasing pleasure. Spark seemed to know what he was doing as he made my body shudder. Had I known he could make me feel like this I would have fucked him my second week in. I couldn't help but voice my pleasure in whines and moans. It lasted for a while. Orgasm, orgasm, orgasm... I felt as though I had just won the test even if there wasn't a test. It was still unclear.

I never gave much thought about how my first time would go, but what played out had to be better than average. It seemed like he really wanted to connect, but something was still off as my brain toyed with my emotions.

We passed out after an hour or so.

When I woke up Spark and his dumb red shoe-laced Vans were gone. There was a note in his place.

It said:

Goodbye, Francesca.

You've officially graduated. You'll be a great Striker. Don't forget it. You're never alone.

Love,

Spark.

P.S. Sorry I snagged your virginity.

Wow, I thought. As thrilling as the evening was, Spark Dawson ended up being a tad too cliché. I crumpled up the note and tossed it in the trash.

At least this time, I wasn't the disappointment.

Elegantly Wasted

Chapter Ten

Katharine was drunk at the funeral. She had downed three bottles of chardonnay the night before, and I was willing to bet she polished off a couple of glasses before getting in the car that morning. She had no intention of showing up to the services sober. Katharine became an aspiring alcoholic four years ago when she caught her husband cheating with another man.

Katharine Fairholm had been born with an innate ability to turn heads. Kat was a true beauty. Addi and I looked a bit plain next to her—Kat had definitely emerged victorious in the battle of the gene pool. She always had her incredible body and people skills to live on, and her good looks and materialistic, but cute, personality had only failed her once in her life.

She had been raised to marry rich and highly influential. Her life had been set in stone the moment she was born.

We were all blessed with parents who were absolutely certain they knew what was best for us, but Kat's parents were the worst. They had her husband picked out even before she could form full sentences. Katharine got married when she was twenty. I was in high school at the time and was privileged enough to experience the full blown bridezilla she became.

She married Charles McCormick while I stood by in an uncomfortably tight bridesmaid's dress. I didn't think much of any of it. On top of being a teenager who already didn't give a fuck, I didn't give a fuck. Kat treated her marriage like everything else in her life— like a material possession. Everyone knows those are the kinds that don't last.

Kat's world came crashing down in a relatively poetic fashion when I was in Italy. She had come home early one rainy summer day. Apparently there was only so much of the Mediterranean she could take with her snotty, self-indulgent girlfriends. She had come home to find her wonderful husband in bed with his best friend, Josh. He was the bottom, too.

Years of college, love, trust, and a pricey Vivienne Westwood wedding dress, all deemed useless in that moment of realization.

Embarrassment was the worst for a Fairholm—and Joan went as far as to act like it was Kat's fault her husband turned out gay.

"You must have made him that way," she told her. "You must have done something to him."

My grandmother was amazing. Even more amazing was the fact that at her funeral, the priest was downright lying about her.

"Joan was loved by all of those around her, especially her four wonderful daughters and their children."

The silicon extruding from Katharine's chest didn't so much as budge as she let loose a low, inebriated chuckle.

I had to scrunch my face to keep from joining her, and I noticed a few heads begin to turn and cast critical looks our way.

I finally elbowed her in the ribs, which caused her to snort in shock and made the priest pause and look at us. I did a quick glance to my right and noticed that Addi had a smirk on her face as well.

Oh, for Christ's sake. I held my breath and bowed my head, trying not to laugh myself.

Kat only smiled to the priest and waved him to continue. She then shifted her weight, making her enormous, black, Jackie O bereavement hat knock into the side of my head.

I threw her an irritated look that was returned with her trademark jackal of a smile, which consisted of a million unnaturally white teeth that made even the best TV personalities rear in jealousy. She picked an invisible piece of lint from her wrinkle-free Versace pants.

On top of the alcoholism, Kat had OCD that materialized after her divorce. She should have been the serial killer of the family, but she had never hurt a fly—she'd just argue one to death. I had an argument with her that morning about her bed—the bed that I took extra pains to make for her since she woke up naked and confused in her closet.

Her bed was riddled with pillows, and each color was coordinated by density. Who the fuck does that? I hadn't put them on right. I just put the fucking cases on whatever pillow I grabbed—huge mistake.

"I don't want to struggle with which pillow is soft, medium, or hard. I want to have the same color pillowcase on the same density of pillows," Kat said, using her hands for emphasis, and I could tell the alcohol was wearing off.

"So I can organize them accordingly. I can reach for a color and know which pillow it is. I can fully justify why it's okay. I'm not nuts, you are nuts for not thinking like me."

"Yeah see, that's why you're crazy—because you're trying too hard to justify it." I rolled my eyes.

"Yellow is hard, crème is medium, and brown is soft." She shrugged, glancing into a mirror for the first time and wiping some smudged lipstick from her face. "Why is that difficult?"

"And I'm the one with the personality disorder," I muttered. I felt bad for Kat. She didn't like what I did at all. It made her extremely uncomfortable, and she most likely drank more because of our situation.

By all accounts Katharine is crazier than I am, trying so hard to deal with simply being herself.

Turning back to the priest as he unknowingly spewed a slew of lies, I couldn't help but think of the days before my cousins were involved with Osiris. Before Kat was on the verge of a nervous breakdown. When things were, ironically, easier. The first step was getting back home.

By the time Spark left me high and wet in Prague, Kat had risen above the vacuous persona her mother had instilled in her and started a finishing school for all ages.

Elegance, Inc. was a grammar and etiquette school that was mainly for foreign dignitaries' children. It also focused on teaching any run-of-the-mill housewife how to have manners.

Realistically, she was trying to prove that she was more than just an amazing boob job and dazzling smile. Kat was a major salesman. She could sweet-talk a Mormon into giving Scientology a try. She put it all to use and started what became one of the most successful businesses in Phoenix. She bought her own house on the outskirts of Scottsdale and a very large great dane she named Bodhi who slobbered and farted and knocked you over if you weren't paying attention.

I didn't know quite what to do once I was solo. I got a call from Judah when I got back to the states and found Spark's Long Beach pad empty except for my stuff. I felt like I had been dumped. It was so silly of me.

"Stop being ridiculous." Judah could tell I was upset. I was trying not to sound overly depressed, but he picked up on it anyway.

"It's just another lesson," he went on. "You don't fucking get attached. You better wise up little girl, or you're not going to last."

Surrounded by douche bags.

"I know." I tried to sound confident. "I'm good at this, Judah. I can do it."

"That's what I want to hear," he responded. "Now get your shit and go back home."

I blinked. "What?"

"Your cousin," he paused. "Katharine. She owns a business off Thunderbird Road in Scottsdale, yes?"

I didn't like where this was going.

"Yes."

"The boss would like you to move back to Phoenix and live as low key as possible," Judah said. "We think your best option is to move in with Katharine and work for her."

"Work for her?" I stuttered. "What do you want me to do? Fetch her coffee? Send her faxes? Wax her unusually thick eyebrows? You realize I joined a society of contract killers to get away from my family, right?"

Talk about a slap in the face—invited to experience the impossible and get dumped right back where you started.

"Look, the company is going through some changes and we have a few higher profile cases that will be easier to handle if we have an agent in Phoenix. Just do it until we can iron out the kinks. You need to appear like you live a normal life."

"So then let me work a desk job in Ohio," I retorted.

"This isn't up for negotiation," Judah said.

My entire body burned with embarrassment and anger. "This is bullshit. I don't deserve to be thrown right back to the lions. I'm better than that."

"Regardless," Judah said, keeping his voice calm. "You will be inconspicuous and easy to keep track of. This is what's been asked of you. Follow your orders. I expect you to be back there, situated, and ready for assignment in a week."

That was it. I sat, dumbfounded, on the back porch of Spark's now-vacant house. A white unmarked van had come by an hour prior and taken all of my luggage and guns—to be delivered to Kat's upon my return— assuming she'd even speak to me.

I tapped my foot erratically on the steps.

I should have run screaming the other way. I thought I deserved more than what was just proposed, but as long as they felt I was a capable killer, I didn't care. I eventually got myself off the porch and went to the airport.

It was well after eleven pm when I stood at my boarding gate at the Long Beach Airport with my one duffle bag. The ticket in my hand would get me back to Phoenix.

I called Katharine, hoping that maybe she wouldn't pick up.

"Hello?"

"Hey," I said, not sure what to say next.

"Frankie?" She was surprised. I heard her drink from what I assumed was wine. "What's wrong?"

"I'm boarding a plane to Phoenix," I said. "I'll be in around one. Terminal Three. Do you mind picking me up? I'm sorry for the short notice."

"Of course," Kat said without hesitating. "Are you okay?"

I heard a clang of glass being set on the counter. Definitely wine.

"Yeah," I said. "I just... I had a bad break up with my boyfriend, and I need to get out of this town. I figured maybe I could stay with you for a while and figure some stuff out."

"Oh?" Kat's voice rose. "A while? Wow, I wasn't expecting this, you know, at all, but you're welcome to stay here as long as you need... as long as you have a job."

There was the Kat I knew—little verbal jabs interlaced with kindness. She learned it from her mother.

"I have a weekend travel job, and I can pay you rent," I said. "Maybe if you have any openings at your school..."

Kat was silent for a moment. I could hear her soft intakes of breath probably weighed down a tad with a bottle of wine she was in the process of polishing off.

"Oh..." she started. "I don't... I mean, Greta won't like that. Well, maybe it's fine. I actually am suddenly down a teacher for the semester."

I snorted. "Overkill. I was thinking janitor."

"No, really," Kat huffed. "I have a lot going on right now and it's getting worse. I'm planning a massive benefit in a few months with Greta for the Ellingsons. Richard and Tricia, you remember them?"

"No," I lied. They were Greta's people. Elitist white privilege assholes who threw their money around and wanted the less fortunate to see. I could care less what Kat was doing for them.

"Anyway, she's one of my investors so I kind of have to do what she says."

"That sounds awful," I snorted.

"So," she ignored me, "of course my assistant up and quit a week ago—no notice. I'm training a new one, but it's taking up all my time. Then the best private English tutor in Britain *canceled* on me last minute with no explanation! She said something came up. I feel like everything is going wrong. Take the teaching job until after the benefit and I can breathe a little."

"Kat..." I knew this was a bad idea.

"Just let me handle this," she said, ignoring me again. "You want a favor, so I'm asking for one in return. I'll see you soon!"

Kat ended the call.

I looked at my phone and almost immediately received a text from an unknown number.

Take the job, it read.

I rolled my eyes and prepared to board the plane.

When Kat's black Escalade pulled up to the curb at Sky Harbor, I threw my carry-on bag into the back and climbed in.

We rode in silence for a few minutes before she cleared her throat.

"Nice to see you," she said. "It's been awhile."

"I know." I didn't make eye contact. "I'm sorry. Guess I needed a break from everything."

"Kind of a long break," she said. "We thought you were gone for good like the twins. Does your mom know you're in town?"

"I'll call her soon," I said. "I just want to sleep. I should be getting some boxes from a moving company tomorrow. I won't take up much space."

"Whatever you need," she said. "I'm just glad you're back."

The warm welcome wasn't expected, but I'd take it. Katharine wasn't opposed to me being her new roommate. The house was large, and my room was on the opposite side of the house from hers. Kat was too self-involved to be nosy, so I felt fine about keeping a locked case of guns under my bed—just my personal favorites. I kept my entire backup, and my secret identity, in a storage locker close to Elegance, Inc.

Katharine also put me to work right away, since I technically had a degree and was raised by etiquette Nazis.

She gave me a simple regimen of teaching three days a week, two classes a day. My students were all adults and mostly foreign dignitaries or some sort of royalty aside from a peppy, southern red head named Emma who was a talkative heir to an oil gazillionaire.

Kat introduced me to other staff members, but I didn't bother learning their names. Except I somewhat liked her new assistant, Gretchen, who was either a nun or a dominatrix and I couldn't figure out which.

Greta was indeed not amused with my return, although I wasn't around to see her face when Kat told her. Kat seemed a little worried because Greta's money helped keep Elegance, Inc. going, and with a flick of her check-writing wrist, it could be all gone. Kat said she appeased our jerk aunt with the assurance that my new job wouldn't be a long-term position. I was more than fine with it, knowing I was the last person in the solar system who should be teaching other people manners.

I told Katharine that I had a freelance photography gig that would keep me occupied on weekends, but as long as I showed up to the grammar classes I had to teach and paid her rent, she didn't care. Careless Katharine just wanted some company. She was awfully lonely in her large house. Bodhi wasn't the best conversationalist, but he certainly knew all of my secrets once I moved in. He was the only one I could talk to. His judicious eyes seemed to know that I was up to no good.

Katharine had rules, rules which had to be followed. First was my work uniform: Prada black scoop-neck dress with a red belt. My shoes could be any brand as long as they were high heels. Katharine bought me five of the same dress, because if I showed up in anything but what was specified, she'd have a heart attack. This was just the surface of how controlling Kat could be. It was a trait I liked to fuck with as often as possible.

Sometimes I would wear my black and white Converse to work just to see how long it would be before Katharine noticed and started having a sneezing fit because she was allergic to anything tacky.

She even adopted a sort of "Lumbergh from Office Space" voice when she addressed my work faults.

"Yeah, I'm going to need you to change your shoes. You know we don't wear tennis shoes here."

"These are Converse," I argued. "They're special edition."

"There are some Kate Spades in my office. Wear those."

That was my life—grammar Nazi by day, freelance contract killer by night. My texts came twice a month, sometimes back-to-back, which was a real pain in the ass. I had an expense account for travel.

Francesca Fairholm was now ready for her first contract.

Elegantly Wasted

Chapter Eleven

I wasn't settled for five minutes before the first hit was texted to me.

I smiled at the phone.

I stood there staring at the link. It meant something special—my very first solo kill. A rush settled in.

This one was mine.

No extremely annoying—yet sexy—trainer's eye boring into the back of my skull waiting for me to fail.

This was just me and my instructions.

These instructions were emailed a few hours later, and to my surprise I was to use Set... in public, something Spark had loved to do.

"Where are you off to?" Katharine asked when I set my camera bag and suitcase down in the foyer.

I walked into the kitchen and grabbed a Diet Coke for the road.

"New York," I responded. "I'm shooting a few restaurants and owners for a travel magazine."

She scrunched her face up. "New York by yourself? Sounds dangerous."

"I'm not twelve. I think I can handle it," I chuckled. "Besides, a producer always meets me on site."

Maybe I should start telling her more low-key destinations like Bastrop, Texas.

"Remember the Ellingson benefit is in two weeks and we need to do a walkthrough of the—"

"I'll be back Sunday," I said as I picked up my bags. "Plenty of time to help you or bounce Greta away."

I wanted to add that I couldn't forget the Ellingson benefit because Kat wouldn't shut the hell up about it. They were invested in Elegance, Inc. Greta was, too. I understood this was all Kat had at the moment and kissing ass was just a drawback to achieving a dream.

"Be careful," she called after me. "I love you."

This was a new development in our relationship. Kat had started saying this to me the moment I moved in, and my first few responses were awkward and low.

Our family had never been big on hugs, kisses and I love you.

I decided that when I said it I sounded even more like a creepy serial killer, so I found it more soothing to respond in a different language.

"Je t'aime," I called back.

By the time I boarded the plane I was overly calm. Alice Stewart was always calm.

I sat next to a nun—fucking figures. She was cute, old and loved her some God. Oh, the things I could tell her…

My mark was a guy named Omar Roads, a shady corporate head. I loved titles like that. It opened up my imagination as to what exactly they headed.

This guy had his hands in a lot of cookie jars. He was married to his fourth wife and working on his sixth kid. He also had an underage gay lover named Manny on the side.

I think the main reason I was killing him was money laundering, but he was a huge douche lord so I didn't look much further than "pedophile."

I checked into my hotel and opened my travel itinerary. Inside, there was a ticket to a huge benefit at the Met the next night. I took out my medicine kit with three vials of the Osiris trademark poison, Set, marked as insulin.

Set was lethal at even a small dose. This worked out great for me, since I had fashioned one of the Set cartridges into a charm for my Tiffany charm bracelet.

Spark taught me one brassy move—just walk up to a mark like you knew them, and as they are thrown off, you hug them and stick them in the back of the neck with the tiny syringe. This smaller dose took longer to take effect, and I could slip far away, back into a crowd, before the mark even went into cardiac arrest.

"Poor bastards don't even know what hits them," Spark had said. "Just move on like you see someone else you know and wait for someone to yell for a doctor."

I liked Set for its convenience. I hated it for its close contact range. Again, I was born to be a sniper. It kept me far away from people. It was hard for me to socialize—it was a total act, hiding behind my alias, wearing fancy dresses and gobs of makeup. Wigs were an option too, but I looked ridiculous in anything but dark hair. I was uncomfortable... but learning quickly how to fake a smile, a laugh, even an entire persona.

I spent Saturday walking around Manhattan. I enjoyed the hours leading up to a hit.

I took the time out to take photos of my destination city. I was becoming a pretty good photographer, and I liked looking at the world through a lens—another great hiding place.

Plus a photographer's lingo was similar to a contract killer's.

I brushed by the Met—had to at least see the place I would be doing my first job. I didn't linger long. I tried not to stay in one place for very long when I was on assignment. I could take my time that night.

I stopped by a few restaurants and snapped some photos, mingled a little with some pretentious chefs—some of my photography had to look legit in case Kat asked to see. It was an extra precaution on my part, because I didn't know how nosy Kat was yet. Addi was the nosy one and thankfully not around a lot. Either way there was an ulterior motive to my photography. It went in hand with rule number two: cover your tracks.

By the time evening rolled around, I was ready to mingle with the elites. My dark makeup and hair were done, my black Versace dress was fitting just right and I slipped on my favorite pair of Jimmy Choo's.

I aged a few years when I played dress up.

Once I was ready, I gave Kat a quick call to inform her I wasn't raped and beaten to death in an alley.

I gave myself a once over and then made my way to the Met, with the deadly poison secured safely in my charm bracelet—so small, so deadly, so me.

This was New York's wealthy; not rich, but wealthy —huge difference.

I knew most of the faces just from training. That's how important these people were. All of them in some way hoped and prayed I didn't show up on their doorstep looking for them. I was a shark in a pool of golden seals.

This was where the power trip kicked in, allowing me to do my job with confidence. Because no matter how much wealth and power these assholes had, Osiris agents could take it away. There were two people at work in my head: Alice and Francesca. Osiris trained me to embrace an alias like it was another person. I wasn't some split personality, but I was crazy enough to put on such an act that I changed myself completely and embraced the lie that was my alias.

I had conflicting thoughts as a side effect. I wasn't paranoid or unsure of myself, but there was also the thought that I was about to take someone's life for money.

My surroundings helped to ease the conflict I felt.

The New York Metropolitan Museum of Art was— as of that moment—a favorite place of mine. People mingled through the vast main area and into the Egyptian wing.

The benefit was set up around the Temple of Isis and a large banner depicting Set.

What a cruel irony.

It took me a bit to locate Omar. When in doubt—try the open bars. Sure enough there he was, drowning himself in brandy.

I took a moment to retrieve the vial of Set and popped the syringe out. Set was now safely in my hand.

I smiled to the CEO of Aetna, Inc. and quickly walked up to Omar after I snagged a glass of champagne from a waiter.

"Omar Roads! How amazing it is to see you here tonight!"

I had to work fast, because obviously my amazing personality would have no effect on him—he preferred boys.

He glanced up, surprised.

Always act a little tipsy—hence the champagne. People always sympathized with the slightly drunk, no matter what.

I wrapped my arm around him, injected him with the poison and pulled back out of the hug. One smooth motion and he was a dead man walking.

He flinched and reached for his neck.

"Oh, silly me," I drawled. "I caught my bracelet on your neck hair. I am so sorry!" I shook the charms obnoxiously at him.

"Quite alright..." He was still trying to figure out who I was.

"You tell Lisa I said, 'hello.'" I poked him and took a swig of champagne. "I hope her pregnancy is going well."

He tried to answer, but I turned around quickly and waved across the room—pretending to see someone else.

A smile crept onto my face as I made my way back to the museum entrance. I would lose my line of sight —Omar was in another room, but all I had to do was listen...

Five minutes passed as I sipped on my champagne. Five minutes before some Wall Street tycoon yelled for someone to call an ambulance, is there a doctor in the house, and did anyone by chance know CPR?

"I can't believe they pay me for this shit," I muttered under my breath. *Too easy. Take that, Spark Dawson.*

I stood there for a while, watching the chaos unfold. I listened to the whispers and watched the EMS crew show up and try to revive Omar.

Good luck with that.

Finally they wheeled him off to the hospital. He was dead before they arrived, but protocol is protocol I suppose. I pursed my lips together and tried to seem concerned, but I felt out of place, so I made my way out of the benefit.

I flew back home the next morning.

First job completed. Just like that.

Not too shabby. This was cake.

My hubris started to get ahead of me, because the next few jobs went well, too. I suppose anyone can get that annoying sophomoric attitude when they think they've finally found the perfect talent. I was young and cocky. I could do anything.

Then I screwed up.

Elegantly Wasted

Chapter Twelve

Addison Fairholm was born to be a doctor. Luckily she was good at it, because her mother, Bette wouldn't have stood for anything else. It was a smart choice really, because the moment she was capable, she applied for Doctors without Borders and made her escape.

Avoid the family—be a trauma surgeon in Southern Sudan or Burundi. Addi could spend her life helping other people and not once bat an eye toward any of us. Addi was ten years older than I and five years older than Katharine. She was closed off and rigid when she was younger, and it didn't get much better under the training of her astringent mother.

Although Addi and I both had the same insistent need to cut ourselves off from most of the family, Addi did it with unrelenting persistence and spectacularly negative undertones.

What was peculiar about Addi was that she was like two people. She did anything for those people in Africa. She braved HIV, Ebola, war and famine to help them. She spoke vehemently on their behalf and dedicated her life to causes like the Smile Train... but if Joan wanted her at a family function, she'd gladly tell the woman to go fuck herself.

The other person wanted nothing more than her mother's acceptance—and although she was a world traveler, Bette's extensive reach still controlled her. Bette often backed her financially. While Addi had her own money, she didn't know how to manage it, so Bette did that as well. While Bette often got angry with her daughter, she still held tightly to a string of love that kept them together. Luckily, Bette disliked Joan and stopped caring about being in her will long ago. That was the only reason Addi got to act the way she did. The rest of us had to "respect" Joan.

She did her best to give off a rebel vibe. She was an extreme liberal—the opposite of Joan and Greta. Joan called her an undermining pacifist.

Addi was very outspoken when it came to her rights and her beliefs... all of which had no religious base whatsoever. All of us had been forced to attend Catholic school all the way through to college. In tenth grade, Addi had gotten herself expelled for reasons unknown to me. People whispered that it had something to do with sex in the auditorium. That was Addi's style. She loathed organized religion, stating that it produced the world's largest concentration of "shitbag hypocrites."

It was a better alternative to Joan's way of thinking, which centered on not even befriending anyone who was a different religion, because they're going to hell and you might catch it.

Addi traveled—a lot. I didn't recall a full year when she was consistently at home.

Addi wasn't given the gift of warmth. She was exactly like me in that way. She wanted to be a caring person, but she couldn't quite make the connection when it came to people.

Her two personas were constantly at war with each other.

If it had been anyone else, all of the charity work and helping others would've been fulfilling. It would have been the end-all-be-all of someone's reason for living. Addi just couldn't think about it that way. She hated herself too much. No matter how much she did, in the end she was just trying to win her mother's acceptance... acceptance she'd never get, because that wasn't Bette's style. In Addi's world, Bette was infallible. Bette couldn't find time to care much for anyone but herself and the dead people she was paid to examine, so Addi was a manic-depressive, and for good reason.

She had been home for a week, which was not her style. She claimed she was there for moral support as Kat prepared for the stupid Ellingson Benefit.

I tried ignoring it as best I could, but Kat roped me into helping as well to appease Greta, who indeed was not happy with my return.

Addi owned her own home in central Phoenix, three blocks from her mother, but she usually just crashed at Kat's house when she was in town. The moment she arrived she was eying me with concern. She followed me everywhere, to the point that I thought I might turn and slap her.

"What is your problem?" I asked her.

"What do you mean?" She seemed stumped.

"If I stop short, your head will go up my ass. Back off, will ya?"

She pursed her thin lips. "You've been a ghost for years. I just want to know what you're up to. You didn't even really give me an explanation as to why you moved back here."

Addi was ruining her Fairholm reputation by acting concerned. Katharine didn't care, so why should she?

"Was I supposed to send out a memo? I was tired of California and Kat needed a beginning English teacher because her British nanny quit or whatever."

"You want to teach..."

"Why not? My weekend photography job isn't enough." I tried to keep my back to her while folding my laundry. "Maybe grammar and etiquette are also my calling."

"Where did you run off to over the weekend when I first got here?"

"Sedona," I replied.

It was not Sedona, it was Portland.

"There was a restaurant opening," I lied. "The chef is a friend from high school."

She eyed me critically. "You had friends in high school?"

Holy Christ this is awkward. I felt like she was boring into my brain.

"Don't you have a world to save or something?" I dramatically shook the static out of some pants that were most likely dry-clean only. *Whoops.*

"I'm just wondering what you're up to, is all."

I kill people, I thought. *I don't even really know for whom.*

"Just teaching a little English diction and pursuing a career with a food magazine."

Addi smiled. It didn't fit her. Addi had an unnatural smile. I called it the Hannibal Lecter smile. "That's good, Frankie."

"What? Do you think that I'm hiding bodies in my closet?"

She didn't respond. I didn't like the way she was looking at me. She was thinking about something. Addi was exceptionally smart. She had a minor in psychology, so I always feared that she could see through me. I was afraid that she knew who I really was. Her mother, a forensics specialist, definitely could, so I stayed far away.

Addi sat down at the kitchen table, picked up a newspaper and dropped the conversation.

She looked like her mother, right down to her short fake-blond hair. I wasn't sure Addi was aware of it.

Bette often just looked at you, judged you and labeled you without saying a word. I learned a long time ago to stay the hell out of Bette's way and out of her all-seeing gaze. She worked around dead people for a living, yet still managed to read people with startling accuracy.

Bette could've been categorized as a humorless ice queen. What set her apart from the likes of Greta was that she enjoyed life in her own way. If she thought no one was watching, she would be nice to me and I appreciated it. Bette had life to her... and she struggled like the rest of us. Bette liked to pretend she was different—something that rubbed off on Addi in an extremely negative way.

Joan was never kind to Bette or my mother. She favored Greta and Audrey and didn't care who knew it.

Bette had managed to turn her years of neglect and ridicule into a weapon of mass destruction. Bette tolerated her mother; she didn't stand up to her, but didn't kiss her ass either. Her major flaw was that she loved money over everything else—even Addi. She wouldn't admit it, but she learned all her life tricks from Joan: including how to control people with money.

She tried to bestow these lessons upon Addi, and instead she just got a negative, demeaning, muddled reflection of herself. Addi wasn't nice. She was, at times, unreasonable and vindictive.

My point is, I never thought in a million years that my life would be in her hands. I also never thought I would ruin the ever living fuck out of Kat's benefit.

It started like any other week. I was still getting used to it all. I couldn't tell a soul when the texts came through. I couldn't vent to anyone about my moral dilemmas or my dark side. The jobs came and I was alone—weaving my way through politicians and royal families—making it back to Katharine's by the start of the week. No one suspected a thing. No one knew that I was taking lives.

As a contract killer, you learn that no one is off the table if someone has the money. I didn't think that the circles my family ran in had that kind of money. They were all targets and clients, but for what reason, I would never want to know.

The Benefit was a Friday. Jobs didn't come through until Friday, so I figured I was safe to volunteer and keep Kat off my case. However, the day before the benefit, I got a text message. I looked at the clock: almost midnight. Later than usual and a day early. I wanted to throw the phone. A day early meant I'd have to wake up at dawn, secure a flight to who-knows-where and piss Kat off by leaving—maybe eternally piss off since she was big on follow through.

I hadn't been sleeping well, and every little thing was irritating me. I hoped it wasn't a job that required guns. Traveling with guns was so much more arduous —wait a day for the shippers, who secured your cargo in an unnamed aircraft and delivered it to your hotel room before you needed them to "handle" someone.

I looked at the text which had a link to my hit, styled like a sick invitation.

Tricia Ellingson. Phoenix, Arizona. Hyatt Regency room 523. Window 6:30pm to 6:45pm.

I snapped awake with a start and turned on my bedside lamp. The words faded from the screen, but they were burned well into my memory.

"No," I breathed. "No, no…" I ran a hand through my hair, letting the phone drop to the floor.

I squeezed my fists tight and mouthed 'fuck,' super hard into the room, letting out a very hard realization.

The good news, I didn't have to travel. The bad news was self-explanatory. This was a friend of the family. A shitty, self-absorbed family, but my family nonetheless.

For the first time I immediately wondered why. Why her? Tricia Ellingson was a socialite and an old friend of Greta's. Her husband, Richard, was a politician, the representative for Scottsdale's congressional district. He was running for a senate seat in November. A blaring alarm sounded in my head as I waded through the stored memories of things I hadn't yet blocked as mental trauma.

Politicians. They were the worst. I had to kill them, kill because of them, or kill for them. Which was this? Certainly not the first one.

It didn't matter why. I'd have to do this. There wasn't some number I could call, no Osiris hotline where I could file a grievance. *Hey, Francesca Fairholm here, sorry, but you've scheduled a hit of the wife of someone for whom I'm helping my cousin throw a party. Gonna have to hard pass.*

This was really bad.

My anxiety must have been clear on my face because the next morning Kat knew something was up.

"What on Earth is wrong with you?" She tilted her head as she entered the kitchen with her mousy assistant, Gretchen, trailing behind her, holding mail and a clipboard.

"Nothing, why?" I said, too shrilly.

Gretchen Pierce blinked at me and narrowed her eyes a little. She set down the mail she held and handed me a padded envelope.

"You better not be getting sick." Kat placed a cold hand on my forehead. "You feel warm."

"I'm fine." I sat back, trying to relax my expression.

Kat stared at me a moment before rolling her eyes. "Pick up my dry cleaning before five. We have to be at the Hyatt banquet hall no later than seven."

"What's her job, again?" I gestured to the cute little pixie wearing a red cardigan buttoned all the way up to her neck.

Gretchen pursed her lips. Her vibrant makeup was flawless, and her short, spiky hair was never out of place. She never said much—at least not to me, but I'm pretty sure she muttered obscenities under her breath a lot.

"Gretchen has plenty to do," Kat assured me.

I stared at the envelope with my name and address typed on the front. This was different. These usually just waited for me under my alias at my hotel, because I usually worked in other cities and didn't murder people I knew.

What. The. Actual. Fuck?

Someone definitely wanted to screw with me. This had to be a test. I didn't put it past my enigmatic employer to keep me on my toes.

"Aye, Cap'n." I laughed, a forced, nervous laugh. Both women glanced at each other then back to me with concern.

"I can't have anything go wrong tonight," Kat reiterated for the five-hundredth time that week.

I pursed my lips and nodded. Grasping the envelope, I got up and took my half-eaten bowl of cereal to the sink.

Something would go wrong. Very, very wrong.

Once I was safely back in my room, I opened the padded envelope. Inside was a maintenance keycard and a typed note: *Locker 5*.

This meant I would have to go into maintenance and look for locker five; there would be a uniform so I could blend in, and the weapon of choice for the hit. If targets were in a hotel room with no opposite roof access, there was more or less a scavenger hunt to get all the information. It was tedious, detailed, and kind of stupid, but it was more or less a paint by numbers for a hit. Someone really wanted this one to go a specific way. Let the game begin.

The rest of the afternoon was spent pacing my room thinking about how bold of a flex this hit was becoming. The benefit started at 7:30pm. I'd have to figure out a way to avoid Kat for an hour, take care of Tricia, cover my tracks, get down to the benefit, and act like nothing was wrong. One would think this may seem easy, but they don't know the nagging power of Katharine Fairholm.

Whoever secured the hit also did not know or they hated me.

Dry Cleaning, I remembered. I'd create some drama with the dry cleaning. I'd forget and have to rush to get it. It would buy me time, and Kat would be two glasses in and forget when she saw her walk-in closet full of clothes.

Time to make myself scarce. I dressed in a black lace cocktail dress, pulled my hair back into a bun, put some makeup and emergency hitman gear in a bag, adorned my chucks, and left the house early enough for Kat not to notice.

I picked up the dry cleaning and put it in my trunk. Then I stopped by my mom's house on the way to the Hyatt just to chat. Things like me stopping by made her feel better. Marlene didn't want to go to the benefit, but I knew she'd attend anyway and it would help my story along. I promptly pretended to forget the dry cleaning and rush out.

The next hour was a blur. Anxiety threatened my brain. I hoped the contents of locker five held a syringe and a dose of Set. I wanted this to be quick and painless since I already convinced myself that, for whatever reason, Tricia had to die.

I neared the maintenance area from a back stairwell, and realized the lockers were all off to the left with no one nearby. I quickly slid the key card to unlock the door and let myself in.

Inside the locker were black overalls with a dirty nametag reading "Stevie," a worn baseball cap, plastic gloves, and a black box.

Inside the black box was a M9A3 Berretta and a silencer.

"Goddammit," I swore.

The hope this would be clean and quick faded. Someone wanted her shot to death.

Cool, I guess I'll just avoid a hundred cameras on the way up and hope for the best. My irritation grew by the moment.

I shimmied the coveralls over my dress, donned the hat and gloves, secured the weapon, placed my phone in the breast pocket, and made my way to the service elevator.

Piece of cake.

As I reached to press the 'up' button, my phone buzzed. I retrieved my phone to look at the text.

You have six minutes.

Before I could question the words, I heard the familiar sound of electricity powering down and then the lights went out.

Elegantly Wasted

Chapter Thirteen

Most people panic during a power outage, but I wanted to give myself a hug.

Emergency lights along the floor lit a path to the stairwell. *Six minutes before surveillance is back*, I guessed.

I had to move quick. I was grateful Tricia's room was on the fifth floor of the twenty-four-floor hotel. It was doubtful Judah or anyone at Osiris would be happy with my lack of cardio work as of late.

The time to stop thinking about my actions approached. I made a mental note of what song to sing to myself. It was silly, but having a song in my head helped me focus before a hit. This nervous habit didn't arise until I was solo. Tonight, it was The Killers. I didn't feel remorse, but I did like a little distraction and cruel irony.

As I approached the fifth floor, I reminded myself that the Ellingsons had to be dirty. Even if they weren't, they were the kind of people who treated wait staff like shit.

I walked down the darkened hall to room 523.

This was easy—in, out and done. Just smile, shoot her in the head, and leave.

I've got soul, but I'm not a soldier, Brandon Flowers' voice echoed in my head.

Through the door, I could hear Tricia's voice. It made me pause.

"Is that what you're calling bribery these days, Rich?"

There was no response.

I waited a moment, vaguely aware that my six minutes ticked down quick.

"I'm not afraid of you!" Tricia went on. "If you don't sign those papers, your career is over just like our marriage!"

More silence.

Phone call, I hoped.

I knocked. "Maintenance."

I brought out my weapon, clicked off the safety.

Marriage counselor, I thought to myself, moments before the door opened.

Tricia stood dressed in a pink silk bathrobe. Her reddish blonde hair was styled in an up-do, and her makeup was fresh. She looked confused.

"Yes?" she asked.

There was definite distrust in her voice. Or, maybe I imagined it.

A glimmer of recognition crossed her face as I raised the gun.

I could only take one shot. It better count.

Even with the extra precautions we took to keep ourselves nameless, it was part of the Osiris credo. We were killers with standards—high standards. Judah said one shot was all it took.

I pulled the trigger.

As the muffled shot sounded, Tricia's head snapped back and a spray of blood erupted from the back of her head. Usually, I diverted my attention once I hit a mark, but this time I stood there and watched her body fall. Her eyes remained opened, unblinking. I breathed in hard from my nose, panic rising quick.

I was fairly certain this woman was at my graduation party.

A flash of a memory forced its way to the surface.

Uncle Anthony sitting in his chair with a bullet wound in his head.

I blinked it away, closed the door, and headed back to the stairwell. My breathing grew more and more agitated. I couldn't shake the feeling I had just done something extremely fucked up on the contract killer spectrum.

My phone buzzed again. Kat called at the worst possible time. I ignored it.

I secured my weapon and made my way back downstairs.

Something was off. I didn't know if I saw an odd shadow or it was just my instincts, but I felt the urge to run. I passed the maintenance floor to get to the parking garage. Once I got to the bottom I looked up and saw the flash of a person in a black suit a floor above.

Someone followed me.

My reflexes kicked in the split second before it happened. I pushed the door open.

A shot rang out, echoing down the stairwell, and a sharp stinging bolted up my arm as I fell forward through the door, landing on hard asphalt. Stunned, I reached over to my arm. It was wet with blood. Pain rocked through me. I knew immediately I had been shot.

Mother fucker. I winced.

I got myself up, stumbling to a pillar near the edge of the garage. I wanted to stay there and bleed, but the lights flickered back on. I didn't hesitate and ran the opposite direction into the alleyway, careful to keep my head down. Pain aside, I didn't think about anything but getting out of the area. I hurried down the street to another parking garage, and stopped on the side of the building out of the streetlight's reach. I could feel blood running down my arm, and I knew I had to do something quickly.

I escaped to an alley wall between two sour-smelling trash cans, and I took a deep breath. I tried to look at the damage, but only succeeded in making myself cringe in pain. I hadn't been shot before. Judah said it would happen eventually. It was only a matter of time.

My phone buzzed again. Kat.

Shit. Fuck. Goddamnit.

"What?" I answered.

"Where the hell are you?" Kat's voice shrilled.

"I forgot the dry cleaning," I muttered. Things were getting a little fuzzy.

"Your mom said that an hour ago!" Kat yelled. "Everyone is here! If you don't walk through the doors in five minutes you're fired."

A laugh burst from my mouth, echoing into the alley.

The ridiculousness of the situation, or the blood loss, got to me quick.

"I'll be right there," I slurred.

"Are you drunk?" Kat asked.

I hung up.

Kat and her benefit was officially the least of my worries.

I glanced up at the looming buildings above and took a deep breath. I managed to remove the coveralls from my upper body and examine my arm. I was hoping for a graze but no such luck—a clean shot right through the upper arm. The hole wasn't from anything larger than a 9mm, so it had been pretty close range. Someone had fucking shot me. *Brilliant. Fan-fucking-tastic.*

I wasn't sure what to do. Panicking was out of the question. My mind raced with thoughts. Whoever had shot me was either stupid or meant to just maim me. Both scenarios irritated me. At least it was my left arm, and I was right-handed. *Thanks, fucker.*

I tore some of the ruined sleeve from my dress, wrapped it around my arm, then struggled to tighten it by holding one end with my teeth. I fumbled for my cell phone. I texted a code that signified I needed medical attention. Judah would get it and be angry of course, but it was the least of my worries.

One of the Osiris Stoppers was supposed to call and tell me my safe phrase: "suicide blonde was the color of her hair." I had a thing for INXS. They would then tell me their location, and I'd make my way there. The phrase granted them my full trust while I was under their care.

Time went by. I have no idea how much, but no one returned my call. I knew I needed to get back to my car which was parked five blocks away.

I felt claustrophobic despite the cool, open air around me. The adrenaline was long gone. Now it just hurt like a bitch.

I jumped as my phone buzzed.

This time, it was Addison.

"Hello?" I answered.

There was no sound for a moment, yet I could hear her soft breathing.

"Hello?" I said louder.

"Frankie," Addi's voice cracked.

Fuck, it wasn't a Stopper. I was becoming increasingly irritated.

"Yeah," I answered.

"Where are you?"

"Can—can I call you back?" I asked. My voice sounded raspy in my head.

"Are you okay?" She asked.

My mind started to race. Nausea rose up quick, and my vision blurred. There was no way I could make it five blocks. I was fucked. What was I going to do? I needed a doctor. Addi was a doctor.

"Addi, I need help," I said quickly.

"Tell me where you are!" She didn't hesitate, which I found very odd.

I did my best to tell her where I was. She didn't seem to question it.

"I'll find you," she said and ended the call.

Good. I let out a breath of relief, relief I knew wouldn't last once Kat's benefit was ruined and news broke about Tricia Ellingson. I'm not even sure I didn't bleed in the garage. It didn't much matter now.

A car door slamming shut sounded into the alley followed by the clack of high heels.

For some reason there was a slight smile on my face, but I couldn't look at Addi as she approached.

I focused on her shoes.

"I don't think I'm making it to the benefit," I chuckled.

"Oh, Frankie." Addi's voice was sympathetic. I figured the hallucinations kicked in. Sympathy was something Addi would tell you to find in a medical dictionary, somewhere between anti-psychotic and Xanax.

I tried to speak, but couldn't. Everything finally caught up to me.

I blacked out.

Elegantly Wasted

Chapter Fourteen

I woke from a haze of what I assumed were amazing drugs. Addi didn't fuck around when it came to medicating.

It took me a moment to focus on my own bedroom. It took me another moment to realize I didn't feel all too bad. The clock on my nightstand told me it was only nine in the evening. Kat would fire me for sure.

"What the hell are you thinking?" Addi's high-pitched shriek ruined my buzz and jolted me further out of my haze.

"I feel okay." I turned and looked at her looming frame in the doorway.

"No, I mean what... what are you doing with your life?"

Holy shit here we go. What lies could I make up to pacify the pacifist?

I opened my mouth to speak, but she held up her hand. "No, you don't get to talk yet."

"But you asked me a question," I complained.

"I don't understand how this happened. Why you?" Addi seemed to be talking to herself more than me.

I sat up and swung my legs around. She had put my arm in a sling.

"I'm not dealing drugs if that's what you're afraid of," I chuckled awkwardly. "It was just an accident."

As I looked at my surroundings, I went cold all over again. My gun case was wide open at the foot of my bed... and empty. My eyes darted around the room to see the contents placed around the room.

What. The. Fuck.

I threw Addi a look of sheer disbelief. She crossed her bony arms in front of her.

"I know you're not a drug dealer, Frankie." Addi seemed insulted. "You're much worse, aren't you?"

My mind began to spin. Like a cornered cat, I felt my anger rise. I leapt up quickly—ignoring the pain I felt jolt up my arm.

"What have you done?" my voice cracked.

Addi sensed my anger and panic. Her demeanor changed. She took a step toward me, but I reached out quickly for the .45 she had placed on my dresser. Rule number seven: if someone discovered who I am, I had to kill them. *Shit. Shit. Shit.* I raised my right hand up even to Addi's head. Good thing my right arm worked.

"Wait, Frankie—" she held out her hands. I could see the fear in her face, but her voice was calm.

We stood there a moment not saying anything. My hand was steady. I was about to squeeze the trigger.

"Stupid nosy bitch," I fumed. God, Addi was nosy. She got that shit from her mother—snoop around into everyone's business, so you can have something to hold over their heads. Well now it was going to get hers shot the fuck off.

My mind was strikingly clear—it was like I was programmed to protect myself, even if it meant killing someone close to me. I stepped up to her and put the gun close to her face.

Addi squeezed her eyes shut, covered her head instinctively and a jumble of words quickly came out of her mouth.

I stopped breathing.

"What did you say?"

She kept her eyes shut tight.

"I said 'suicide blond was the color of her hair!' Please don't kill me, Agent twenty-two—I'm just a Stopper. I'm not trained to defend myself!"

There was no way—no way—my own cousin just recited my safe phrase.

"Agent twenty-two..." My eyes narrowed. She knew my ID number.

She opened her eyes, hoping I understood. "Your ID number is twenty-two. Your distress text came through, to my phone. Imagine my surprise when you were at the other end of the number I called."

I kept the gun raised, but my hand started to shake. I felt so utterly exhausted with everything. "So, then you brought me back here and spent all your time cracking the combination on my gun case."

"No," she breathed. "That part was easy. It's your mom's birthday."

"You're an asshole, Addi." I shook my head.

"I had this suspicion when you disappeared for so long," Addi whispered. "But I didn't want to think it was true. I didn't want to think that you were a..."

She couldn't bring herself to say "killer."

"Did you know I was the Striker you had to treat?"

"No," she started. "We only see your ID numbers, and of course all the phone numbers are redirected, so it's not like I saw it was your phone number. You picked up my call and it nearly broke my heart right then. I didn't even want to admit it was your voice on the other end of the phone call."

I looked at her strangely. Addi worked for Osiris. She was one of the medical agents. She was a Stopper.

That meant she didn't kill people, but was involved nonetheless.

"I'm sorry," I said.

Addi let out a laugh. "To be fair, I was glad to get out of that wretched benefit too. Kat is probably having kittens about now."

"Oh, I think this will be the least of her worries soon." I clenched my jaw.

"What?" Addi frowned.

"How long have you been with Osiris?" I asked, wanting to chang the subject.

"Since my attending years," she answered, calming down a little. "Long before you were ever involved. The traveling I've been doing with DWB is more or less a way for me to travel to where agents can use me. Can you put the gun down now?"

I lowered it to my side, but didn't drop it.

Straight-as-nails, cold-as-ice Addison Fairholm worked for an organization of contract killers. That fit.

"You're shitting me," I finally said.

Addi tried to relax her face. "Hey, it's justifiable work. Osiris has a pretty strict client list, and you're backed by the government. The benefits are great, too."

"I don't get it." My mind was still racing.

"What I don't get is why you didn't just go to college," Addi said, her voice back to normal. "Don't think I'm not aware of the entire process and why they pick the people they do."

"I'm not some crazed murderer," I retorted. "I'm a contract killer. There's a difference."

"What's the fucking difference?"

"One's a job and the other is a cerebral defect."

"You think you don't have a problem?" Addi gave a short laugh. "Come on Frankie, you've been weird since you were a kid. They picked you because of your mental condition. You have to be off to do what you do. You hate being around us—you're quiet and reserved, and you don't like to be touched. Yet I'm willing to bet you move around those yachts and parties like nothing, smiling and chatting away until you have your target where you need him."

I looked at the ground.

"Am I right?"

"Yeah, but…"

"But what? Just because these people are corrupt doesn't mean they should be killed. Or at least it doesn't mean you should be the one killing them! You had a paid way to college. You're lucky your mom doesn't know what you do. I don't think being a hired hitman is the right path for you."

"And what is the right path, Addison Fairholm?" I felt myself getting angry again. "Owing Joan my soul? Doing what my mommy wants me to do just so I make her proud? I see how well it's worked out for you— your mother is so important to you that she's made you try to kill yourself!"

Addi's eyes widened, and I immediately regretted saying the words. She didn't know I knew. I had overheard her mother and mine talking shortly after Uncle Anthony's suicide.

Bette had moved her and Addi to New York to be with Bette's third husband, and Addi was miserable. Bette's husband was abusive toward Addi—in what way, I'll probably never know.

At fifteen, Addi tried to kill herself by swallowing whatever types of medication she could find in her mother's medicine cabinet—half for attention that Bette never gave her and half out of depression. Bette refused to believe her husband was in the wrong and blamed the incident on Addi's manic-depression—something she's been on medication for since. Bette shipped her back to Arizona to live with Audrey and Katharine before she divorced the guy a year later for sleeping with an eighteen-year-old.

Regardless, Bette never apologized to Addi. It wasn't in her nature.

Addi's face fell a bit, as if a realization hit her. "You're right. I have a shitty mother who never hugs me and forced me into medicine. If our family is so fucked up that you're now a contract killer for Osiris, then I don't know what else to say."

"Say you understand," I pleaded. "Say you know that we're all fucked up and there's no logic in what any of us do—namely me, who's killing people for a living."

"Frankie," she sighed. "You got shot. Tell me how this is working out well for you."

Movement from the doorway made me stop talking. Katharine was standing behind Addi. Her expression lie somewhere between furious and terrified. She must have come home with a plan to berate me, yet her brain needed to process the new information. I think she was trying to figure out if what she was hearing was true, yet her eyes just kept getting wider with realization as she looked around the gun-strewn room.

Addi turned herself around quickly.

"Kat," we both said in unison.

She looked at us strangely. "What the fuck?"

I reminded myself that the pistol was still in my hand. Addi might've been working for Osiris, but there was no way in hell Kat would've even been allowed to fetch coffee in my world. I'd have to threaten her, and perhaps worse.

"How long were you listening?" Addi asked her.

"I—I—I—" Katharine was stuttering trying to find her words. "What the fuck?"

"Listen," I held a hand up, "I can explain."

"Explain..." Kat took a deep breath.

Katharine did the only logical thing she could at the moment. She took off running down the hall.

My reflexes forced me to take off after her. "Where are you going?"

"You said you killed people! I'm calling the cops!"

"Katharine!" Addi yelled from behind me. "Don't you dare!"

I caught up to Kat, and ignoring my bum arm, I tackled her to the ground before she reached the stairs. She let out a frightened yip as I straddled her and pointed the gun at her head. Somewhere in the house, Bodhi started to bark.

"You're crazy!" she screamed.

"Katharine," I breathed, "stop it. Calm down."

"You're trying to kill me." She struggled against me.

"No, I'm not," I argued. "But if you fucking touch that phone I will have to. Do you understand me? I'll have to kill you, if you call anyone or tell anyone what you just saw."

I spoke a bit slower and emphasized my words so she'd understand.

Bodhi bounded his way up the stairs, but stopped short when he saw the both of us on the floor. He cocked his head, wondering if he should be concerned or not.

She processed what I told her and let out an aggravated sigh. "Get off of me."

"Say you understand!"

"Yes! I understand, Frankie! Now let me up!"

Addi's hand reached down to help me up. I winced in pain, having used my bad arm to tackle my idiot cousin.

"Well, that was eventful." Addi rolled her eyes as I moved out of the way.

"I don't even…" Kat begrudgingly took Addi's arm for help as well. "You two better explain this right fucking now. You up and abandon me when I need you, —I had to deal with Greta all night…"

Kat started to sob. "I never even spoke to Rich. People showed up and rushed him out."

"Well, do you want the whole story, or just want me to sum up?" I began to walk downstairs.

"Who did you kill? More importantly, *why*?" Kat was right behind me. "Why did you go kill someone when I needed you at the benefit?"

"Oh, for the love of Christ," I moaned. "Say 'benefit' one more time!"

My phone buzzed. I entered the living room and answered.

"What?" I yelled.

There was a moment of silence. "Francesca," Judah sighed.

"Yeah," I seethed. "Lay it on me."

"X is aware of the situation at hand and wanted to make sure it's rectified to their specifications before you make any of your own rash decisions."

X can fuck off, I thought.

Mr. X—in all his or her cliché glory—was a higher-up that Judah reported to. I had never heard or seen them, which left me to fantasize that they were like Dr. Claw from Inspector Gadget.

"I'm listening," I answered.

"That was messy," Judah started. "But I knew it would be."

"Did you?" I spat.

"We're sending an agent over to explain everything. She knows about what happened tonight and has extensive information on your situation. You and your family will be safe."

I glanced at my cousins. "You promise?"

"No," came the reply. "They will have to cooperate. I'll contact you again soon."

"I understand."

"You may want to watch the news," Judah suggested.

Oh, great.

The call ended and I put the phone away. "Someone's coming over."

"They're not going to kill Katharine, are they?"

Kat's mouth dropped open wide. "Excuse me? What the fuck are you two involved in? Am I in danger? Should I get a drink? I don't want to die sober."

"I'm glad you're concerned with a little bit of everything." I frowned at her.

I reached for the remote to turn on the TV.

Katharine's phone rang. She looked at it. "It's my mom. It's after six so she's probably drunk. I don't want to talk to her."

She looked at me again as the phone went silent. "But if I'm going to die, I probably should."

"You're not going to die, Katharine. Jesus..." I started to register the pain in my arm. "Speaking of dying, is my arm alright? I kind of need it in my line of work."

Addi took in a deep breath, as if she had stopped breathing for the entire ordeal. "Yeah. At least I think so. Whoever hit you knew the perfect spot, or you're just incredibly lucky. I got to it before there was any serious infection."

"You were shot?" Katharine chirped.

Oh my god, Katharine, welcome to an adult conversation.

"Yeah." I turned the channel to the local news.

I didn't know what I could and couldn't say at this point, but two out of the three people in the house worked for Osiris, so it wasn't too concerning.

"The congressman hasn't been reached for comment," the newscaster said. "But we are getting reports that Phoenix philanthropist, Patricia Ellingson was found dead in her hotel room earlier tonight. The cause of death has not yet been released."

Foul play, I let out an awkward laugh.

Both Kat and Addi listened intently, unmoving. Addi scrunched her face in thought and opened her mouth to say something.

Kat turned on her heel and grabbed a bottle of wine then a bottle opener. She opened the wine and began to drink straight from the bottle.

"Wait—" Addi pointed at the TV. "You killed Tricia?"

"Tricia Ellingson was my contract, yes." I nodded.

It should have been harder to say out loud, but instead it brought this overwhelming sense of relief.

Katharine's face was blank.

"You murdered the wife of a congressman," Addi reiterated.

Kat stopped drinking. "Are you *fucking* kidding me? What?"

"I had a contract from my employer to kill Tricia Ellingson." It was getting easier to say.

"No." She shook her head. "That's *not* a thing. That can't be a thing!"

"Well," I started, but Kat held up a hand.

"Shut up," she barked. She began to pace around the room. "You two left me to fend for myself tonight! I have been working on this... charitable affair for months! It wasn't just for Rich, it was for Bloom— Tricia's main charity. She's one of my investors!"

Addi slowly sank down onto the couch with me, eyeing Kat.

"And you're telling me that Tricia is dead, and you killed her?" Her voice was stern and calm.

A chill ran up my spine and I swallowed. "Correct."

Fuck, maybe I should've questioned this hit. Kat was laying a lot of need-to-know information on me.

"Why?" she seethed.

Addi turned her attention to me, waiting for my answer.

"Because someone put a hit out on her." I spoke the words slowly. "I'm a hit man—woman. Whatever. I kill people for money. A contract killer."

That word she understood: killer. I could see it register, and her upper lip twitched.

She took another long swig of wine. Her gulps were methodically pounding in my ears.

"So, you've been lying to me," she said as she came up for air.

"We both have," Addi spoke up. "We work for a company called Osiris. I am a doctor who treats Strikers —killers in the field—should they need it. I didn't know Frankie was involved until she needed my help."

I patted my arm.

"Strikers," Katharine muttered in disbelief.

Addi snapped her fingers at me.

"I want you to rest, Frankie. You're not indestructible, you know."

I threw her a look as she awkwardly put her hand on my shoulder. "I gave you a decent amount of pain killers and antibiotics, so that should hold you for a while, but let me know when the pain gets bad again. I'll get you some water."

Addi rose from the couch and walked to the open kitchen. I watched her grab a glass and fill it with filtered water.

"Osiris knows we're family," I said.

Kat walked over to sit down across from me. She took another long swig from the bottle. It was now almost empty.

Bodhi paced back and forth like a deranged lunatic. He periodically put his head in my lap. Poor guy was confused. He didn't like tension or elevated voices.

"I can't help but feel this was personal," I went on.

"No shit." Kat clenched her jaw. "Feels pretty personal to me right now."

Addi brought the glass of water to me and sat down. I took a drink, realizing I was thirstier than Kat.

"I think I was told to move back here to I could carry out this hit," I said.

"Frankie," Addi sighed, "Rich Ellingson—"

"Had his wife killed I'm pretty sure," I interrupted.

I knew what Addi wanted to say. Rich Ellingson was a Democrat. Rich Ellingson was a philanthropist. Rich Ellingson was a nice guy.

"One of them has to be dirty," I went on. "If not both, but none of it matters because I can't ask fucking questions."

The doorbell rang. Katharine paled a little and finished off her bottle.

"They're not going to kill you," I assured her.

Addi sighed and got up to answer the door, with Bodhi trailing on her heels. From the foyer, I could hear an unusually cheerful feminine voice say hello and comment immediately on Bodhi's size.

"Do you have a saddle for that dog?"

Congrats on being the eleven-millionth person to say that, I thought.

I also knew immediately who it was just from the overly bubbly southern drawl.

Addi led the woman into the living room.

I gazed at Emma from my "Modern Etiquette for Beginners" class.

I figured she was a Wingback—the business-minded damage-control people: information seekers. The ones who left the notes, and tracked hit movements prior to death days. She had an overly skinny frame, but was cute with red hair pulled back in a neat ponytail. She had taste in clothes—black business attire with some amazing red Marc Jacobs shoes.

Maybe Kat has conditioned me more than Osiris.

"I'm Emma," she said. "I'm with the Osiris Condition Control Department. I hear we had a bit of a hiccup."

Oh good, they had an entire department assigned to deal with people like me—complete with the letters OCD. *Swell.*

"Is Frankie in trouble?" Addi asked.

"Oh lord no." Emma was way too cheerful to be working for Osiris... maybe that was her mental condition. "I'm here to negotiate the conditions of employing all three of you lovely ladies with Osiris."

Katharine peered at Emma as if she were looking at a complex scientific equation.

"You," Kat said, "you're one of my students. Emma Duncan. I thought you were Kal Duncan's daughter..."

Nothing was clicking in that brain of hers. *Frankie kills people for a living and works for a big bad hit-man company... and in walks its representative, Emma Fucking Sunshine.*

Emma threw her a sympathetic smile. "No, that was all utter bullshit. I have—"

"Been attending Elegance, Inc. to get information on us," I said, eying her.

Emma cleared her throat. "Mr. Cohen is your chief mentor, Ms. Fairholm. Is that correct?"

"Yes," I replied. Judah was the guy responsible for me if things go wrong. It's basically both our asses if I screw up, so the fact he sounded calm over the phone rang an inner alarm.

"I bet he's pretty proud of you," she smiled. "Not everyone passes their trials without having a full breakdown. Let alone have to move back home."

"Trials?" I narrowed my eyes at her as she brought out an iPad mini and began to scroll.

"Yes." Emma nodded. "Once your trainer thinks you're ready, they send you on a lone mission and shoot you, leaving you to fend for yourself. Only..."

She frowned at the screen. "That's odd."

"I've been on my own for months," I said.

Emma smirked at the screen. "Yes, looks like your trainer wouldn't initiate your trial, so X did instead."

Oh, my trainer initiated something, alright, I wanted to strangle Spark with his red shoelaces.

Emma tsk'd as she sat down on one of the other chairs so she could address all of us. "It looks like there were a few mistakes on the administrative end and we don't want to lose two very valuable agents.

"Mistakes?" Kat's voice rose. "Your people had my cousin kill a perfectly nice woman!"

Emma cocked her head to the side. "Oh, I wouldn't call Tricia Ellingson nice."

Kat opened her mouth a couple of times, but said nothing.

"Anyway, Mr. Cohen proposed bringing you three on as a family unit and running things a bit differently from here on out. The heads of Osiris are in agreement with the proposal and want to implement it immediately."

Addi narrowed one eye and straightened herself up even more. "What runs differently?"

"Well, obviously Francesca will be out for a bit with her arm," Emma responded. "You will continue working for Osiris as a Stopper. However, they would like for Francesca and I to train you to be a back-up Striker. Katharine ideally would be the family operational Wingback, but I will have to assess her after training."

Addi's eyes went from narrow and skeptical to surprised, and Katharine's usual sun-drenched skin continued to grow more ashen.

"The business that Katharine runs is a perfect front for what you do. Eventually there will be jobs that all three of you will have to pull off. Our client base is rising with all the political turmoil, and it's proving more difficult to keep to our current 'stand alone' policy."

Emma paused, looking up from her iPad. "We actually lost an agent last week." Emma shook her head sadly. "A great agent, but a little reckless."

I felt panic rise up and tried to utter a very disinterested "Who?"

"James," Emma said, and I immediately felt relief. "James Burke—I doubt you've met him. You'd know if you did."

She let out a sigh and I had the quick thought Emma had a crush on the dead guy.

Emma went back to her iPad. "There's a big chess game going on right now with the Sinaloa drug cartel.

It's why you were tapped to kill Ellingson and why we now believe we should team a few groups of agents."

Emma chattered on as if she were gossiping with girlfriends.

"Excuse me?" Kat leaned forward. "Tricia Ellingson was involved with a drug cartel?"

"Yes," Emma stated. "There's a Mexican congressman who heads up a large front for arms and drug dealing out of Mexico. Tricia filtered money from her various charities to help it along."

That was an interesting twist I could get behind. I felt much better about killing her.

"Wait," Kat held up her hand, "are you saying there's drug money in Elegance, Inc.?"

"Big deal," I snorted. "My dad used to work for Barry Seal."

"Also, not okay!" Kat yelled.

She dramatically fell back into the chair and covered her face with her hands.

"This is not happening," she stressed.

"Elegance, Inc. will now begin transitioning into a front for Osiris," Emma moved on without a thought. "We will have to do extensive background checks on all your teachers and staff to ensure there is no threat for leaks. Be prepared to lose some people and have us replace them in due time. In exchange for your cooperation, of course you will be well compensated. You won't miss Tricia's contributions."

Never mind that we would be a threat to anyone who worked at the school. Turn Elegance, Inc. into a front for an Osiris Striker ring? Seemed ludicrous to me. It also seemed unfair to take something Kat had worked so hard on and put it in indefinite jeopardy.

Surprisingly, losing her business to X and his non-sensical ideas didn't make Kat scream her head off.

"You..." Kat stared at the ceiling. "You want me to hand over my entire life to your contract killer cult. I can't..."

Katharine Fairholm wasn't aware that Emma wasn't asking, but at least she wouldn't die sober.

Emma only smiled in return. "Think of Elegance, Inc. as collateral. We won't interfere much as long as you cooperate."

Kat's jaw clenched and she sat up to stare at Emma.

"Fuck off," she said. "You can't... I won't..."

"We realize this must be a lot for you to take in Ms. Fairholm." Emma gave Kat's hand a reassuring pat. "I understand that finding out your little cousin is a contract hitter is hard to take."

"What you're talking about is murder," Kat finally said. "You murder people, Frankie!"

I cringed. Coming from her, it actually sounded bad.

"We normalize potentially harmful political and economic situations," Emma interjected. "Our client list is very specialized and we only carry out hits on people who are proving to be a hazard to global peace interactions and social growth with the United States."

"Yeah, what she said." I gave Kat a huge fake smile. It was also a huge load of bullshit, but I wasn't going to say anything.

Addi threw me a look, and I knew she knew the line was crap too.

"Since I'm Frankie's assigned Wingback, I will be overseeing your transitions."

Ah hell, I groaned inwardly. Cheerful McCheery was going to be around for a while. Teaching Kat about the dark underworld of Osiris seemed like a job Emma was born to do—like a twisted nanny.

"We are economizing some of our processes, switching around some management, and hopefully taking on some new investors who are open to these fresh ideas. In this special case, we will keep training to a minimum and have Francesca work with you as you go along—sort of an extended shadow program. You will have a secure warehouse for weapons training and tactics."

She turned to me. "And you will receive a pay increase for the added hazards."

This night didn't go as planned. *Get shot, get promoted.* I was starting to like Osiris again. *Wait— what was the catch? There was always a catch.*

Addison, Katharine and I looked at each other. Addi knew there wasn't much of a choice. Kat couldn't process the choice. I was already in it.

Fantastic.

Elegantly Wasted

Chapter Fifteen

Emma was interesting. I liked her after the first day, once I realized she wasn't exactly the happy persona she conveyed. There was a definite reason to her cheerful disposition, and that reason was insanity. She was a loon.

She lived a relatively normal Osiris existence in Tempe—just moved from Chicago (but was born and raised in Alabama).

Emma did a great job taking care of me while having patience with Kat and Addi.

Emma talked a lot, which she did in class too, so it wasn't a shock.

She was four years older than I and, surprisingly enough, was a trained Striker who got demoted to Wingback over what Emma called 'a technicality.'

It was my job to observe her while she trained Kat and Addi. It wasn't an easy job since Kat whined about literally everything—including losing her beauty sleep.

During one of the many late night dinners after we trained Addi and Kat at "the Warehouse" outside of town, she opened up a bit and told us she used her skills to torture and kill a cheating boyfriend, so she was downgraded to the Wingback position. She ended up liking the job much better.

"We all make mistakes," she told me. "I think part of me likes the super spy aspect, but I can't be trusted with death."

Emma Jolene Wake was finished killing for the time being.

"I was just attracted to the wrong men with these nut-bar personality disorders," she blurted out over dinner, one evening. "My ex—he was a total loser,—lived a double life and everything, but worse than mine. Compulsive liar, cheater, and come to find out, rapist. I was so consumed with disbelief and anger that I tortured him without even thinking. I made a bad judgment call. I let my dark side take over. I hurt people in the process. He had a family he was hiding from me. I didn't mean to destroy them as well."

"Sounds like you did them all a favor," I said. One less bad answer. Maybe that's why Osiris didn't kill her. They knew that we were unstable. They had to know what we were capable of.

The days after the big event dragged on as I sat on the couch and played Xbox. I had to deal with a few visits from my mother who was told I had been in a car accident on the way to the benefit, but that I walked away with just a few bumps and bruises. My dad called to make sure the Mustang wasn't wrecked.

I'm fine, Daniel, thanks for asking.

Emma made me exercise my arm, she involved me with the meals she cooked and even asked about video games. I had made my first real friend. It was odd. I think I really did want to be social, but I held myself back. I blamed Joan for that, too.

Judah finally called back. He had good news and bad news.

The good news was that the spectacle of Tricia Ellingson's death was blamed on a Sinaloa Sicario named Victor Reyes. I was also correct in assuming Rich Ellingson paid for the hit. His wife was treading through territory that could lose him the election. His secret was safe with me, however Judah said it was far from over.

"Unfortunately, Tricia was involved with a man named Rico Escandon. He's a suspected head of the Sinaloa drug cartel and has other operations and connections with a bigger crime lord putting other hit factions at risk... even the Sha Lù," Judah revealed.

"And I care because..." I pressed.

The Sha Lù were a Chinese faction. They were extremely dangerous and we rarely tread on their Hong Kong territory unless the job was lower-profile. They weren't important in my circle, but I respected and maybe even feared them a bit.

I heard Judah chuckle. "You know Tricia was your aunt's good friend. You know her money is in your cousin's school. Right now, the news is just poor Tricia getting killed because her charity work was putting a dent in the human trafficking highway. Poor Rich, let's get him sympathy votes for a Senate seat. If her secrets are found out, everyone loses—everyone finds out that Elegance, Inc. was partially funded with cartel money, and your family will be disgraced. There are ends to sever, and you have the scissors."

The news was becoming worse. Goddamn Kat and her need to involve "influential" people in her endeavors.

"So, you put me here on purpose," I sighed.

"I can't go into detail," Judah said. "But please try to trust me, just a little."

"Speaking of trust," I said, "who the hell did you send to shoot me?"

"*I* didn't send anyone." Judah sounded dejected. "Spark was supposed to complete that training exercise. However, it appears he didn't follow through and X felt the need to spin some extravagant mind game to lead us here."

"You sound angry," I observed.

"I have my reasons," Judah replied. "None of which is your concern. I'm just glad you're okay."

I was silent for a moment.

"Why didn't Spark shoot me when he was supposed to?"

"You know why." Judah sounded irritated. He hung up.

Great, I thought. Everyone knew he overstepped into my pants.

My arm prevented me from doing much of anything for a few weeks, so I used the time to step up my game at Elegance, Inc. Kat needed all the sleep she could get.

Kat's prestigious school was off of Thunderbird Road in North Scottsdale. When I was a kid, nothing had been out there but ranch homes, now it was more or less trendy businesses. Elegance, Inc. stood out.

Kat wanted a unique building and had spent a good penny building an industrial-style warehouse. It was three stories high, and the inside was spacious and decorated retro-chic; lots of red brick, metal and glass went into its creation.

Katharine had a staff of about sixty people. Her mother, Audrey, wasn't a paid employee, but was always there for some reason... most likely because her life was devoid of anything else.

"What did you do to your arm?" was her first question, when I walked in the door one morning.

"I'm fine, thanks, Audrey," I retorted. "How are you?"

"Does Kat know you're wearing *those*?"

Audrey pointed to my worn chucks.

Why did I even bother coming in?

"Does Katharine know you're here?" I inquired sweetly. Audrey knew that she wasn't supposed to be there in her daughter's absence. She had the tendency to help herself to Kat's wine stock and pick on staff until they quit, which caused problems for the business.

"Well, I have no idea, seeing as how she hasn't called me." Audrey pursed her lips. "Honestly, we have so much to discuss with what happened to Tricia. Greta is beside herself."

I rolled my eyes.

Audrey squinted at me, teetering on her heels. She smelled like wine.

"You should go comfort your sister and let Gretchen and me handle things," I responded.

"Gretchen." Audrey scoffed. "The business would go under if she were left in charge. I miss the other girl... Renee. No. Rebecka. Whatever. I'm going to grab a drink."

Nice attitude. Audrey didn't actually care where Kat was. She just wanted to complain. I could feel my hackles go up as Audrey helped herself to more wine. Wine was always in stock. Katharine had a wine cellar put in under the building for wine tasting and sommelier classes. We were a long way from Sonoma. We also used it for dinner etiquette lessons, but Audrey and Katharine also used it as an excuse to drink on the job.

"How did you hurt yourself? Trip and fall over your dry wit?"

You can't kill your own aunt, I kept reminding myself.

"Car accident," I responded. "I thought Katharine had told you. That's why I didn't show up to the Ellingson benefit."

"Oh, right." She waved her hand carelessly. "Joan and Greta weren't happy with you. Not that they ever are."

Really, it was a relatively short drive to get my gun and silencer...

"I'm glad you weren't hurt," Audrey went on. "But you certainly didn't win back brownie points with the family. You really should start behaving."

Oh my God, please leave.

Audrey's responses were so rehearsed, like she said things because she knew she probably should—not because she cared. It also physically pained her to give a compliment unless she followed it with an insult.

I hadn't been in the building five minutes, and I wanted out. That was the power of a Fairholm. I couldn't wait for Kat to be back full time, once Emma decided exactly where she fit in. I doubted she would fit in at all.

When my arm was healed, Kat seemed a little more accepting to the whole deal. She hadn't said much to me in the weeks that followed the benefit. I didn't blame her. Killing Tricia, while just a job, hit too close to home. It would make Greta even more of an insufferable bog witch.

On top of having to quickly adjust to a new life, Emma monitored Kat's alcohol intake while "in training." There were also dark circles under Kat's eyes, evidence that Emma had purged the drug cabinet of the sleeping aides Kat depended on for rest.

"She'll be your Wingback," Emma said, as I walked in the door.

I dropped my messenger back and threw her a look. "Isn't that your job?"

"I'm needed elsewhere." Emma smiled. "Although I'll remain here in town indefinitely. We still need to have training sessions at the Warehouse now that you're better. Addi is ready to help you, too. I think she will make a rather proficient killer. Kat, not so much."

Katharine wasn't like me or Addi—definitely not like me. Deep down, she knew what compassion was. She was a snobby social butterfly on the surface, but Katharine cared about people—she cared about us. She was the most vulnerable. I suppose Wingback would fit her nicely.

Addi already spoke to me about her willingness to move forward. She liked that she had more control over the 'Frankie kills people for a living' scenario. Addi lived for control.

"This is a good thing," Emma reminded me. "A family unit isn't anything we've had before in my time at Osiris."

I wanted to tell Emma she didn't know my family.

I didn't buy it. *How was making a hit nest of dysfunctional lushes and borderlines a smart and economical move?*

Kat closed herself in her room in the evenings. It was her way of telling me she didn't want to be bothered. That night, I chose to ignore the passive aggressiveness.

I quietly opened Katharine's door and stepped in the darkened room. Bodhi took up more than half the bed, sleeping soundly.

Kat was curled up on her small portion of bed, hugging a pillow. She sensed my presence and sat up.

She looked at me almost as if I were a stranger, and that stung.

I sat down on the edge of the bed and took a deep breath.

"Remember when we were kids," I started, "and we would play hide and go seek at Joan's mansion?"

Kat sniffed and nodded.

"Addi and Nero were too old to have fun," I chuckled. "So, Lex was usually it and you and I were pretty great at never being found."

A sad smile graced Kat's pretty face. "We always snuck back to base."

I reached out and grabbed her hand. "That was all you. You guided me. You had the plans. You won those games for us every time."

"This isn't hide and seek, Frankie." Kat's face fell.

"I'm sorry," I said quietly. "I really didn't mean for any of this to happen."

"How could you keep something like this from me?" she asked.

"Same reason Addi was, we aren't allowed to say anything," I responded.

"Addi wasn't doing terrible things—she was being a doctor like we all thought. It's not the same." She looked at me with tearing eyes.

"I'm sorry I lied to you," I said. "But just know some of these terrible things include killing a German international real estate multi-millionaire. He had a basement in his Switzerland estate that was filled with young girls— girls who he had his way with and took pictures and video of... he beat them and cut them... and people would pay to watch. He deserved much worse than what I gave him."

Katharine looked down; tears were pooling in her eyes.

"Just because I kill people doesn't make me a bad person. Some people deserve to die."

"You were sick. I knew it and your mom knew it, but we just ignored it." Her lips began to shake as she spoke. "Maybe if we had said or done something... we didn't want you to end up like..."

"Like what?" I asked.

There was a long silence, as Kat stared off into nothing. Bohdi's incessant whines behind the door got louder before she finally replied.

"Nothing," Kat shook it off. "I just don't want you to get hurt. I want you to be okay."

"I am okay." I tried to smile. "Osiris taught me to utilize my dark side. I don't do anything I'm not paid to do. Everything is fine."

"It's not fine, Frankie." Katharine shook her head. "It's so not fine. Your poor mom... if she would have just addressed your trauma early on."

"This isn't anyone's fault," I said, pushing myself off the bed. "I chose this. This is who I am, and I happen to love my job. I didn't plan on you finding all of this out, but you're either with me or you're against me."

Katharine jumped up as well and hugged me. Her arms were tight. I could smell her vanilla perfume as she spoke into my ear. "I'm not against you, but I don't understand this version of you."

I hugged her back. "I get it."

"I need time," she continued. "I'm not sure how I even fit into this. I can't kill a person, and I certainly do not want to watch someone die."

That may be unavoidable.

"I also need you to be honest with me from now on. Let me know the real you. It's the only way I may begin to understand all this."

I looked down at my chucks. I wondered if she could at least understand that the real me didn't wear heels.

"I'll do my best."

"I know we're a fucked-up entitled family," she said. "I know our parents don't exactly teach us to be warm and fuzzy, and they've fucked us up.."

I sighed. "At some point we have to start taking responsibility for ourselves. This path is how I'm choosing to start."

Kat pursed her lips and sat back down on the bed.

"I need to get some rest," Kat said. "You should try and do the same."

Rest. Luck. Therapy. We would need it all.

I shut the door and walked down the stairs, to the kitchen. Addi stood at the counter, holding a bag of pre-made salad.

"She'll come around," Addi said, as she began to pour the lettuce into a bowl.

I sunk down into a chair at the kitchen table. I figured Addi had been listening. She couldn't control herself.

"What if she doesn't?"

Addi looked over at me with a sympathetic gaze, but didn't have an answer.

Elegantly Wasted

Chapter Sixteen

Katharine had a few strikes against her in the hit man business. First, she was too girlie. That was her mother's fault. She was raised to be pretty, not to be practical.

Second was that aside from impeccable English, she only knew how to speak French and a little high school Spanish.

So when the time came for us to infiltrate a drug cartel in Mexico, I figured we were screwed.

But let me back up just a tad.

Three months had gone by since I was shot, and not much had changed with Katharine's views on killing— she still detested the idea. Her moral compass was her third strike. While mine pointed anywhere but North, Katharine had a decent grip on hers that came from pouring over mountains of etiquette books since she hit puberty.

She was the perfect Wingback. All she needed was to learn every little thing about my world.

"What is this?" I held up a nine-millimeter.

"A gun." Katharine was filing her nails.

"What type of gun?" I was irritated to say the least.

"A shiny one," she spat. "Why do I need to know about your guns?"

I held my breath and counted to ten a lot. "Because, Wingbacks need to use all their assets to get information."

We congregated at the Glendale warehouse. For four nights a week, this was our routine. It was after ten p.m., and Katharine was cranky, as usual. "What does that even mean?" Kat asked.

"It means you have great tits and a killer personality." I aimed my gun above her, something she hated. "You can use them to get information from people—Jesus Christ, Kat, watch *The Long Kiss Goodnight* or something."

"I am one of the most successful entrepreneurs on the West Coast! I have philanthropy awards on my wall! I don't need to be devalued like this!"

"Devalue this," I said, and flipped her off. "We're never going to get anywhere if you keep bitching about every little thing."

"I think Kat just needs to be taken on assignment," Addi said, trying to dissolve the argument. "I'll let Emma know we need a fairly easy task."

Addi fled up to the small office that overlooked the vacant building. I could tell she was growing tired of my cynicism and Kat's attitude. It was probably wearing her out.

"This isn't me." Kat shook her head.

"You haven't even tried anything yet!"

"I know it's not me! I am a socialite with no defensive skills! How on Earth would I be useful in a world of assassins?"

I rolled my eyes. "First off, we aren't assassins. Being an assassin requires great skill, willingness to obey, patience and dietary discipline—none of which I have. Second, your social skill is what is required for this job. You're a great actress, you're a salesman and you are beautiful. You can get what you want from people. All I'm asking for is for you to understand the difference of weapons so I don't walk into an AR-15 situation with a pocket knife."

It wasn't easy giving Kat the right kind of confidence. If she was sure her life wasn't in danger, she had all the confidence in the world, but shake her ground up a little, and she crumbled. I didn't get it.

"I just..." Katharine seemed totally unsure of herself. I wasn't used to this Katharine. It would have annoyed me, but she looked so helpless that I couldn't help feeling bad for her.

"Look..." I reached out and awkwardly touched her arm. I wasn't the best at comfort. "I know you can do this. You have to put that fear behind you and just act the part. Addi and I will always be two steps away from rescuing you if something goes wrong. All you're doing is hooking the target and assessing danger."

Katharine let out a heavy breath. "That does about nothing to make me feel better. I don't think I thought this whole thing through. Everything happened so fast, I just jumped on board, but did we stop to think that I'm not built to be in serious situations? I like being the owner of Elegance, Inc. I don't like watching my cousin get texts with names on it—names of soon-to-be-dead people. I'm a socialite, not a sociopath."

"This isn't any different for you," I reasoned, trying to ignore her last remark. "You're a socialite who just happens to be conversing with people marked for death. You're not killing them. Half of them aren't even dangerous to you."

Kat seemed to consider this. "And you'll always be there?"

"Absolutely," I responded. "As long as you don't wander off."

Kat stood up a bit straighter.

"Alrighty!" Emma's high-pitched voice rang out from above us.

I looked up to the office area where Emma and Addi descended the stairs.

"I arranged a transaction for the group this weekend." Emma clapped cheerfully. "I think it will be a great starting-off point!"

"Where?" I asked.

Emma skipped down the stairs and waved a paper at me enthusiastically. "Vegas!"

I inwardly groaned as Kat's eyes lit up and her demeanor snapped back to attention like a druggie that had just been handed free crack.

Sometimes Emma was the biggest idiot.

I snatched the orders from her and scanned the details. It didn't seem too bad... similar to my first solo job and not nearly as complicated. This would be a good place for Kat to start.

Or so I thought.

Elegantly Wasted

Chapter Seventeen

Apparently I need work on assessing situations, because I didn't see Vegas going as badly as it did... or perhaps as well, depending on your point of view.

The weekend—which Addi had dubbed "the Incident"—started off as well as any other hit. The first of a few "loose ends" I was tying up in the wake of Tricia Ellingson's death.

Isa Kadir Sa'idi was a young renegade heir to the Al Bu Sa'idi dynasty of Oman. He had laundered millions from his Sultan father during the ten years prior, starting at the age of sixteen (with help from an overly-smart servant who was later executed), and then he fled the country. He managed to lay low in Britain for years before relocating to Las Vegas with assistance from Rico Escandon in return for opening up more trafficking highways.

He now went by the name Elliot Malak. He invested his hardly-earned money early and was beginning to draw unwanted attention to himself by buying up land on the US/Mexico border, then running guns and people into the states to be distributed to the highest bidders in Vegas.

He was one more pin in Osiris's "global economic safety" crap. Katharine had decided that Ketel-One was more of a concern anyway.

The good news was that Elliot was young, impressionable and loved hot women. He held permanent residence at the top of Caesar's Hotel and was notorious for seeking out different women weekly —or nightly. Obvious STDs aside, he'd be easy prey for Katharine, if she could suck it up and relax. This guy wasn't dangerous. His hired bodyguards might be

—but Emma's side note stated that they were often dismissed before the night really got started.

Sounded easy enough. Now to factor in Katharine's alcoholism, her ADD concerning all things shiny and her overstimulated nerves... pray to Allah that this went off without a hitch.

My nerves were raw, and my inner thoughts mocked me the entire four-hour drive to Vegas. This was my first mission with baggage—a term Spark liked to use in reference to me. Not only did I have to watch out for myself, I had to keep a watchful eye on two idiosyncratic cousins whose mothers would be furious with me if I got them killed.

Katharine wanted to fly. She didn't like the idea of wasting time in her SUV, having to talk shop with me the entire trip... but she had no choice. It was my call. Plus, the case of knives Addi wanted to bring as her weapons of choice traveled much easier in a vehicle.

The sun was setting as we pulled up to the hotel valet.

It didn't take long to check into our suite, get situated and head back down to the casino floor, where I could watch Kat frolic in a drunken state of ostentatious glee. She brought a flask for the drive and then cracked open the mini-bar in our room with the skill of Thomas Crown before I even blinked.

This might be a long night.

I had to admit it was amusing to watch Kat try and cope with a dangerous situation. She got herself drunk in public. There was no mother to prove anything to here—she was elated and probably trying her best not to think about her impending tasks.

My amusement turned to concern when I spotted our mark. True to the intel given to me, he was sitting at one of the casino bars, conversing with a female bartender. He looked younger than I expected, but then again he was only twenty-five. We could have gone to high school together. Maybe Kat looked too old for him. Maybe her nervous laughter would raise alarm. Maybe she'd throw up all the rum and coke she'd had in his lap.

I felt Addi's presence beside me and glanced her way. She looked suspicious. The scowl that was permanently fixed on her face was glaring at our target, and she was dressed dramatically all in black. I nudged her and shook my head. Her face relaxed and she shifted her rigid posture to a left slump.

Suddenly I wished I was alone. The impending pooch screw that could be this mission was starting to depress me. Maybe I'd go back to the room and occupy my mind by teaching Addi how not to dress like a CIA agent. I could go to bed early and wake up hoping Kat hadn't been disposed of in the trash room. I could call Judah crying and say that this wasn't working, that I should be put back into my secluded bubble. Contract killers totally cried to get their way.

Addi touched my shoulder, bringing me out of my thoughts. She nodded toward the bar and I stared for a moment to make sure what I saw was real.

Kat had positioned herself next to Elliot and was in a full-on conversation with him, giggling, flirting and throwing him dazzling smiles. She seemed to have the corrupt little shit's full attention.

Addi gently guided me to a couple of lounge chairs in full view of Kat. I sank down, still perplexed by the sight.

"Maybe Emma did a better job with her than I thought," I said.

Kat seemed totally at ease; there was no trace of fear in her voice. She reached out to touch him playfully at all the right moments. It was like the hit man gods had blessed my luck.

"I think that she listens to you and is determined to make a good first impression on Judah," Addi responded. "If you give Katharine something to prove... she'll prove it."

The stress I endured since leaving lifted. Addi seemed to notice.

"You know she'll be fine. I'll keep an eye on her for a while. You should get some rest." Addi smiled. "You've been anxious all day."

Kat didn't have a time frame for talking to Elliot, but as long as she got his schedule for tomorrow, I didn't care. I nodded and headed toward the elevator bank without as much as a glance back in Kat's direction.

When I opened the door to the room, I saw an envelope on the floor. My defenses flared slightly, and I quickly locked the door.

I snatched the envelope up and tore it open.

Frankenstein,

Grats on your promotion. Make me proud. Don't let the hot one drink.

Yours,

S.

I instinctively crushed the note and felt my anger boil up. Just when I was forgetting about him too. *What a jerk.*

Half of me wanted to hunt him down and shoot him in the face, and half of me hoped he was lurking in the shadows of the room—ready for another sexual romp.

Wishful thinking: the room was empty.

I sighed and sank down into one of the couches that faced the door. Never mind the view—I should always be on high alert. Never mind that either... I drifted off to sleep.

Addi called me two hours later. I jumped at the sound of my phone.

"Hey," I said groggily.

"I'm sorry to wake you up, but I need some help," Addi replied, sounding like she was struggling with something heavy.

"What is it?"

"Kat," she said. "She's being ridiculous."

I could hear Kat's loud voice in the background, singing "1999" by Prince... very poorly.

"I'm trying to get her into the elevator now, but she needs to be carried. Can you wait for us at the elevator banks?"

I sighed. "Did she even get information from the guy?"

"Oh yeah... I would guess lots. Between her musical numbers she starts hitting me and crying about killing her friend."

"Oh lord." I jumped up and headed out the door.

"The guy left when she got too drunk. I guess he has some standards about not raping drunk women. But she went pretty nuts after that, and it involves tequila."

"I'll be waiting at the elevators."

I rushed down the hall with Spark's note in my mind and impatiently eyed the elevator doors. We were on the twentieth floor—it would take a moment. It felt like forever.

The door gave a cheerful ring and opened to Addi's irritated face—no Katharine.

I opened my mouth to question her, but she held up her hand.

"Don't ask!" She started pressing buttons in the elevator. "That little weasel sidestepped me and bolted when a group of Asian tourists got on. Now I have NO clue where she is! They all got off on the floor below and didn't understand 'excuse me.' I figured punching them out of my way would draw attention."

Fantastic. Now we technically had a rogue drunk agent possibly spilling her stupid mouth to any Ed Hardy-wearing asshole she could find. This wasn't good.

I wanted to believe that Kat wasn't this dumb, that she was simply drunk and wouldn't ruin everything for us. Then I thought that no self-respecting contract-killing agency would allow an alcoholic agent.

"I'm going to go back down," Addi said.

"Do you need help?"

Don't let the hot one drink.

"Nah—this is pretty much Kat's senior prom night revisited, minus the whole marked-for-death-guy scenario. Just wait here until I call you."

I was still trying to sort out the entire thing, so I just nodded. Staying in one place sounded good.

I checked my phone. It was just past one in the morning.

Twenty minutes later, the elevator behind me and farthest away dinged. I quickly turned toward it.

"Get your hands off me!" I knew that drunken slur anywhere.

I started to walk toward the door, when Kat tumbled out and landed head-over-heels in a heap on the floor. I rushed over to her and tried to glance into the elevator, but it was shutting swiftly. I caught a glimpse of a dark suit. That was it.

My brain immediately flashed back to the night of the benefit—a flash of a dark suit above me in the stairway.

I looked down at Kat, who was laughing on the floor. She was clutching one of her shoes in her hand, and her sweater was awkwardly wrapped around her body.

"Stupid Asian douche bag," Kat muttered.

I assumed her racial slur was aimed at whomever threw her out of the elevator.

I reached down to help her up, and I suddenly realized that her sweater looked funny because it was on inside out... and backwards... and upside-down.

I really don't want to know.

"Frankie you're such a shithead," she giggled. "This whole killer thing doesn't suit you. Remember your painting phase in high school? You should have stuck with that."

"Shut up, Kat," I seethed. "Shut your mouth until I get you back into the room."

"Oooh," she put all her body weight against me, and I had to use the wall for support as I texted Addi real quick.

"You left me..." she poked my chest. "So this is all your fault."

She blew me a raspberry, and I winced at her tequila-infused breath.

"Walk," I ordered. "You're not a fucking child."

"I was dreaming when I wrote this, so sue me if I go too fast, but life is just a party, and parties weren't meant to laaaaaaast!"

She was swaying back and forth, and stopping every two steps, but we made it back to our room just as Addi came charging down the hall.

"Are you completely insane or just suicidal?" She grabbed Kat's hair, dragging her into the room.

"Ouch! Let go of me you bitch!" Kat tried in vain to slap at Addi's hands, dropping her lone shoe in the process.

I quietly closed and locked the door, and followed an enraged Addi into the bathroom. She flung Kat into the square glass shower stall and turned the water on full blast.

Kat shrieked from the onslaught of cold water. She couldn't manage to scamper out before Addi closed her in and held the door.

"Let me out! This isn't funny! This is brand-new Prada!"

"You'll stay in there until I decide to let you out," Addi spat.

Kat struggled a bit against the door before she started crying.

I watched the scene with displaced intrigue.

The water must have started to get warmer, because Kat sat back against the shower wall and let the water soak her. She looked defeated as she continued to whimper and cry.

"Both of you go to hell," she said quietly.

Addi let out a loud sigh of frustration and then stormed out of the bathroom.

I watched Kat weep in the shower like a stray dog caught in the rain. She was so small and fragile to me now—a significant change from the ball-busting career woman I grew to love. I did love her. I cared how she felt, and it honestly hurt a bit to see her so upset.

My phone rang. I hastily answered it.

"Yes?"

"Is there a problem, Francesca?"

Shit. It was Judah. This guy was good, or he had spies in the hotel.

"Everything is fine," I snapped and hung up.

I didn't have time for this. Somehow he knew Kat was causing problems. That was a very bad thing.

I opened the shower and turned off the water.

Grabbing a towel, I knelt down to look at Kat. She looked up at me in a drunken haze of sadness.

"Why do you have to be a killer, Frankie? Of all the professions in the world..."

I sighed as I began to undress her and cover her up with the towel.

"The profession chose me," I said.

"And you didn't think that it could so negatively affect my life!" Kat didn't struggle as I lifted her up and guided her out toward a bed.

"Nope, can't say I did," I muttered. I could have rattled off what a self-centered, drunken dick Kat was being, but what was the point? She wouldn't remember it tomorrow.

"Get in bed." I shoved her down. "Sleep it all off. If you try to get up—I'll pistol whip you."

Kat looked too defeated to retort, and she simply closed her eyes.

Out in the other room, Addi was standing at one of the large windows, looking out. "Maybe this isn't working."

"What did either of us expect?" I frowned. "Kat is different. She won't magically be able to be on my level."

"She doesn't have to be. Wingbacks are social information gatherers. They don't follow the same rule set at Strikers. Kat just has to focus and not let alcohol buffer her job. She certainly doesn't show up drunk to Elegance, Inc."

"She loves Elegance, Inc. She doesn't need to drink to cope with it... much."

Addi turned to me. "Well, we can't force her to do this. Maybe I can be your Wingback."

I cringed a bit. Addi's people skills were limited to socially awkward contract killers, and even they were told to "shut the fuck up," in no uncertain terms.

"What about Emma?"

Addi shook her head. "She's tending to other stuff —Strikers—I don't know."

"What? There are no more fucking Wingbacks in this company?"

Addi shrugged. "I think the point is to be a family unit with a foundation of trust. I mean, we don't trust our mothers all too often, but I don't think I've ever not trusted you or Kat."

"If we can't do this job together, then it won't work. If it doesn't work, we're dead. Judah is nuts if he thinks this is anything but added anxiety."

"You're right." Addi shook her head. "There could be some underlying psychological issues that prohibit us from being a good unit. Trust might be less of an issue, but confidence is an issue. You were doing fine on your own and we are a hindrance."

"Osiris likes psychological problems." I walked over to my backpack, where I kept a small black box. Inside, neatly arranged, were some vials of insulin, a syringe, and my special Set cartridges. I took out the small silver bullet of Set and secured it to my bracelet.

"What are you going to do?" Addi asked me.

"My job," I said, and walked toward the door.

"You're going to execute him early?" Addi seemed alarmed. Osiris wasn't the only one who liked to obsessively stick to plans.

I opened the door.

"You're not a hindrance," I said. "Either of you. This might be tough, but so am I."

The door closed quietly behind me.

Elegantly Wasted

Chapter Eighteen

I rode the elevator downstairs and started to walk around the hotel and casino. I was looking for Elliot Malak, but I used the time to calm my nerves. It was well past two in the morning, but the hotel was still in full swing. I walked by the main bar, and there was no sign of the mark. I wasn't sure what I was doing anyway.

Osiris insisted that we keep to their schedule. Staying behind a day after a mark was killed wasn't on our list. I wasn't thinking anything through, but the less Kat had to deal with right now, the better. She had drunk herself into a dangerous stupor—and I'd have to deal with that once I got home.

The strange thing was my fear that the whole Kat and Addi thing wouldn't work out. I had been surprisingly calm since they found me out. It was refreshing. I had dreaded going home from the start, because I was losing an environment where someone understood me. I wanted to be the one in the family who got away; I felt like my life had depended on it for so long. It surprised me that I now felt comfortable at home. My own cousins knew who I was... I didn't need Spark to feel like I fit in anymore.

I immediately started to think about his note again. It was silly of me, but I felt a pang of abandonment reading it, and I couldn't shake it. Sure, he screwed me and then disappeared—that happens to just about everyone at some point in their lives. But for a moment I had thought this guy really understood me. No—I was certain he did. There was something there. So why such harsh treatment? Was he just a huge asshole, or was Osiris that anal about training exercises? Were Addi and Kat a transition into a larger company? Addi had already been involved with Osiris for years. Did that mean I was chosen for a reason?

Too many thoughts clouded my head. I wasn't focused. That would make for a bad hit. Mr. Malak would have to wait until tomorrow. I returned to the elevator lobby, surprisingly empty. I got into the elevator and pressed the button for the twentieth floor.

I saw this whole weekend going to crap, and I wasn't any sort of leader. I was an atomic introvert, trying to make sense of the last couple years.

I was so lost in my thoughts that I didn't notice the passenger who ran to get into the elevator behind me. My face automatically turned toward him as the elevator rose.

Smiling back at me was Elliot Malak.

I instinctively brought my hand to my bracelet where I kept the Set, looking awkward as I tried to smile back. "Are you having a good time in Vegas?" he asked me.

Typical male. Trying to start a conversation on a thirty-second elevator ride. That's all the time I had to form any thoughts in my head... thirty seconds.

"I suppose." I shrugged. I lifted my eyes quickly to the elevator cameras. I couldn't let him pick me up. I couldn't leave this elevator with him. "It's a little too flashy for me."

My mind raced. Whatever issues I had before dissipated into the form of my mark. It was like he was being presented to me as a sacrifice. We were alone in an elevator in the early hours of irony.

The elevator was moving fast. It had sped past the jump floors and was beginning to ding...fifteen... sixteen...

"I'm sure a pretty lady like you can have this entire city." he winked.

Who is he trying to kid?

I smiled and batted my eyelashes a little. "Thanks so much."

Giggle, giggle, shift, shift... yeah buddy you're so smooth.

"You remind me of someone," he said.

"What?" I reacted a bit too nervously as I quickly extracted the Set needle on the bullet charm. When I unfastened the clasp on my bracelet, it fell to the floor in a shimmery mess near Malak's feet.

He was quick to swoop down and pick it up. *What a gentleman.*

I watched as he winced slightly and briefly dropped the bracelet again, before picking it up more carefully.

"One of your charms seems to be broken," he said as he rose to give it back to me. "It stuck me good."

He started to examine it, but I plucked it away and retracted the needle as the elevator slowed to a halt at the twentieth floor.

I stepped out hastily as the doors opened and turned back to face him. I wasn't a coward.

"I'm sorry," I said. There was no right thing to say.

A strange look crossed his face as the doors closed. It was sadness and a sort of understanding. He couldn't have known who I was or that I had just put the end of his life in motion... but still. My whole body shuddered. I stood there stunned for a moment, looking at the closed elevator doors. That last look showed a hint of sadness coming from the face of a kid who would be dead in the next ten to fifteen minutes.

I broke away from my trance and started walking back toward the room.

This was the second kill where I felt a pang of sympathy. It crept up and made my neck itch. I wasn't used to feeling this. It was a weakness. I never felt much of anything when it came to hits.

Goddamn Tricia and her cartel-meddling bullshit.

I wondered if Kat's reaction to everything had softened my stance on the whole hit: young kid trying to escape his undoubtedly overbearing father, killed in his prime because he wanted to be free. It was kind of fucked up... and uncomfortably close to home.

I let myself back into the suite, which was silent and dimly lit. Addi and Kat were both soundly sleeping.

I sat down on one of the couches, and before I could process any more of my stupid feelings, I passed out...

And woke up to Kat's face leering down at me.

It shocked the hell out of me, because I was dreaming that Judah had her kidnapped, killed and buried in the desert, and our grandmother was upset because she had been buried with her ten-karat ruby brooch. I woke up thinking, *why the hell would Kat be wearing that thing anyway?* Like it was the biggest concern.

"What the fuck is your problem?" I waved her face away.

"I'm ready to do this job right," she answered back.

"What fucking time is it?"

"Quarter past eleven," she said. "Time to wake up."

"I hate you," I mumbled and tried to sink back into a comfortable position on the couch.

"Why did you sleep out here?" She shoved me up and aside to sit herself down. "You missed breakfast."

"I don't give a rat's ass."

"I ordered fruit, pancakes, danishes and orange juice. But it's been sitting for two hours."

I sat up straight. "WHY ARE YOU EVEN UP?"

Kat blinked her eyes at me. "I felt bad about last night. I thought I was doing okay, and then at some point, I drank too much and lost control. I woke up this morning without a hangover for the first time in who-knows-how-long and it hit me that I could have seriously fucked us all."

"Well luckily you didn't." I could now feel the knot in my neck from sleeping wrong.

"You've just been working hard trying to get me into the swing of things, and I haven't been very receptive."

"No shit?" I rolled my eyes.

"I'm sorry," she said. "I want to try harder. I'll do my best tonight."

"It's most likely not necessary," I yawned.

"What?"

"Malak's dead," Addi said as she shuffled into the room in a robe, her hair wet. "Frankie offed him last night, according to my morning texts. Hopefully it wasn't suspicious."

"You mean I wasn't supposed to stab him to death in the elevator?" I retorted.

Addi's face remained blank.

"It was fine," I said. "In fact, I think it worked out perfectly."

"What happened?" Kat look genuinely disappointed. She was probably realizing that this whole trip did nothing to prove her worth.

"I left the room with the intent to kill him. I packed the Set around my wrist and headed down to the casino. But once I was down there, my head was clouded with all this bullshit conflict. I was worried about everything and I was just..."

My voice faded, and Kat reached out to pat my knee. "Conflict is good Frankie. It means you're not a psychopath."

I told them, in full detail, everything that transpired in the elevator. Then I was silent for a moment.

"Bodyguard found him this morning," Addi said. "Maybe we should think about getting out of here."

"Is there a reason for them to be suspicious?" I asked.

"No," Addi said. "I don't think so. But the job didn't go as planned, so I think it's best we leave."

"It didn't go as planned, but it still worked," I said.

"I feel like a big dumb animal," Kat sulked.

"Stop with the self-loathing," I said. "You're more tolerable when you're trying to blame everyone else for your actions."

"When do I do that?" She seemed shocked.

"When do you not do that?" Addi chuckled.

Kat was about to answer when there was a loud knock at the door.

I jumped up and motioned for Kat and Addi to be quiet and go into the bedroom area. I crept up to the door and looked out of the peephole.

It was a big dude: nice suit, serious looking, no name tag.

I knew I shouldn't answer. It could be nothing, or it could be something. I didn't want to jeopardize our departure from the hotel, so I slouched a bit and squinted my eyes before opening the door slowly.

I yawned and peered out at the man. "Yes?"

He sized me up. My inner alarm was ringing, because this guy already looked at me with suspicion, and all I did was sleepily answer the door. I kept my cool.

"Is 'ere a Natalie Stewart stayin' in this room, love?" he asked in a thick Cockney accent.

Kat's alias. Shit. She must have told Malak her name or room number.

"Sure." I nodded. "But she passed out last night and isn't up yet. She's deep in with Prince Ambien and a vodka chaser."

I leaned out a bit and whispered, "Drinking problem."

He cocked his head slightly, relaxing his posture. He was definitely a bodyguard—they have a certain douchey mama's-boy air to them.

He most likely was the head bodyguard, judging from his expensive attire.

"Can I give her a message or have her contact you later?"

"I'd just like to ask 'er a few questions concernin' my employer," he responded.

"Is there some sort of problem? If she's caused anyone grief, I should tell you she's very rude and insolent when she's drunk... she'll be quick to apologize once sober."

He hesitated. "No, no, love, I'm jes questionin' everyone who was wit' my employer las' night. Have 'er call me."

He handed me his card.

"Benjamin Parrish," I said. "I'll pass this along to her."

I stepped back to close the door when he placed his hand on it, stopping me.

I looked up at him, surprised.

"I didn' catch your name, love." He cracked a sleazy smile.

"You didn't ask for it." I smirked back, closing the door.

I let out a soft breath and closed my eyes. He could be a problem if he checked the surveillance tapes. Or maybe he already did, and he was assessing the situation. Either way—not good.

I hurried back into the room where Kat was standing there with her hands on her hips.

"Drinking problem?"

"Shut up." I rushed past her. "We need to get out of here."

"Should I tell Judah about that guy?" Addi was right behind me, one of her he-knives in hand. *Over protective, much?*

I didn't really have the chance to unpack, so I closed my Set kit and then grabbed a clean shirt.

"I don't think we should bother," I said finally. "Call the valet for the car. Check out over the phone once we're on the road."

I don't know why I was panicking like this, but something told me Mr. Parrish wasn't someone I wanted to mess with. If money could buy you anything, it could buy amazing protection. He was like eight feet taller than me. I liked having the upper hand. I liked being invisible. Kat made that impossible.

"It'll be fine," Addi said, packing up her array of safety measures in their leather case. "I think he was just being precautionary. Natalie Stewart doesn't exist once we check out. You know that."

"She still said too much," I whispered harshly. "This would have been fine if—"

"It is fine," Addi quieted me down. "Get packed and meet me downstairs. I'll take the first round of luggage to the car."

I stole a glance toward a packing Katharine. She pretended not to overhear, but the look on her face let me know she had.

Kat didn't utter a word as she gathered the rest of her belongings, put on one of her ridiculous hats and large sunglasses, and stormed out the door.

I trailed behind her and rode the elevator in silence… although she gave two irritated bitch sighs.

Kat's black Escalade was waiting for us down at the valet with Addi nestled in the back, looking at her phone. I threw my bag into the back seat with Addi and walked around to the driver's side.

Kat kept her head pointed out her window as I took off toward the 215.

Elegantly Wasted

Chapter Nineteen

Safely on the highway, I let out a sigh of relief.

"Look," I said. "Crisis averted. We're all fine. We did fine. There's no reason to be angry or hurt."

"I know I didn't do a great job," Kat said. "But I'm learning. This isn't a job that I can just take to, you know. I'm not..."

"You're not a killer," I finished for her. "I know that."

"You just need to be more mindful of your task," Addi spoke up from the darkened rear of the SUV, covering her always-cold ass with a blanket. "Maybe we need to limit your alcohol."

Kat pursed her lips. She was starting to get real touchy about her vice, which meant she knew she had a problem.

"I agree," I said. "But this is also largely my fault. I don't have control over either of you, and I need to in these situations. When we get home we will come up with a plan to stay more focused, and we can negotiate compromises. But you will have to start listening to me."

This seemed to placate Katharine, because she seemed to relax a little and throw her hat in the back seat and lean back.

"I did okay at first," she said softly. "I found out a lot about him. Useful stuff. Not that any of it ended up mattering."

It would have mattered if I waited.

"You know he hated that Escargot guy," Kat said.

"Escandon," I corrected.

"Yeah, him." Kat rolled her eyes. "He mentioned him by name. I remember that clearly. He said he was doing what he could to bring him down. It was almost like he knew I was there for information."

I didn't know what to say. I felt the same pang of sadness as when I glimpsed Malak's face for the last time.

"That's weird," I tried not to think too much on it.

We rode in silence until we were well on the way toward Phoenix, past Kingman... when Kat started to complain about her pea-sized bladder.

I hated stopping on road trips. I hated it even more when I was trying to get as much distance between me and the city of sin as possible. It left a bad taste in my mouth.

Katharine would have peed herself if I didn't stop, so I pulled off the 93 into what appeared to be the thriving metropolis of Wikieup, Arizona. It had one gas station... and very few cars. If Arizona had a lot of something, it was creepy little towns.

"Go quickly," I muttered. "You want anything to drink?"

"Water," Addi sounded off from the back seat. *Great, so we could stop to pee again.*

I opened the car door into the blazing sun. Limo tint really made you forget about the safety of your retinas. I made my way toward the run-down mini-mart as a car pulled out and another one pulled in—kicking up dust.

Totally happening hot spot, I thought sourly to myself.

I bought Addi's water, checked my phone and then walked outside toward the bathrooms... Kat hadn't emerged yet—I'm sure she was negotiating the dirty floors and was hovering as high as she could above the toilet seat.

I stopped short. There it was again—that feeling. Something wasn't right.

The door to the bathroom opened and Kat emerged, straightening out her dress.

"Disgusting." She looked up and her eyes focused behind me and squinted.

"What is she..."

Kat stopped talking, and I could see immediate panic register on her face.

A few moments later the sun was blocked out, and I instinctively whirled around into the broad chest of one Benjamin Parrish.

Kat let out some sort of choked agitated animal sound behind me and I looked up, raising my eyebrow.

"May I help you?"

He smiled down at me. I heard the click of his gun, felt it in jab my stomach a second later.

I rolled my eyes. "Really?"

"Stop wastin' my time, Ms. Stewart. Both of ya. Get back into your car. You drive." He gestured to me with his gun.

Was no one seeing this? The old fart behind the minimart counter could at least alert the local cop that my rights were being violated. This is when I got to play out the innocent card. Who would believe some huge slimy dude was hunting down a female contract killer who killed his boss? *No one in Wikieup, that's for sure. Definitely rape waiting to happen. I bet they praise rapists in these here parts.* I debated screaming.

He shoved me forward into Katharine, then grabbed her by the arm.

"What do you think you're doing?" She gave him her best Fairholm evil scowl.

He guided us back to the SUV, shoved Kat into the backseat and watched as I tentatively rounded the car and climbed into the front. I threw the water bottle into the passenger seat.

Kat was whimpering as the doors closed and we were submerged in the darkness of the limo tint. *This might suck.*

"I don't understand what you want," she said.

"Quit jerkin' my chain now, love." He tapped his gun on my seat.

I started the car and gave him a quick glance in the rear-view mirror.

"Drive," he said.

I'm not sure why I spaced Addi out of this equation completely until I was back on the road, but it suddenly hit me that she was nowhere to be seen. The car swerved a bit in my moment of realization, which made Parrish point the gun at me.

"Best not to upset me, or I'll shoot your sister here," he grunted.

I recovered and swallowed hard. Had he gotten rid of Addi before he approached us, or was she hiding? I tried to peer behind Parrish's head in the rear view, but I couldn't see anything.

I drove in silence for a bit before I attempted to talk out the situation.

"What the fuck do you want?" I tried to focus on the road and not my missing cousin.

"Malak came back to 'is room last night talkin' about running into two birds who seemed ta look alike stayin' on the same floor. He said 'e felt strange and 'e thought one 'a them drugged 'im. I didn' think much 's his ramblings at the time. Bugger, he knew how to down a few. But when I found 'im dead this mornin' I got ta thinkin.'."

He seemed genuinely upset—most likely because I relieved him of a rather large monthly check.

"At first I figured 'is old man had a hit called on 'im. I knew the old trap had a vendetta for 'is boy. Tha's why he hired me. But never in a million years would he send a woman to kill him. Arabs are damn traditional that way. Nah. You were sent by Rico."

I blinked. My shock came out in an awkward laugh. "No, pretty sure that dude is next on my list."

"Don't jerk my dick, missy," Parrish spat. "Rico is pissed at Malak for screwing things up—for screwing his rich bitch mistress who ended up dead last month."

Well that was too much a coincidence. Seems like Tricia was getting around.

I couldn't entirely see Kat in my rear view, but I could feel her pressing into my seat. It was slow and methodical, not panicked—a message.

"I'm actually impressed," he said. "I can tell this one's clumsy. She don't pose much of a threat."

He reached out and grabbed Kat's chin. "I don't have to worry much about her, do I, when I dump yer corpses in the desert. But you," he looked back to me, "yer a handful, aren't ya, love?"

He chuckled to himself. He thought he was pretty funny. I liked that about big, dumb body guards... they were just full of shit.

"I'll most likely 'ave some fun with which one o' ya I kill last," he went on. "Any volunteers?"

Good to know he's an upstanding citizen. My eyes moved to a shadow behind him in the rear of the car.

There was a series of swift motions as Addi grabbed his head, ran a large knife along the length of his neck and pulled back hard on his hair, making blood spray everywhere, including onto Katharine and the window behind her.

"Me," she seethed into his ear. "You fucking prick."

I slammed on the brakes, and the car skidded off the road to the shoulder. It almost did a full circle before I got the car to a stop in a huge jolt. I could hear the knife drop somewhere behind me.

Katharine screamed loudly as Parrish's mouth opened and closed like a fish out of water. His eyes were understandably surprised. He slumped over into her lap.

There was silence in the car as I assessed the situation and the dirt settled from my sudden stop.

"Frankie!" Katharine yelled. "Get him off of me!"

I leaped out of the car and opened the back door, dragging Katharine out onto the dirt.

She scrambled over to a small cluster of dead bushes and started to puke on all fours.

I stood there, watching in a trance for a moment before I heard a car passing slowly. I turned toward the road, where I saw an older couple slowing to a stop. I waved them on, hoping I didn't seem too panicked. No one consciously wanted to stop for anyone who was hoarking in the bushes, so they waved and sped up. *Don't mind us. Just killing a loose end.*

Once Katharine was done, she turned to me and sat down in the gravel, trying to wipe blood from her face.

I wrinkled my nose, grabbed Addi's blanket and threw it over Katharine before another car passed.

"Stay here," I ordered. "I can't drag a body out of the car in broad daylight, and you look like a horror movie."

I looked in at Addi.

"Fuck me, I thought he killed you before he got to us," I breathed out.

"Please," Addi pulled herself into the backseat and climbed out of the car, careful to avoid Parrish's body. "You didn't even see him pull up behind you?"

"I didn't think to pay attention," I huffed. "I didn't think he'd fucking follow us out here!"

Addi reached back into her purse, pulled out some makeup wipes and began to clean the blood from her hands. "That was all pure luck. I saw him pull up in a small sedan. I had to bank on him using the Escalade for his getaway, although causing a scene in bum-fuck nowhere probably would have been just fine."

"How did he not even know about you?" I breathed.

"He never saw me." Addi looked back at Parrish's body. "He must have had no idea there was a third hitter. I call that extreme luck—I mean we walked out in broad daylight."

"He wasn't that smart," I said. "You left first, maybe he just missed ever seeing you."

I turned and looked down at Kat, who hadn't said anything but was sitting on the gravel with the blanket around her in the extreme heat.

Addi handed me a few wipes and motioned her head toward Kat.

"You okay, Kat?" I asked.

"Two shirts," she said wiping blood from her face with the blanket corner. "Two perfectly good designer shirts. Ruined! On one trip!"

"I think she's fine." I said, and surveyed the area. "I think there's an access road halfway between here and Wickenburg. We should drive out there and wait til sunset. Then hide the body."

Katharine stumbled to her feet. "I am not hiding a fucking body, Frankie!"

"You'll do what I tell you to do." I threw her a look and handed her the wipes. "Change if you have to, but shut the fuck up and deal with this situation."

Addi smiled over at me before shoving Parrish's body over.

"Give me that blanket," she said. "There's a lot of blood."

"My car!" Kat shrieked, realization dawning on her. "Are you fucking kidding me? Frankie! This is total bullshit! He's ruined my car! I can't exactly take it to be detailed!"

I held up my hand. "Relax. I'll call Judah and explain what happened. He'll send someone to come take the car from the house tomorrow, and you'll get a new one."

"And that just fixes everything? I bought this car with my own money!"

"And you'll get a new one free of charge," I said through clenched teeth. "You can take it up with Judah later, but for now change your clothes and let's get going."

Elegantly Wasted

Kat stormed to the back of the car and opened the hatch. "Really, Addi? You had to slice his throat in front of me? What the fuck is wrong with you?"

"I couldn't get the bigger knife out," she reasoned. "I thought about stabbing him through the seat, but I didn't want him to shoot you. I needed quick and painless."

This is a perfectly normal conversation.

"I asked one simple thing," Kat muttered while thrashing through her clothes and angrily putting on a new shirt. "I said don't kill anyone in front of me. Pretty simple request. What's the first thing that happens? My other cousin opens someone's jugular in my fucking face."

She wiped her face clean, slammed the back shut and marched to the front passenger side.

"Both of you..." She waved her arms. "Both of you are lunatics."

Addi smiled slightly and shook her head before jumping into the back seat, covering the rest of Parrish with the blanket.

I secured myself into the front seat, letting the whole ordeal settle.

"Unbelievable," Kat kept muttering.

"How about a thank you?" I asked her.

"What?" Kat seemed appalled.

"Addi saved your life," I said. "I'm pretty sure that fucker was going to rape you."

"Excuse me, Thelma and Louise," Kat said, turning to face us, "I have a man's blood in my hair. I'm not thanking anyone until we are home, and I have had a bath and a doctor's appointment."

Addi snickered from the back seat. I caught a glance of her face and started to chuckle too. Katharine looked at us both like we were crazy before her face cracked into a smile.

After a few moments we were all laughing—dead guy in the back seat and all. Team Fairholm might work well after all.

Elegantly Wasted

Chapter Twenty

"And then we dumped him in a cactus patch ten miles off the ninety-three in the middle of nowhere," Katharine said. "Between two large boulders."

Emma blinked and then looked at me. I nodded.

"Wow," she muttered. "That's probably the worst hit story I've ever heard. And I've heard a lot. Two agents once had to rescue another agent from a Haitian voodoo cult."

I rolled my eyes. "Judah thought so, too. I think I rendered him speechless with the story."

"You just left him there?" Emma asked.

"Why not?" Katharine yawned. "His blood ruined my car."

"The info dump on Malak said he was an under-the-table sort of guy, so if his bodyguard followed us, he was someone who probably doesn't have any family and was most likely a criminal. I know I'm trying to make the situation sound better, but his body is hidden from view. The desert is a cruel mistress."

"Hope the coyotes eat his dead carcass," Kat spat. "He was disgusting. I should have just stayed married to my gay husband. At least he never would have hurt me."

"Shut up," I rolled my eyes. "Judging from your OCD and the wine bottles that might as well have nipples secured to the top—I'd say that guy hurt you, too."

That shut her up.

"You completed your own sweep." Emma kept looking back and forth between us. "That's actually pretty impressive."

She was right. We cleaned up our own situation. We tied up our loose ends—rather Benjamin decided to tie them up for us. I wasn't going to be held responsible for the death of a guy who could have just let the whole situation go.

"So the whole thing wasn't a total waste of training me. I learned a lot. I learned that Addi is a crazed lunatic and fits in a lot more than I do. Fabulous. Now what?" Katharine crossed her arms in front of her as a scowl settled on her face.

"Now the real fun begins."

Emma and I turned toward Katharine with smiles on our faces.

The months that followed went a little bit smoother. *I stress "a little bit."*

Kat started to fall into a routine of approaching marks and had a whole stage play she seemed to follow. She was getting more and more easy-going about our business trips, although she tended to get pissy when contracts interfered with her weekend excursions and social digs. Running a contract killing front is tough—especially when you have to juggle a social life.

Addi still disappeared into her charity work from time to time. She was heading a new one called the Wishing Well, which gave education and medical care to children in third-world countries. She hadn't killed anyone since the bodyguard. She simply watched me kill marks. I couldn't decide if that irritated me or gave me the creeps.

It was hard to control them both. They were very much on their own schedule, if I didn't tell them where to be. On top of that, I had to deal with a nagging mother and verbally abusive grandmother, both of whom were drunks. Everyone did little to appease my murderous impulses.

I started to realize I had much more of a problem than I initially thought. I needed to kill. It wasn't just something I happened to be good at. My issues were larger than any personality disorder.

Usually about two weeks passed between jobs. Around the two-week mark, I would get a low buzz in my ears and my irritation level shot through the roof. I'd get antsy and fidgety to the point people noticed.

It only lasted a day or two, because the moment I got a text, I calmed down. Just knowing I would kill someone soon quieted whatever demon was pushing through to the surface.

One particular month was bad. Addi was trying her best to avoid me and my shitty personality. I was going on three weeks without a job, and I was losing it. I was going to shoot a student for writing "your" instead of "you're," and Kat had to relieve me of my classes because I shoved Gretchen for saying "Somebody has a case of the Mondays" to me—which wouldn't have been bad, but we were at the top of the staircase, and had she not caught herself on the rail, she probably would have broken her neck.

It didn't help that Osiris had pretty much taken over Elegance, Inc. earlier in the month by closing off the entire back portion and moving in a construction crew. You couldn't see what they were up to of course—and as far as Kat knew, they were adding to the wine cellar. *Adding what? A bomb shelter?*

The hammering, the sawing, the grinding—I tried to venture over to shut them up, but all I succeeded in doing was getting to the edge of the caution tape before a worker yelled at me to keep back.

Yelled. At me. Don't you know who I am? I'll fucking kill you!

To top off the delicious week, Grandmother summoned Kat and me to have high tea with her. If I was even slightly normal, I would still hate the shit out of high tea. *Who the hell even holds these things anymore? Where are we? Pre-Revolutionary France?*

I didn't say much as I sat at the table with a permanent scowl on my face, occasionally stuffing a scone into it. Whenever Joan spoke, my skin would crawl, and I would start hallucinating about killing her in extravagant ways... in front of all of her ungracefully aging guests.

"Katharine here has a divine little school that helps people with their etiquette and manners," Joan drawled. "Francesca is one of the teachers. Although, I'm hard pressed to think she's any good at teaching manners."

She gave me a condescending look as I smiled and put my elbows on the table.

"This one ran away to Europe after I offered to pay her way through college." Joan kept her vampire glare on me. "As ungrateful as she is, I'm happy to see her applying herself to such a good company. Those who can't do, teach."

My fingers curled and clutched the tablecloth as I thought about the knife I kept secured in my boot (or purse, if I was wearing a skirt). Addi had been showing me a few tricks. Just a flick of the wrist and problem solved. *Kat had to be used to blood being sprayed in her face by now, right? Great idea all around. Anything to stop this buzzing.*

There were only twenty people here tops, and all of them were too old and senile to identify me accurately. *I could get away with this shit. Maybe I could just smash her face into her fine china. That's clean.* I leaned toward Joan with what I'm sure was an evil grin on my face.

Kat suddenly patted my hand, and I was surprised to see a look of worried understanding on her face. She was figuring things out. She had to. It was her job now. Reading people and getting answers was her job.

"Let's go," she mouthed.

As I burst through the doors of her majesty's quarters—not a moment too soon—Kat caught up to my shit-fit, stomping run and whirled me around, grabbing my shoulders.

"Repeat after me," she started.

I stared back at her blankly. The buzzing in my head was now causing a headache.

"I will never hurt a family member."

The buzzing stopped abruptly, replaced by a sharp pain on both sides of my head.

"What?" I was surprised.

"Repeat it to me. Say you promise."

So, she can tell what I am thinking.

Joan really didn't give the girl enough credit.

"It hurts," I said softly, the pain in my head making me wince.

Kat reached up and gently brushed a strand of hair from my face and then placed her hand on my cheek.

"You're trying, Frankie, I know you are, but you need to find some sense of control. I know I haven't done my part in helping you feel accepted. I'll do better by you, but I need you to promise me this one thing."

"I will never hurt a family member," I repeated slowly. "I promise."

Katharine nodded to me. Kat knew I needed to hurt someone to make the pain go away. She knew I was about to hurt our grandmother.

What the fuck is wrong with me?

I needed to get a grip.

"Keep that promise," Kat said.

"I will."

However, I couldn't ensure anyone else's safety if we didn't get a job soon. Thankfully, later that day, Judah called.

This was the big one: Murder Rico Escandon, the asshole drug lord. On paper, we were avenging a Mexican Federal Investigations Agent who was murdered by the Sinaloa drug cartel.

Yes, yes, drug cartel sounds great. Narcotraficantes, whatever—just get me the fuck out of here.

"I don't like it," Judah voiced his opposition. "This feels too soon. But apparently you impressed the upper chain of command by disposing of dead bodies in the desert."

Oh, do I detect a hint of jealousy?

"Stop being so supportive," I quipped. "It's really smothering."

Judah's voice had become somewhat of a comfort to me. I hadn't been in his presence in years, but I still felt close to him. I knew that beneath that calm, irritated exterior lay the heart of one of my more stable father figures. He cared about what happened to me. It was refreshing.

"I'm only concerned," he argued. "There's no one to back you up this time if something goes wrong. You mess up and you're the trophies of whichever cartel member kills you first."

I flinched a little at his words. Katharine would be none too pleased with the prospects of being tortured and mailed back to her parents in pieces. Good thing we had aliases.

Thankfully we weren't going into balls-deep Mexico to take down an entire cartel—it was just one target, with the exception of collateral damage. Basically, we were given free range to kill whomever came at us.

Ricardo "Rico" Esquivel Escandon. I loved names that were more than eighty syllables long. It just insinuated that he was a huge dickhead.

What I had learned since killing Tricia was that Rico was a corrupt congressman from the state of Jalisco who was losing a lot of money due to the undercover work of the now-dead FIA agent Santiago Cantu. Rico orchestrated the graphic murder of Cantu, who had suspected Rico had ties to the Sinaloa cartel, but hadn't been able to prove it. Cantu had been an honest man whose job was to root out corruption in Mexican police and government, specializing in drug cartels.

Cantu eventually snuck a bug into Rico's office and recorded a conversation of the big bad Sinaloan making arrangements to divert a truckload of semiautomatic rifles headed for the army base outside of Puerto Vallarta. With this information, the Mexican DEA intercepted the truck and Rico was out quite a large chunk of money.

On top of that, Cantu had information connecting him to human trafficking. Knowing exactly who was responsible, Rico ordered Cantu kidnapped, tortured and decapitated before any more information was released. Magically, the evidence against Rico disappeared. For added hatred factor, Rico requested Cantu's head be put in a box, wrapped with festive paper and bows, and left on his own doorstep where his kids could open it—special delivery for the Cantu family. I almost liked Rico's style, but supplying weapons to a drug cartel in your country was a no-no, human trafficking even more so. Not to mention I wasn't a fan of parental abandonment and those who caused it.

How Osiris had all this information and the media didn't—well, that was the type of question I never asked. My guess was that this was a big mess that would ruin any hope of Rich Ellingson running for president one day. So... Osiris would quietly end it all.

Later that night, we gathered in the living room. I read off the mission specifics while Addi and Kat gave themselves manicures.

"We're sisters on vacation from Austin, Texas." I rifled through papers on Rico Escandon and key members of the Sinaloa cartel. "Rico is spending his weekends at his oceanfront mansion on the cliffs south of Puerto Vallarta. The area is thick with cliffside rentals, and I have one picked out for us to vacation at. October is ending, so there will be some Dia De Los Muertos festivities. It will be a good chance to mingle and poke around."

"I have such a bad southern accent," Katharine complained, filing her nails.

"That's really the least of your worries," Addi whispered to her. "You don't have to have an accent, but we should decide on that before we leave. It's a little Three Stooges for only one of us to have a bad accent."

"I'll take the target out Sunday night," I went on, ignoring them. "He's got guards and a family. It's unclear if the family is around, so we're going to have to spend a good portion of Friday and Saturday staking the place out. I'd like to try to only kill the mark."

I paused for a few moments. Kat put the nail file down and grabbed the paperwork.

"This FIA guy was decapitated?" Katharine's voice rose. "Are you kidding me?"

"It's a drug cartel." Addi shrugged. "They dismember people who get in their way."

"I don't want to go." Katharine crossed her arms in front of her. "This is bullshit, and I don't need to be a part of it."

Apparently Princess Katharine had some issues with big bad drug kingpins. *There's a shocker.*

"It's not as complicated as it sounds," I reasoned. "It's just the one guy and, quite frankly, he's a congressman—not really a drug lord, I don't think. He can't be that dangerous."

"Fuck you, Frankie! You always say that. He's not THAT dangerous," she mocked. "Then all of a sudden a huge English bodyguard is trying to rape me! This guy has armed fucking guards and is tied to a drug cartel. Ergo, he's fucking dangerous!"

I felt my hackles go up. I had to bite my lip to keep from screaming at Kat that danger was a part of the whole fucking job. *Really—contract killing is totally safe, bring the kids along.*

"Look, Kat," I said, trying to keep my voice normal, "all jobs are dangerous. There isn't a safety regulation on hits. We don't answer to a union. I need your help, and if you won't listen to some comforting facts then I have nothing but the Tank for you."

Katharine clenched her jaw and rolled her eyes. I wanted to tell her that she looked exactly like her mother when she did that, but I remained silent.

After Vegas, Judah came up with the Tank. It was an add-on to the Glendale warehouse. It consisted of a dark room with no windows. It was solitary confinement, where Kat had to watch horrible movies over and over. It did an okay job at leveling out her alcoholism and getting her to focus more on the missions.

"Fine, I'll go," she said finally. "But I swear to God if they cut my head off..."

"Come on, a pretty girl like you will be sold into sex slavery."

Elegantly Wasted

Chapter Twenty-One

Katharine and Addi were anything but subtle. They stepped off the plane in two very different grand fashions.

Katharine looked like a Dolce & Gabbana billboard. She had the idea that we were going on a Mexican safari into the deep jungle—so she looked like Anna Wintour and Panama Jack had a kid. She was adorned in a crème satin blouse, matching slacks and a white fedora. Her oversized purse was also white, matching her pumps. I couldn't wait until the humidity got to her royal highness.

Addi, on the other hand, had taken a vacation from her usual rigid corporate attire and embraced the Mexican culture in full force. She looked like a flamenco dancer had thrown up on her. If there was a loud color available in the world, I'm pretty sure it was on Addi at the moment.

I smiled at the back of their heads. I wandered behind them in my white tank top and jeans. My flashiest item was a pair of black Fendi sunglasses— their main purpose was to keep my long hair out of my face.

I gave a sideways glance to another, much smaller, plane that was arriving at the open tarmac of the Puerto Vallarta airport. The jet was private and unmarked. I hoped it was my artillery. We weren't allowed to travel with weapons of any kind. Osiris set up a separate transport, funded by whichever government agency liked to deny its existence.

I didn't have to worry about how it got to me, it just did—usually before I even checked into a hotel.

This stay was different. It was longer—Thursday through Sunday—and we were staying in a vacation rental villa. That would mean lots of places to hide my guns. I didn't need many, but my orders were to execute Rico with a point-blank shot to the head—no sniper and no Set. Someone wanted it to be personal, *again*.

I wondered who exactly was behind this order, because the Cantu family was humble and couldn't afford the likes of me. I didn't need a degree in economics to know that Cantu was a scapegoat.

Once we got through customs and into the rental car place, I was exhausted. Katharine kept chattering in an over-done Southern accent, and it was starting to make my eye twitch. "You don't need to have an accent, Katharine."

"But it's fun!"

"Oh, well, as long as you're having fun," I muttered.

"Yeah! Let's party like Mexican rock stars, if they existed!" she said, much too loudly.

She made a disapproving noise as she noticed the available cars.

"Why can't I hire a driver and a decent car?"

"And draw even more attention to yourself?" I eyed her cryptically.

"That one." She pointed to a black H2.

"Your carbon footprint must be huge," Addi sighed.

"Whatever, I wear a size six," Katharine spat back. "I refuse—refuse—to be stuck in this... " She tried to find the name of the tiny car. "...Chevy-Chevy for four days."

I was about to lose it. "There," I said, pointing, "a Jeep Wrangler. I found the middle ground. Crisis averted."

Addi drove to Mismaloya. She was used to driving in other countries and could negotiate the lack of road rules in Mexico. *Did you know you have to get into the far right lane to turn left? Sheer brilliance.*

"Just get me somewhere I can drink a margarita and sleep in a bathing suit," Kat directed.

It was quiet in Mismaloya and the surrounding areas. The jungle had one road in and one road out.

The weather wasn't too bad for the end of October. Our rental was a new villa built on the opposite cliffside from the Escandon Estate. There was a cove in between us that I probably would have appreciated more if I wasn't on assignment.

Katharine disappeared right away and reemerged a few minutes later wearing a pink bikini, white high-heeled sandals and a large white hat. "I'm off to the pool."

"I need you back here at six o'clock. We're going to a bar down the coast a bit. I'll need you at your best, so no drinking until you get there. You can't be drunk on this trip."

"What kind of vacation is this?" Kat frowned.

I knocked her hat off her head. "The kind where we kill people."

I wasn't sure how safe Mexican fireworks were, but watching children run down the street practically on fire made me a little uneasy. They seemed to be having fun though—they were shrieking, with large smiles on their dirty faces. Kids had it so easy. If someone like me ran screaming up and down the street with sparklers and no shirt on—I'd be arrested—or filmed.

I turned my attention to the people in the bar where I was sitting. None of the establishments had many walls. Almost everything was open, which kept my claustrophobia at bay. It wasn't a huge issue, but there was a definite reason I opted to snipe marks from rooftops rather than getting up close and personal.

Four tourists from Boston, a gay couple from San Francisco now holding permanent residence in Puerto Vallarta and a group of college kids from San Diego currently occupied the bar's tables, scattered in the shade. I now knew all of them.

"Hi, nice to meet you, my name is Alice."

It was fairly easy to make friends in vacation areas, because everyone was so happy to be away from their nowhere lives... well with the exception of Mr. and Mr. Simon-Napp. Those two were rich and retired.

In this touristy town, why did I choose this bar? Rico owned it. Presently he was upstairs with Katharine. She caught the eye of one of his bodyguards right away—just as planned.

I ordered a beer and then walked to the seaside part of the establishment, where I could hear the waves lapping against the rocks.

I could also hear Katharine laughing upstairs. She was hard at work. Her laughter held traces of nervousness in it, and I made a mental note to slap her later. I was probably too hard on her, but she had to get over the severity of the situation and focus on seducing the enemy.

I sat down at a table nestled in the corner, where I had a clear view of the ocean and I could slightly overhear what Kat was up to. Addi had come down with a migraine, so I let her sleep. It wasn't imperative that she stake out anything tonight anyway. I could sit on my own and read. It was Mexico—no one really questioned your actions.

I opened The Bell Jar by Sylvia Plath, good reading for someone of my psychological state.

I felt a wet nose nudge my leg. I looked down at the bar's bouncer—a mexi-mutt named Sweetie. She was a medium-sized black dog with a small head. Her gigantic ears were torn, marking her street status.

"Hola, Niña," I cooed to her. If our parents taught us anything, it was to love animals and hate humans. I was so busy fussing over the awkward animal that I didn't notice Rico approach me.

The dog suddenly growled in his direction and I looked up, surprised.

"Señorita." He tilted his head in greeting.

Ricardo Escandon looked much younger than his thirty-seven years. He smiled at me when I didn't answer.

"It's a beautiful evening," he tried again to speak to me.

Fuck. Why is he trying to talk to me? Where is Kat?

"Yeah," I said.

Lame. Lame. Lame.

Sweetie barked at Rico, and he threw the dog a nasty look.

"Salgate de mi bar, mestizo," he snarled.

"Hey," I frowned. "I like her."

He smiled at me, and I realized he was pretty fucking good looking.

"She doesn't like me."

"She has standards," I retorted.

"You don't like me," he concluded.

"I don't know you." I rolled my eyes.

Seriously, what was going on? I gave the bar a quick sweep with my eyes. Katharine hadn't come downstairs, and I couldn't hear her voice anymore.

He sat down at my table and extended his hand to me.

"I'm Rico," he said. "I own this bar."

I looked at his hand a moment before taking it.

"Alice."

"Hello, Alice," he said in his accent-ridden voice. *Damn, he was extremely good looking (my final verdict).* He had dark, ominous eyes that only slightly concerned me, a nice husky build, well-kept dark hair and a crooked smile.

I went back to my book. I was trying feverishly to figure out what to do without drawing too much attention to myself.

"Your sister," Rico went on. "She talks a lot more than you."

I slammed the book down. "There's a reason. Why don't you go bug her?"

His expression darkened for a moment. I could tell he was getting frustrated with me, but I didn't care. I was pissed off. I didn't want to converse with this guy. I had to kill him in a few days.

"You caught my eye," he said. "I wanted to meet you."

Caught his eye? My messy, brown hair; my lack of make up; my white, Target-bought tank top; my cargo khakis; my worn sandals and permanent toe ring caught his eye?

Give me a break.

Oh wait—boobs. Sometimes I forgot how much they preceded me.

"Well, you met me." I gave him a tight smile.

Sweetie suddenly gave a high-pitched bark and took off out the doorway to chase a slow-moving vehicle. *Great. No more protection against the bad guy.*

"Can I buy you a drink?"

I got up quickly and banged my knee on the table, making everyone in the bar turn and look. *Perfect.*

"I have to go, actually," I stuttered. "Nice to meet you."

I could feel his gaze on me as I hurried out of the bar. I took off running up toward the villa (all uphill) and didn't stop until I collapsed in a heap on one of the deck chaises. I stayed there for about ten minutes as the sky finally went dark.

Addi shuffled out and turned on the porch light. "What are you doing?"

"I had to get out of there."

"Did you just leave Kat? What did you see?"

Oh, oops. Guess leaving her in a bar with criminals is pretty shitty.

I got up and walked to the porch railing, gazing out into the darkening ocean. Across the way, I could see Rico's sprawling villa lighting up the peninsula.

"I tell you what I didn't see. I didn't see Kat doing her fucking job."

Addi walked over to me, concern showing on her face.

"Why, what happened?"

"Rico came up to me. He talked to me."

"That's it?" Addi yawned. "That's good. You can get close to him if he's interested."

"That's Kat's job!"

"In this case, I don't think it matters who gets his attention as long as someone does," Addi pointed out. "If he's taken an interest in you, then go with it."

Addi turned to the sound of the front door opening and slamming. The entire back wall of the condo was an open door that ran into the deck—Mismaloya was big on utilizing their tropical weather.

"What the hell?" Kat was breathing hard. "Frankie just left me."

I turned toward her. "What were you doing? I was at the bar and the mark came to talk to me."

Kat shook her head in aggravation. "He wouldn't even look twice at me. I was stuck trying to get rid of one of his stupid bodyguards. I must attract them with my perfume or something. Once you left, Rico grilled me for your information. I had to practically escape myself. I told him we'd be back later."

Addi smirked. Apparently she liked the idea of Kat not being able to seduce someone. Moreover she was probably dying, thinking that Kat's charms didn't work and my lack of charm did.

"Ha," Addi said. "Rico likes Frankie."

"So, he has bad taste." I shrugged. "Not my problem."

"Oh, it is your problem, because none of those hardened criminal nut bars would tell me a damn thing," Kat huffed. "But Rico seems pretty darn interested in you. You have the bigger boobs, so he must be a tit man."

I shook my head. *Absolutely unbelievable.*

On top of Kat's wonder powers not working, Rico tried to pick me up. The guy had a family and yet that didn't seem to matter. He didn't even seem broken up about the loss of good 'ol Tricia. Rico was probably just used to getting his way. *What a shit head.*

"I can't socialize with a hit," I said. "It's against rule ten."

"Fuck your rule ten," Kat replied.

"Okay fine," I said. "I'll just go case his hacienda by myself later. You'll still need to try and get some numbers for me. How many bodyguards, what kind of artillery, keep them talking..."

Kat glanced at the clock. It was only eight o'clock.

"In that case, dinner and drinks on me." She smirked.

Kat loved her alcohol. She had me wondering if she just didn't try very hard to talk to Rico—that maybe she even told him to come talk to me. I wanted to ask her, but if she had, I would have been forced to beat her over the head with my gun—and I promised not to hurt family members.

I watched her pop open a bottle of Chardonnay almost instantaneously and give me a huge grin.

"I'd appreciate you retaining some of your wits," I told Kat. "Because if shit goes down you will need to defend yourself—or, heaven forbid, one of us."

She eyed the bottle of wine. "Shit won't go down for a couple of days. Can't I enjoy myself tonight? Then I'll ease up until Sunday."

Aspiring alcoholics always made such good compromises.

Addi took the moment to grab two beers from the fridge. "Well, we all might as well relax. No sense in being all pent up and nervous for the whole weekend. That will attract the wrong attention."

She handed me one of the bottles. I had always preferred beer over wine—maybe it was the fact that almost the entire family drank wine and, in some twisted reasoning, I thought if I stayed away from wine, I wouldn't become an alcoholic. Deep down I knew that was a stupid way to think.

I downed the beer, but I didn't relax.

Once Kat finished her wine, we headed back out for dinner. I lagged behind the half mile down the hill to the small bar.

"Cheer up, small fry," Addi chirped. She hadn't called me that since I was a kid. I hated it. *Black sheep, small fry, cupcake, Frankenstein... nicknames were stupid.* I didn't understand their necessity.

We entered the bar. Rico was bartending for some strange reason. He noted our arrival and waved with a stupid grin on his face.

Kat returned his wave with equal enthusiasm, and I just nodded. She pinched me.

"Stop being Frankie. Start being Alice," she whispered.

As we sat down, Rico waved my book over his head. He jumped over the bar and shuffled up to our table.

"You left this here," he smiled, extremely proud of himself. "I wanted to return it."

"Thanks," I grabbed it and tried my best to smile. "Didn't know you also worked here."

Rico kept his smile. "I do what I want."

He winked at me. *I wonder if this was the smoothness Tricia fell for.*

"Another sister?" He glanced at Addi.

"Veronica," Addi drawled and held out her hand. "I'm the oldest and the least fun."

He sized her up and nodded. "Alice, Veronica and..." he tilted his head at Kat. "Natalie."

Kat waved the wine glass that she had brought from the house. "Chardonnay," she ordered—no reason to be sweet when the guy wasn't interested.

He didn't lose his smooth disposition as he took the glass from her and made his way back to the bar.

"I'm telling you," Kat said. "Just sweet talk that guy a bit and get all the information you need. If Osiris can turn our lives upside down, we can adjust their rules."

Osiris would have to make a special rule set just for Kat, with footnotes.

"I don't want to admit it," Addi nudged me. "But she's right."

God, I hated them at the moment. I got up and threw them both ugly looks that were ignored.

Rico had given the glass to the actual bartender and said a slew of words in Spanish too quickly for me to catch.

"Hi," I over-emphasized as I approached the bar.

He winked at me. "Following me?"

Oh fuck you. "Yes." I smiled. "Since this is your bar, what do you suggest?"

He visually accosted me for the fifth time that day. "Let me get you the house specialty."

I sat down at the bar and clutched my book in my hands.

He nodded to my hands. "Why Sylvia Plath? Isn't she... depresiva?"

"Maybe I like depressing."

He studied me. "No, I don't think so."

"No?" *The audacity of this guy.*

"Your eyes... don't speak of depression."

Oh, so Ricardo Escandon was a shrink. He was a bar owner, congressman, drug trafficker and mental health advocate. Lucky me. If I didn't have to kill him I could have married him and made my mother extremely proud.

Oh wait, he was already married.

"Aren't you observant," I answered. "I like Plath. She's dark. I like dark, no matter how non-depressive my eyes are."

Truthfully I didn't know what this guy was talking about. My eyes were brown and boring... and they saw a lot of death.

"Dark Alice," he chuckled. He passed me a large margarita with a pink straw. *House specialty—of course it was.*

I took a long sip from the straw. "So, what else do you do besides run a bar?"

He wiped the counter with a rag. "This is my vacation area. I actually live in Puerto Vallarta. I'm a Jalisco congressman."

"You bartend on weekends?" I cocked my head to the side. "Interesting."

"Mexico runs a bit different than America," he said.

Yeah, no shit, Captain Obvious. "So, you're a politician."

"Yes, does that impress you?"

"Not really." I smiled.

He never took his eyes off me, which was starting to make me uneasy. "I'd like to make love to you."

I swallowed hastily and coughed. *Subtle.*

"How romantic." I tried to look insulted.

He reached out and touched my hands, which were still grasping The Bell Jar. "I am sorry for being forward."

I had him. This was it. Frankie 1 – Rico 0. He just sealed his fate by hitting on his hitter. Only I wasn't supposed to kill him tonight. *Guess I'll do other things.*

"Fine. Wanna get out of here?" I asked as I downed the last of the margarita. "Show me your casita."

For the record, if a shrink had to diagnose me, I wouldn't want to know what the ever-living fuck was wrong with me.

"I have just the place." He grinned back.

Ugh. He was really good looking. Rule ten was making more and more sense.

I got up and waved to my cousins. Addi nodded at me. It was time for her to go to work. She would have to follow us—if not physically, she would have to go back to the house and scope out his estate from our end of the cliffside.

Rico led me outside and down the side of the cliff to a decent-sized motor boat. He unhooked it from the dock and hopped aboard before offering his hand to help me on.

"Where are we going? I can't just disappear with a stranger," I said. "My sisters will call out the guards."

As if on cue, Addi called out from the top of the cliff. "Oh Alice, dear, where are you going?"

I looked up at her. "With Rico."

"Where are you taking her, Rico?"

He pointed to his estate in the cove. "Casa La Vista. Number eight."

"Very well." She eyed him aggressively. "Keep her safe or I'll kill you."

Funny joke.

"I'll keep her perfectly safe." He grinned back up to her.

"Don't stay out all night." Addi switched her gaze to me.

Now she sounded concerned for my safety, but it was absolutely too late.

Elegantly Wasted

Chapter Twenty-Two

I woke with a start. That's usually how it happens. Bad girls have to wake with starts—sitting up in bed gasping, clutching the sheets and acting like they don't know full well what they did the night before... and the following morning.

I looked down to my right. Rico still slept soundly.

Bad. Badbadbadbadbad. Malo!

The sun blared in at me from a large open window.

I jumped out of the very comfortable bed and was relieved to find out I had the initiative to put my bra and panties back on after our vicious rounds of love making.

Latin lovers—not really a myth. Rico stirred, but didn't wake.

It was like a bad telenovela playing out, and I was the star.

Stupid gringa.

I whirled around and located my tank top and khakis. Two seconds and dressed—*way to go, Frankie!*

I tiptoed out into the massive hallway and surveyed my surroundings. I wasn't sure which way to go from here.

Rico had shown me around briefly before he had me bent over his kitchen table. The margarita had just enough Don Julio in it for me to not object. Apparently his wife hadn't joined her husband on this trip. In fact, the entire mansion was pretty vacant, minus the casually dressed guards walking the grounds. I think there might have been a wedding photo on the wall in the living room, but I tried not to look too hard.

Telling myself to calm down, I did what I came to do in the first place. I walked the length of hallway and noted that the house was a large square with a courtyard in the middle, branching off into sections upstairs. I quietly made my way to the second floor. It was much more complicated up there. There were hallways leading in different directions and an entire area that looked like it was built over the ocean. I didn't go far, because a sound from one of the rooms made me rethink my scouting mission. I threw up my arms, pretending to be confused, then made my way back downstairs and jetted out into the morning light.

Touchdown—crowd goes wild.

It was only Friday. I had a night and day to think about my dirty night sleeping with the enemy. *God.* I was sick.

No one was more upset than Addi. She was waiting for me at the door. She was more than upset—she was downright disgusted.

"Day one and you have sex with the mark?" She was trying to keep her voice as normal as she could. "Are you completely insane, Francesca Beatrice Fairholm?"

Fuck, she hit me with the full name shit.

She looked at me critically. "Don't answer that."

"I got myself in there," I said.

"Literally." Kat chuckled from under her hangover.

"What on earth is wrong with you?" Addi shook her head in disapproval. "We have been worried sick!"

I had to admit I kind of felt bad. I didn't like disappointing either of them. As time passed, Addi began to see more and more of who I really was, and it continued to shock her.

Suddenly Kat blew a raspberry and laughed. "Give me a break, Addi. I've witnessed many mornings with you doing the walk of shame after going home with some guy at a bar."

"That's not the same thing." Addi crossed her arms in front of her chest. "I didn't sleep with them and then kill them two days later like a praying mantis."

"Or black widow," I muttered.

"You know how disturbing this is," Addi said to Kat. "She has to kill him. She's becoming more and more sociopathic."

Maybe I just needed to have sex and the best option is someone who definitely won't call again.

Kat considered Addi's words. "I think Frankie knows what she's doing."

"Yeah, your job," I retorted.

"I wouldn't have slept with him." she smirked. "Oh, that's a lie. I totally would have. He is fine. How was he?"

"I've had better." I briefly thought about my last careless romp in the sack with Spark as I walked up the stairs.

"I need a shower."

A nice, long, scalding shower. I scrubbed myself as if it would undo what I did. He used protection, but his tongue was pretty much everywhere. *I'm really an idiot sometimes.*

When I was done refreshing myself and trying to block out my night of debauchery, Kat was back out at the pool and Addi was reading.

She looked up from behind her book.

"I think Rico had one of his men scope out our place last night," Addi said.

I poured myself some orange juice. "What makes you say that?"

"I saw someone," she said. "I didn't get a good look. He was pretty quick to hide. Do you think Rico is onto us already?"

"Doubt it."

"It made me even more paranoid than usual." Addi shivered. "I turned the flood lights on afterwards."

"We have nothing to hide," I pointed out. "The guns are locked away tight, and we don't use the phone lines. Every tourist has binoculars for oceanfront views."

"I still think you should be extra careful," Addi said. "I just have a bad feeling."

"Noted." I drank the juice and then flung my purse over my shoulder. "I'm going to drive into the city and find Uly."

Uly Vega was the only other Osiris agent I knew outside my family other than Emma, Spark and Judah. He had a reputation for being a wildcard, but I only knew him as reliable. He was a great resource. He moved guns, distributed fake identification and who knows what else. When he wasn't playing counter-terrorist—something he claimed to have a degree in, he was a Chilean fisherman with an array of boats—one of which was a speed boat. He brought it down from Mazatlan just for us.

We needed a boat for Sunday. It was the easiest route of escape.

I planned to take my time. The longer I was gone the less chance I had of running into Rico.

Puerto Vallarta buzzed with activity. It was the day before Halloween, so there was more going on than usual. Mexicans took their festivals seriously. There was no rhyme or reason to the city—just celebration and color.

"Hey, Uly." I waved to the camo-clad bundle of misplaced energy. He even had a red bandana on his head.

"Ay, gringuita," he responded. "Whatchu doin' all dressed like it's a funeral? It's almost Dia de los Muertos! Wear some pink and turquoise!"

Uly laughed as a frown hardened my face. "Why are you always dressed like Rambo?"

Uly considered this. "Good point, gringuita."

"Esta listo el barco?" I got to the point.

"Si, your boat will be delivered tomorrow, to the address Emma gave me." His English was clean and clear even with the heavy accent.

"Thanks." I smiled.

"Mexico is alive with activity this week," he commented, looking out into the crowds. "I love this time of year."

"Maybe one of these days we'll get a real vacation." I winked.

"No rest for us wicked," he responded. "You're also not my type."

"I didn't mean…" I rolled my eyes. "Shut up."

"I kid," Uly said. "You kind of scare me, anyway."

I was about to answer him, but something strange caught my eye. I blinked and he was gone. *Dark suit,* my voice echoed into my head. The comedic scene of Kat being dumped out of the elevator in Vegas also pushed into my brain, connecting a few instances. A man wearing a dark suit.

No, I thought as I stepped passed Uly and strained my eyes. The man had disappeared behind a building. He was quick.

"Something wrong?" Uly asked.

"No," I said, distracted. "No... I just thought I saw someone."

I quickly excused myself, thanking Uly for his help. As I walked away, he began to sing "Glory of Love" by Peter Cetera.

I tried not to appear visibly shaken, but I couldn't help but think back to my other missions. Someone was always watching, lurking in the shadows... "You're never alone," Spark's note had said. Was that a threat or a reassurance?

I kept alert, but casually walked around the port town for a long time, walking in and out of shops, bartering for colorful bracelets that Addi said she wanted. Hours passed before I started to get that feeling again. It was denser than the late October humidity. It was an instinct, according to Judah. I felt him watching me.

The sun would be setting soon, so I picked up my pace, hurrying past a large group of loud teenage boys to get back to the Jeep, which was parked a little too close to an alley.

That's when I saw him.

I saw the back of his black-haired head—he was in front of me, walking toward the street where I parked the Jeep.

He might be one of Rico's men, I wanted to tell myself, but noting the quality of his designer suit, and the easy glide of his steps, I knew better. He was a killer.

As I struggled to get out of the crowded streets and back to the Jeep, I took a sharp turn into a side alley and started to walk faster. I felt trapped. I felt panic rise in my throat. I managed to trip over a curb and scrape my knee before I had to stop and collect myself.

Just breathe, Frankie, I told myself. Panicking wouldn't solve anything. It would just get me killed. I sighed heavily, trying to calm myself down before I began to walk again. The Jeep was the next street over; I could make it.

A hand reached out and yanked me, hard, into an empty restaurant.

The man whirled me around to face him.

I was staring dead into the face of Johnny Yeh.

Surprise!

Sometimes I hate being right.

You should know a few things about Johnny Yeh. One, he was one of the most lethal and successful assassins in recent history. Judah once quizzed me on the almost fifty-page accomplishment document on Yeh. Two, he was with the Sha Lù, until he went rogue. He now considered himself a free agent, which made him dangerous and unpredictable.

"Good evening, small fry." He smirked.

And three, *I was going to kick his ass.*

"What do you want, Yeh?" I snorted.

My mind was racing, but I wasn't about to appear flustered in front of this maniac.

He shrugged carelessly. "Street tacos. Have a seat."

He pulled a chair out for me. I eyed him warily in the poor light of the restaurant, but sat down.

Across the room, an ancient refrigerator kicked over a horrible grinding noise, making the walls shake. There were two disinterested patrons sitting in the far corner.

I took in everything, inwardly panicking, yet trying to size up this new development.

Yeh was in his late thirties, and he was rather out of place in nice slacks and a Gucci button-up shirt. He had a pair of dark sunglasses on that made him look like he was auditioning for the next James Bond villain.

Note that no formal introductions were uttered. We couldn't waste time with stuff like that. He was too "mysterious" to introduce himself, and it was obvious he knew who I was, so why bother.

"You've been following me," I said.

"I have, and it has been such an amusing trip." Yeh was a low-talker, so trying to understand him correctly with his slight accent and a dying refrigerator in the background was challenging to say the least. I had to concentrate closely on a guy like this, not only because he was lethal, but if I was going to throw down with Yeh in a foreign bar, with the chance of taking a bullet or three, I wanted to make sure he said 'it's been such an amusing trip' rather than 'you're such a stupid bitch.'

"You know my mark?"

"I do."

"Are you countering?" I frowned. Countering would imply that Rico has become aware of a hit against him and ordered another contract to protect him. It was a very expensive move. But then again—a free agent wasn't tied to any group that wanted to keep in good standing with other agencies, and I haven't heard of any agencies countering in my years with the company.

"No," he responded. "I am babysitting."

"Me?"

"You catch on quick." He rolled his eyes.

Dickhead.

"Well, what the hell?" I tried to give him as much attitude as I could. "You're getting paid to just lurk in the shadows behind me?"

As soon as I said it, something clicked: Yeh and his shadow lurking—like a Gucci-clad ninja, always around, but never quite seen.

Stupid Asian douche bag, Katharine's voice echoed into my head.

The guy in the elevator... and the shadow in the stairwell of the Hyatt.

"You mother fuck," I spat. "You're the one who shot me."

He smiled again. "One of my more enjoyable tasks."

"Oh yeah?" I challenged.

"Oh yes. I enjoy shooting you, Francesca."

No past tense. Har-fucking-har. I briefly entertained lunging at him. I doubt the oblivious pair in the corner would care if I started some shit.

But this was a highly trained killer. I had a fifty-fifty shot of bringing him down, and if he was half as good as the rumors I'm sure he started—I'd be pretty dead.

"Go fuck yourself." I smiled.

"Such a pretty mouth. No wonder I have to watch you."

"Osiris hired you?"

"Three times now." He winked at me.

"Can I get a name with those orders?" I spat.

"You know that I have no idea who gave the order." He rolled his eyes. "It was not Judah Cohen, if that is what you are worried about."

"Well if you have no idea, then how are you sure?"

Yeh had this look on his face... like he was babysitting eight toddlers at Disneyland. I couldn't have been that much of an inconvenience.

"Why so serious?" I mocked him.

"You," he enunciated, "are an unruly little girl with unpredictable baggage. Do me a favor and stop screwing your mark and start killing him. I will be seeing you soon."

He got up and patted me on the back.

I felt my face get red as a surge of anger shot up my spine. He was gone in the blink of an eye. He left me there, dumbfounded. *Slippery little rat.*

So, here was the big question: was I being played?

Yeh shoots me—why? So I would purposefully seek Addi out? Why not just make a call?

Your cousin works for us, too. Just tell me—don't shoot me, it's rude.

Yeh was in Vegas. He threw Katharine out of the elevator before she could say anything stupid. He was protecting her. He was covering for me.

Yeh in Puerto Vallarta—why? Babysitting, he said. More like watching me have sex with a corrupt Mexican congressman who has ties to the Sinaloa.

I wonder when the prestigious job of Osiris Creeper was instated.

Yeh must've been vying for an in with Osiris. Free agents had zero protection. Osiris offered quite a sizable income, protection and all the perks of a Fortune 500 company. Judah was so smooth he could negotiate that the Sha Lù back off. It's the only reason a man of his reputation would jump through ridiculous hoops. Yeh was no spring chicken, and Osiris liked to invest in their killers. He would not only have to prove his own actions, but prove he could control another hitter's actions as well—namely mine, the new kid on the block with liabilities in the form of two dysfunctional cousins. *Oh, the twisted games killers play.*

I was just about done with Mexico, and I had only been there for twenty-four hours.

I got out of the main city as fast as I could.

I threw open the doors to our villa and tossed my bag down, knocking over a large vase of flowers.

"Son of a fucking bitch!" I yelled, and I didn't care who heard me. I really wanted to kill someone. I didn't want to wait.

Addi walked into the room with her usual frown. "What is your problem, Francesca?"

I grabbed my hair in my hands. "We have a situation."

"Everything is a situation," she retorted.

"I mean a bigger one than I thought!"

"Maybe you shouldn't have had a night of mindless sex with the mark."

I threw her a murderous look.

"He even stopped by today... like a lost puppy. You know, we could quit this life of servitude and just live here and take over the drug highways with your golden vajayjay."

"Can you just stop?"

"Stop what?" Katharine breezed into the room.

"Frankie would like me to stop being a bitch," Addi responded.

I suddenly wished I hadn't returned to the villa. I noted the time: almost seven o'clock. This day was over.

"I'll be in my room." I turned to the stairs. "I need to be alone. Don't disturb me until the morning or I'll shoot you in the face."

They didn't say anything in return.

Elegantly Wasted

Chapter Twenty-Three

I liked nights much better than days. It was so much easier to hide at night, so that's when I did all of my killing. Killing—how I missed it. This was the longest vacation of my life.

The sun was setting. It was Saturday. I had slept the entire night and day. Now, I was refreshed. I wanted to get this done. Maybe Osiris wouldn't care if I jumped the gun and killed Rico today instead of Sunday. Sunday was God's day after all, and I didn't like giving God more reasons to throw me into the seventh circle of hell. *Early-Kill Frankie, they'll call me.*

My cell phone rang. It was Katharine.

"You should come down to this bar," she said in a low voice.

"Why?"

"Oh well…" She gave a short laugh. "Remember how you fucked Rico? He keeps asking me questions about you. Questions I don't want to answer, because you don't exist. Get over here and help me out. This is your problem now."

She hung up on me. *Bitch. Seriously why not just pitch a tent and live at the bar?*

I always came up with great things to say a few minutes later.

I grabbed my Heckler & Koch USP Compact .45 pistols and holstered them in my elastic gun belt. It wasn't the most comfortable contraption—it dug into my boobs a little—and I tried to stay inconspicuous under this airy clothing in Mexico, so I certainly didn't need any more attention to my "tit region," as my mother liked to call it.

I ditched my trademark tank top and threw on a loose-fitting white blouse with blue embroidery on it. I made sure that I would be able to draw the guns fairly easily and gave my reflection a once-over in the mirror.

I grabbed my boots—can't be a hired hit in sandals —and secured my frizz ball hair in a tight ponytail.

I marched downstairs and out onto the deck where Addi was sharpening knives in broad daylight.

"Why are you doing this outside?"

She looked up at me. "I didn't think it mattered where I tended to my hobbies."

I bit my lower lip. "I need to tell you something."

Addi smirked. "Falling for your target? That's romantic."

"No," I said defensively. "I don't give a shit about Rico. Stop being so dramatic."

She sensed my aggravation and nodded. "What is it?"

"There's another killer here." I sat down.

"You mean Uly?"

"No." I shook my head. "A free agent, real dangerous. He has a reputation. In fact, I'll go ahead and call him what he is—an assassin."

"Who is he?"

"Johnny Yeh," I said. "Judah used to talk about him like he was a legend. He appeared out of nowhere. He's followed us here on Osiris' orders."

"Johnny Yeh is here?" Addi seemed impressed. "That's random."

"You've heard of him," I stated, not bothered to be surprised.

"Actually, I had to treat him after he left the Sha Lù. He didn't leave them without a fight. Osiris has been watching out for him since then."

"So, he's not a free agent," I muttered.

"Oh, he is," Addi said. "It's kind of like a 'keep your friends close and your enemies closer' type of situation."

"He's the one who shot me the night of the benefit." I placed my hand over my other arm. "He said Osiris paid him to do it."

"I see." Addi's eyes narrowed. "He must have been filling in."

"Filling in?"

Addi sighed. "I treat all kinds of agent gunshot wounds. Getting shot is a number one hazard. An agent needs to know what it feels like without any immediate danger, so your trainer has to shoot you. Your trainer didn't. Yeh must have been tapped."

I felt my cheeks flush. Spark had plenty of opportunities to shoot me. Hell, he most likely wanted to a few times. Spark was supposed to shoot me that night in the Prague. Instead he opted to screw me. That's why I never saw him again.

"As irritated as that idea makes me, it makes sense, but why Yeh?"

"I don't know. Maybe he's proving himself to Judah—or whoever is above Judah."

I looked out over the ocean toward Rico's estate.

"I don't like that he's here," I said. "I don't know what his orders are, and I'm not all that happy with our employer either."

"What do you propose we do?"

"I'm moving up the hit time." I reached out and took one of Addi's knives. It was dangerous-looking, as big as my hand and with a jagged curve. "Tonight. I'm heading over to the bar now. If Osiris wants to keep shit from me, then fuck 'em."

"Sounds a bit rogue..." Addi looked nervous.

"It's not like I'm abandoning the hit. I'm just altering the orders. It'll keep Yeh on his toes."

Addi nodded. "Normally I'd argue, but you have a right to be wary."

"Seriously, what is this one for?" I looked at the ridiculous knife in wonder.

"I'm really not sure, but it skins tomatoes like no one's business." Addi grabbed it from me and headed up the stairs.

"Ten p.m.," I called to her. "Same plan."

"Got it," she called back. The same plan consisted of her piloting the boat around the back way and infiltrating via the cliff side—clearing a path for my escape once Rico was dead.

I needed to tell Kat the plan. She would watch over the boat once Addi was inside. It was a sure-fire way of keeping Her Sweetness out of trouble.

Little did I know that Kat was already in trouble.

Elegantly Wasted

Chapter Twenty-Four

I picked up my pace as I neared the bar. It was twenty past eight already. My plan was to send Kat home and look for Rico—explaining to him that I thought we were moving too fast—or were we? Bat eyes, whine a little, look innocent... and tell him I can make it up to him.

The bar was even more empty than usual. I did a quick sweep with my eyes and then walked over to the bartender. "Is my sister here?"

He stopped what he was doing and tilted his head at me before he smiled. "She went up to the house with Rico."

I paused. *Why would she do that?*

"Rico says you should join them," he added.

"Does he," I muttered.

Way to fuck up my plans, Kat.

I nodded to the bartender.

Once outside, I fumbled for my cell phone and called Addi.

"Kat's up at Rico's," I said.

Addi was silent for a moment. "She wouldn't be that dumb."

"Really." I kept my walking pace steady so I wouldn't draw unwanted attention. "The chick who thinks she's got a size six carbon footprint?"

"There would be no reason for her to go up there," Addi insisted. "Not without telling us what she was up to."

"Maybe she's trying to prove herself."

"Maybe Rico didn't give her a choice."

Fuck. That thought had crossed my mind, but I was hoping for stupidity instead.

"I'm on my way to grab the car," I said, huffing. "I'll get up there, and if you don't get a text from me, speed up your plans."

Goddamn Katharine and her absent-mindedness. She better pray she was kidnapped, because if she took off without telling us I'd be pissed.

I parked the Jeep down the street from the mansion —Kat's comfort over being inconspicuous. *Remind me to bash her over the head with a frying pan later.*

Well I could attack this one of two ways:

1. Act like nothing was wrong until I was balls deep in gunfire; or

2. Go in with my guns drawn—and demand my cousin back.

The first one seemed a bit more logical at this point because, for all I knew, Kat was just having a drink with my leftovers... it certainly wouldn't be the most fucked-up thing she's ever done.

There were armed guards at the front gate. They took one look at me and nodded me in. They didn't shoot at me, which was a good sign.

Rico opened the door.

"Oh there you are, mira." His mouth was twisted in its usual crooked grin. "I was beginning to think that you had forgotten about me."

I winked at him. "Who could forget about you? I just had a case of the typical morning-after regret. I'm usually not that spontaneous."

He motioned me in and closed the large teak doors behind me.

"You shouldn't regret anything you do." He tried to place his hands on my back but I twisted out of the way before he could feel my weapons.

"I heard that my sister was here," I said, getting right to the point. "Veronica needs her, and she's not answering her cell phone."

Rico reached into his pocket and pulled out Kat's cell phone. "She is a little too preoccupied to answer any calls, I'm afraid."

Ah, hell.

I tried to keep my eye from twitching. "I'd appreciate it if I could take her home."

He got close to me and put Kat's cell phone into one of my pants pockets. His eyes didn't leave mine. "You and I both know that won't happen, Francesca."

Oh, he went for the jugular. He knows my real name. Shock me, shock me, shock me.

Well, as it stood, my back was up against a wall. There was a doorway to my right that led to the middle courtyard.

"You really don't think I'd have information on Tricia's killer?" He grinned. "I have friends in the lowest of places—even lower than Osiris."

Responding seemed like a moot point, nor could I think of a one-liner. I remained quiet, keeping my eyes glued to him.

"You don't seem shocked." Rico tilted his head.

I raised both my eyebrows. "What? Like this?"

My hand flew up to my lips, I took in a sharp breath, and I mocked surprise for him.

"Spare me," I said. "Dirty money gets you anything, I guess."

Why did I have to push him? The urge to piss him off just poured over the edge of my sanity. I'd trash his ego before he got the best of me.

"Indeed it does." Rico nodded.

He stepped back and, behind him, four of his armed men appeared from the other side of the room.

I did what any Fairholm would do—I took off running.

The whole house seemed to buzz to life as I escaped through the doorway. Gunfire quickly followed.

I leapt into the courtyard and dove behind a brick island. I quickly grabbed my guns; they felt heavier than usual as I brought them up to a ready position. I looked for a way upstairs. I had no doubt that's where he'd have Kat: cliffside—harder to escape.

Shots rang out over my head, and I peeked around the island.

"Be careful," Rico said from inside the house. "She's dangerous. She knows what she's doing."

Actually, I didn't have a totally set plan, but what they didn't know wouldn't hurt them. I fired two shots into the air to keep them down and bolted into an open doorway that led to the stairs.

I hoped Addi would hear the commotion, climb her skinny ass up that cliff and get to work.

I stayed alert as I made my way to the upper level of the house. They wouldn't be far behind me. I turned at the top of the stairs and fired at the first guy I saw come through the doorway.

The bullet caught him in the shoulder, and he dropped his weapon. There were voices and shouts, but

I didn't pay attention to what was being said. I just kept moving.

There were lots of hallways and doors—it seemed more confusing than the previous morning. A guard appeared at the end of one hall. We exchanged fire until I got the lucky shot.

I ran down one hallway and looked out a window that ran from the floor to the ceiling. It was a long drop down to the water. I kicked in the door nearest to me and began to wade my way through the upstairs maze, searching for Kat.

"Kat!" I yelled, noticing that it was suddenly too quiet. I held one gun in front of me and kept the other trained behind. The rooms were poorly lit, yet connected by bathrooms. I walked quietly and listened for any sound to help me along.

I heard thumping somewhere. Most of the rooms seemed to be connected, so I kept moving. I burst out into the hall, into someone shooting at me from the far hallway. I ducked out of the way and reloaded.

The bullets hit the wall above my head. I looked up, realizing there was a gate to close off the hall I was in. I fired a shot, hitting the guard in the stomach, then reached out to close the gate. I secured the lock and kept running.

Once I neared the next set of doors, someone grabbed me from behind and dragged me into a dark room. The door slammed shut behind us.

I elbowed my assailant, and we toppled over backwards. My guns went flying. I landed on top of him —it was Rico. He looked furious.

He slurred something derogatory in Spanish and punched me in the face.

"Frankie!" Kat yelled from somewhere in the room.

My face hurt—I hated getting punched. It rarely happened, because I shot my goddamn marks from across the street.

I brought my head down quick, smashing my forehead into his nose. He grunted and let me go. I rolled backwards and fumbled around for anything to hit him with.

My hand grazed one of my pistols. *Perfect.*

I brought myself up to a standing position and aimed at Rico. The moonlight from outside gave me enough to see. Kat was tied to a chair. She had been crying. Rico had his own gun pointed at Kat's head. I was happy to note that his nose was bleeding profusely.

"Drop your gun," he said.

I looked down at Kat. She looked terrified. She hadn't really seen me in action before. Serves her right for being at that damn bar by herself.

I tasted blood in my mouth. He had caught me square in the jaw. I'd be paying for that one later.

"It'll be alright," I told my cousin.

"So sure of yourself," Rico chuckled. "I like that in a killer for hire."

"It's honest work." I grit my teeth. "At least you know someone wants you dead before you die."

"There's that confidence again," Rico chuckled. "I'm in politics. Everyone wants me dead. Luckily for me, I kill those people first."

He pressed the gun to Kat's head, making her flinch and whimper. "I did enjoy this, though—an entire family of killers. It's precious."

"She's not involved," I said. "She does paperwork. She's practically my secretary. Just let her go."

My head felt ready to explode. I wanted so badly to lunge at Rico, to tear his heart out for even thinking about threatening my cousin.

"You really think I'm stupid, don't you?" Rico spat.

Don't answer that out loud, I told myself.

The window behind him opened quietly. I tried to keep my attention trained on him.

"You think that I haven't dealt with assassination attempts before? You might be the first woman they've sent after me. Impressive, but no bother. You were a fun night, but I have no issues with killing the both of you and then hunting down that third bitch as well."

Addi popped her perfectly styled head up slightly and surveyed the situation before curving her lips into a sneer at the back of Rico's head. She slinked into the room like a well-dressed cat. Without a sound, she disappeared behind a couch. She was really good at this part.

"So, you're mad I killed your mistress." I knew I had to keep him talking. *Huge egocentric assholes love to keep talking. Anything about how amazing they are or how they always have the upper hand... yada, yada, yada. Snore. Good, tell me more, fuck weasel, gives more time for Addi to execute her sneak attack.*

Rico rolled his eyes. "You practically did me a favor, there. Tricia was a lapse in judgement. I have to watch my ass. I'm deep into Mexican drug, arms... human... trading." He smiled.

He started to pet Kat's head, making her shudder.

"Tricia got between my business associate and I," he went on. "She made things much more difficult."

"Elliot Malak," I guessed.

Rico smiled then chuckled. "Oh yes, him too..."

Confusion must have been easy to read on me because he started laughing harder.

Tears were rolling down Kat's face again as she struggled to keep her breathing regular.

"You know, now that I think of it," he continued, pointing his gun at me, "you're just clueless enough. Must be trained to not ask questions. You should be on my books. My wife keeps my good Sicario in San Miguel."

"You knew I was sent to kill you from the get-go?" I was running out of bad questions.

Rico shrugged. "Like I said, I have—"

"Low friends in high places," I interrupted. "Got it."

I shifted my weight. Waiting on Addi began to raise my anxiety. I needed her to at least distract him if I wanted a safe shot. Part of me wanted to keep asking him what else he knew.

"Plus, I've known too many killers not to recognize you," he said. "I noticed it when you were reading that book in the bar."

"You said my eyes didn't hold depression," I remarked.

"They don't." He smiled. "Yours don't. It's not depression; it's death. A killer's eyes are dark... a killers eyes are dead."

Addi quickly rose up behind him and wrapped her piano wire around his neck, dragging him back. "Kinda like you," she whispered.

He jerked violently, but Addi kept a firm grip on him. Both Kat and I ducked our heads as the gun went off in his hands. I pushed myself forward and fumbled for my knife. *Never leave home without one.*

Rico's gun kept firing in sporadic directions as Addi struggled with him. He slammed her into the wall behind him, and although she gave out a small protest of pain, she held firm. She went dead weight, lifting her feet off the ground.

I cut through the duct tape that had Kat tied to the chair. Once she was free, I grabbed her by the hair and tossed her out of harm's way.

"Stay down," I warned her.

I turned back to Rico and Addi. He was trying his best to keep smashing her into the wall, but he was losing consciousness quickly. His tan face was now purple from a mixture of anger and lack of oxygen. With a lot of effort, he tried to focus on me as he raised his gun.

One last strong tug and the wire cut deep into his neck. He dropped the weapon.

Blood began to gush, and he weakly reached up to grasp his neck.

Addi, breathing hard, let him go and pushed him forward. He collapsed and rolled around onto his back.

"Do the dramatic one-liners help?" I threw Addi a look.

She nodded. "You should try it."

I secured my lone gun and picked up his. I took a long look at it before I pointed it at Rico's head.

He just smiled, a bloody smile. "We can't be stopped."

His voice wasn't more than a whisper followed by a death rattle.

"Later, dude."

It was something Spark always used to say. It conveyed a sense of coolness—like I didn't give a shit that I was putting him out of his trafficking misery.

I pulled the trigger.

Kat jumped, put her hands up to her ears and squeezed her eyes shut.

The bullet went right through Rico's forehead. I take no chances. His head rocked slightly from the blow, his eyes stared at me blankly.

"Now whose eyes are fucking dead?" It was silly, but his words got to me. *I had dead eyes. What the hell did he know?*

I shot him again for good measure. This time Kat started crying again.

Addi, her face riddled with concern, reached out and took the gun from me.

"I think he's dead, Frankie," she said.

I was about to respond, but the far door burst open, flooding the room with light, and someone fired a weapon at us. Instinctively, I grabbed Addi and pushed her into the side room, then dropped down and pulled a now-screaming Katharine's hand over toward me.

More men were advancing quickly. I weighed my options.

My other gun was clutched tightly in Kat's hands. Now, what on earth was she going to do with that?

I pried it from her fingers.

"How many?" Addi called from the other room.

I peeked out from behind the couch. "Five," I counted. I whipped out of my crouch and shot one in the chest, all in a matter of one second. I may have fucked this all up, but there was no one better than me at a blind shot crouched behind a barrier with my HK. Spark always said I shot better when I wasn't looking. The henchman flew back and didn't get up. "Four."

"Get in here!" Addi gestured frantically.

I pushed Kat toward the door. Thankfully she wasn't completely hysterical.

We tumbled into the next room and I locked the door—that would keep them out.

"Shit," I breathed. "We need to move."

"I'm trying," Kat spoke up.

"We're going to go out that door and try to make it back down the stairs," Addi said, pointing. "Keep moving until you get to the courtyard and then jump off the back wall into the ocean. The boat should be right there."

Kat gave her an incredulous look. "Just like that, Wonder Woman?"

"Fucking go!" I pushed her. There was no time to argue over the situation.

The remaining assailants pounded on the door, making the wood splinter. They weren't the smartest of men. They left the hallway wide open... there were more bodies in the hall.

"Jesus Christ, Addi, how many did you kill before you had time to sneak in through the window?" I turned them around. The other men were making their way into the hall.

We sprinted down the hall toward the stairs. Wrong way—more men were coming from that direction. *She didn't take out enough, apparently.*

"I didn't kill these guys!" Her voice was frantic.

"Fuck…" I looked around. *Trapped. This was just great.*

Addi's eyes widened. "Frankie… "

Hands grabbed me. Again.

I was growing tired of being pulled in every direction and fighting my way out of this shit hole.

I whirled around to face Johnny Yeh—who now had a degree in surprising the shit out of me.

"Fucking Gucci Ninja." I rolled my eyes.

"Ninjas are Japanese." He smirked at us. "Grab her hand."

He motioned for Addi to latch onto Katharine.

There was a deep rumbling somewhere in the house. A moment later, the walls started to shake.

"Whatever you do, do not let go." Yeh grabbed my hand and Addi's free hand, and took off sprinting down the side hallway toward the lone window at the end of the hall. "Run."

Bullets began to hit the walls around us. You could hear the men shouting aggravated Spanish. *Oops, did I just kill your boss?*

"Are you fucking kidding me?" Katharine screeched as she realized what Yeh was about to do.

Yeh picked up speed. The walls were definitely shaking. The roaring got louder.

Fire erupted up the stairs behind us. I whipped my head back to look behind me. A fireball was invading the hallway, rushing toward us very quickly.

Yeh was blowing the entire house up.

"This is not happening," Katharine sounded off. "This is not happening!"

"Keep going," Yeh said. I could feel him smiling as we all crashed through the window.

There are only so many situations I can go through without too much reaction. This time—I screamed. The crashing glass splintered and gave way as we fell through into darkness. Kat and Addi matched my screams.

The entire house exploded above us in a spectacular fashion. Fire, wood, rock and glass sprayed out into the warm night air.

I squeezed Yeh's hand tightly as we fell. *Down... down... down... into about forty feet into the ocean.* Hitting the water stung hard, but it also felt warm and oddly inviting. The impact forced my hands to break free, and I sank fast.

Disoriented, but alive, I kicked toward the surface. I could see the light of the flames and the rippling of water as the debris came down.

My head broke out of the water, and I took in a deep breath. Before I had a chance to gather myself, Yeh reached out and grabbed me by the shirt. He gathered all three of us and swam out of harm's way, toward the speedboat that was bobbing out in the water.

Fire engulfed what was once Rico's extravagant hacienda. *That wasn't going to attract the right attention at all.*

A bit wounded, but alive, I pulled myself into the boat and then helped the others aboard. We all collapsed against the sides.

"Holy shit." Kat clutched her chest. "I think I'm having a heart attack."

Addi scooted over and hugged Kat tight. She closed her eyes and began to rock back and forth. *That was a really close call.*

I looked over at Yeh. He looked like a drowned rat. He probably ruined a perfectly good suit helping us out.

Oh, why sugar-coat it? He saved our lives.

I searched for the words to thank him. Nothing came out. I suppose a simple thank you would have sufficed, although "fuck you" would have been fine too, but all I could muster up was a nod.

He nodded back. "You are welcome."

Elegantly Wasted

Chapter Twenty-Five

Yeh steered the boat out to a much larger yacht, which was anchored off the coast of Punta Mita. It hadn't taken him long to gather himself and get the ball rolling.

Calm and collected—I just wasn't sure I could trust him.

Addi and Kat didn't move from their huddle until Yeh tied the boat to the back of the yacht.

"Your boat?" I asked.

"Not exactly." He smiled. "It is the Sweeper's boat."

I guided Kat up to the main ladder and noted the name on the back.

Tripwire

Interesting name for a boat.

"There was a Sweeper?"

"Do you think I am a demolitions expert? Please. I am a Chinese assassin—there is no honor in just blowing things up. That is more you Osiris cowboys."

"Noted." I sat Kat down on the deck of the yacht and began to check her for wounds. She tried to brush me away, but I was persistent. "Will the Sweeper be joining us?"

"No he has other things to tend to."

Like covering our asses up completely. A Sweeper meant that Judah probably suspected I'd screw up. I would have been insulted, but I still managed to do my job at the end.

Kat had some minor scrapes from the glass, but otherwise just seemed shaken up. She surveyed her surroundings and her eyes fell on Yeh.

"I don't know who you are, but thanks for saving us."

See, Kat could do it, why couldn't I?

"I'll take her." Addi took Kat's hand, then turned to us.

"I can take care of myself." Kat pushed Addi away, stumbled forward a bit and then grabbed back onto her.

Addi sighed. "Mind if we go sit down?"

Yeh made a vague hand gesture. "I will be taking the boat to up to Mazatlan to wait for your documents. Make yourself at home."

He meant our passports—that was all in Mismaloya. I'd have to call Judah and tell him what happened.

I reached into my pocket and pulled out a wet cell phone.

"I have already contacted your boss," Yeh said. "They anticipated Rico would find out. Rico has always been a resourceful man. That is why they called me."

"I could have handled it," I said.

"I killed eight armed guards on my way up to you." Yeh's voice wasn't really critical. It was calm and soothing. *Trickery, trickery.*

"Women are such unpredictable killers," he said, shaking his head.

"I'm sorry, Sha Loser," I said, letting out a short laugh, "but which one of us was kicked out of their assassin ring?"

"You know nothing of honor," he stated. "You are merely a mental issue on an ego trip."

"Whatever," I said. I gestured back to the burning estate. "This was fairly honorable. I mean..."

Another explosion from somewhere on the peninsula sounded.

Yeh sighed and walked away from me.

I followed him up to the bridge, where he turned the boat's engines on and retracted the anchor.

"I'm still pretty new," I said. "I mean you're, what? Forty? You have like fourteen years over me."

"I am thirty-six." He threw me a look. I hit a soft spot.

"Got a home life?" I smiled

"No," he responded quickly. "My work is more important than having a double life."

"You mean you can't multi-task," I prodded.

I was starting to break his cool. "You are rude and insolent."

"You're bleeding!" I pointed at his arm. His shirt sleeve was covered in blood. I reached out to give him a hand, but he yanked his arm out of the way.

"I will be fine," he said. "I just saved your ass, and I do not need any favors repaid. I do not need to owe Osiris anything else."

I rolled my eyes. "Man, what's the name of the bitch who fucked you up?"

He didn't respond, and I didn't say anything else while I let him get underway. My silence couldn't last though. I deserved at least some sort of explanation from this guy.

"Why do you owe Osiris?" I leaned against the control panel as the boat began to move steadily through the water. "Why'd you save us? What's in it for you?"

"You ask a lot of questions," he said.

"Yeah, well you shot me. Remember that?"

He kept his eyes forward. "I owed someone a favor."

"So, you shot me?"

"No, that was an order," he said. "I saved you as a favor."

"Come on, Yeh." I smirked. "Spill it."

Oddly enough, he broke a smile. "Petulant child."

"You sound like my Aunt Greta." I chuckled.

Yeh's expression went back to devoid of emotion. "I hope not."

My humor was wasted on the foreign.

More silence—I didn't know what to say to the guy.

Small talk seemed out of the question. *What's your sign? Have any hobbies? How many people have you killed?*

"About ten years ago I ran into a problem in Zurich," he said, finally braking the silence. "I made a few mistakes."

"You?" I feigned shock.

"Do you want to hear this or not?"

I held my finger over my lips, signaling I'd be quiet.

"This young man helps me out. He did not have to. It hurt my pride because he was a kid—younger than you are now. Ten times as annoying."

I could hear Katharine's voice somewhere in the background along with the clinking of wine glasses, which filled me with a sense of normalcy. I began to relax into Yeh's story.

"Gabe." he nodded to me. "Gabe Dawson."

My eye lids flickered slightly. *Spark—that son of a bitch*. Not only did he disappear from my existence, he had the nerve to let me know how incapable he thought I was by sending Yeh to protect me. I fully planned on killing him if I ever saw him again.

"He saved my life. I saved yours," he said. "I paid back my debt to him."

"I see," I whispered.

"He was your trainer." It was a statement more than a question. "He must care what happens to you."

"Why doesn't he look after me himself then?" I frowned.

"He is not permitted to at this time," Yeh responded quickly.

Not permitted. That was a good excuse. The more I thought about it, the angrier I got, so I pushed onto a better subject.

"So then why did you shoot me?" I asked.

He shook his head. "A killer needs to be hurt to feel and understand what they are doing. You must build trust out of uncertainty in a job like ours. We are indeed killers—there are no rights and all wrongs with us. Everything is a test, Francesca. You are supposed to trust your employer. It will be very hard to trust them at times, but you must."

"Easy for you to say," I muttered. My wet clothes felt heavy against my skin. All the adrenaline was leaving, reminding me that I had gotten punched in the face.

"Well, then, you will fail your test. Your company is one of the fastest-growing firms in the world—it has only been around for eleven or so years. The people in charge know what they are doing because they are driven and have specific plans for you."

Yeh's voice was soft and soothing. I felt myself grow sleepy as I contemplated his words.

"Specific plans," I said, finally. "See this is what I'm talking about. How am I supposed to invest my life in something that I know nothing about? I'm just some puppet for them to control."

I didn't like this. I didn't like that Johnny Yeh knew more about my company than I did. It didn't make sense. I didn't like that Spark still had tabs on me. I didn't like the trail of death that led too close to my family. I didn't like that I had almost gotten my cousins killed. *This company was way too careless with my world. I was too careless...*

"Do not fail your test, Francesca," Yeh said. "You have a very special gift. It would be a shame to waste it."

"So... I'm supposed to trust out of nothing?" I threw up my hands.

"Without trust there is nothing," he said.

Elegantly Wasted

Chapter Twenty-Six

November in Phoenix is my favorite time of the year. Mainly because I loved fall—it was my favorite season. I enjoyed it more in places like Spain or France, but in boring, old Phoenix it was still pretty nice, too.

I loved the autumn months because they were colder, but not freezing. I could wear layers. I was more comfortable in layers. I didn't have to wear Katharine's dresses to work. She let me design my own fall uniform: black and black with some grey, black pumps —not high heels. Signature red belt. It was comfortable, and I needed all the comfort I could get.

My birthday was also approaching. I wasn't big on birthdays, but hey, it was nice to grow a year older without dying horribly.

I tried to put Mexico behind me. To my surprise, Yeh had sold Judah on the idea that we had all worked around a solid problem of being identified and still making it out clean.

Ricardo Esquivel Escandon was dead. Santiago Cantu's work wasn't in vain. Whoever had ordered the hit had gotten what they wanted. I hoped.

I tried not to let Rico's last words get to me, but I still told Judah what he said. Judah tried to assure me it was nothing, but his tone suggested otherwise.

I overlooked it because Katharine started drinking more once we got home. It wasn't easy to watch.

I woke up Thursday morning to find her standing in the living room drinking a bottle of Scotch because she was "allergic to hangovers."

On top of this, my mother suddenly wanted to be friends. She was over all the time and, oddly, she was usually cooking.

"Marlene…" I scooted into the kitchen still in pajamas. "What are you doing?"

"Making pancakes," my mom sang. "And call me Mom."

She had discovered the Food Network a few weeks back—along with the internet—and was now convinced she needed to cook everything known to man… as long as Tyler Florence cooked it.

"I'm taking my key back, Mom." I yawned and popped open a can of Diet Coke.

I know—it's disgusting. I'm addicted to caffeine and for some odd reason I didn't like coffee. Addi drank protein shakes, I drank Diet Coke, and Kat drank Scotch. Mornings in the Fairholm household were healthy and happy.

"Is Katharine alright?" Marlene asked lowly. "I mean, I know I'm not one to judge, but I usually wait to drink the hard stuff until I'm alone at night."

Alcohol 101 had now commenced.

"She's fine," I said. "Some complications at the office."

"Well, make sure you help her with them," she said. "You don't have real vanilla? I haven't raised you right."

Yes, my upbringing all rested on the fact that I had shit vanilla flavoring in the house.

"I need to get to work," I said. "I have a class at nine."

"You can eat first." She pointed the spatula at me. "Then later we're going shopping for your birthday. What time are you off work?"

I didn't remember my mother being this chipper.

"Whatever you want, Mom," I answered. "My last class ends at three."

I must have looked irritated, because she reached out and put her hand on my arm.

"I want to spend time with you," she said. "I'm worried about you."

I looked up at her. "Why are you worried?"

She seemed hesitant. "I just keep having bad dreams about you. I figure my brain is telling me that I'm not being as good a mother as I should."

You want to be a good mother now? How does that benefit me? I wanted to say this to her, but in the back of my mind I knew that if I got angry then she'd probably start drinking again. This mom was okay.

"I appreciate the effort, Mom," I muttered.

I welcomed class. I welcomed idiots who didn't know the difference between their, they're and there. Today, I loved it. *Be stupid, let me teach you—get me the fuck away from my suddenly clingy mother and the lingering thought that I had royally fucked up in Mexico.*

Addi called me as I was getting ready to leave and let me know she was supposed to head to Los Angeles that night to solidify funding for the Wishing Well.

"I have to travel with Aunt Greta," she said. "Kill me now. She insists on being involved since Bloom fell through when Tricia died."

"I'm surprised she's even helping you," I said. "She's probably got an ulterior motive."

Having Aunt Greta interested in a charity was like watching a shark circle for food. She had to have an ulterior motive, because the word "giving" wasn't in the bitch's vocabulary.

"I know I'm going to regret this," Addi said, "but she seemed to convey real interest in the charity."

"When you get a chance, we need to talk to Katharine," I said. "She's starting to worry me."

"She'll be fine," Addi said. "I don't understand what's so hard for her to deal with."

"I don't know, Addi, a few months ago she was worrying about what shoes would match her new MiuMiu jacket, and now she's obsessively cleaning other people's blood from her clothes because you keep slitting their throats in front of her. Have some empathy."

Understanding was not an Addison Fairholm trait. If she could cope, then everyone else should be able to—end of story.

"She's at work right? She's functioning?"

"I guess," I sighed. "I'll see you later."

I hung up and immediately felt irritated. The distant hammering from outside my office began to work its way into my head. A moment later there was a low and ominous rumble, and the building shook.

For fuck's sake, I thought.

I peered out into the hallway and smelled smoke. It was near the end of the day—classes were over, but there was still a building full of staff, and I felt the need to worry about their safety.

I marched down the hall toward the caution tape and ran smack into Gretchen, who was walking around the corner looking down at paperwork.

She gasped in her timid fear, dropped the files she was carrying and backed up right away. "Oh, I'm sorry Ms. Fairholm! I didn't see you!"

"It's alright." I eyed her questionably. Gretchen was always playing the shy, timid mousy girl. Always asking questions, always giggling shyly and not making eye contact. It was only in recent months that it appeared fake to me. She was acting.

I watched her pick up her papers. I spotted what looked like an elaborate tattoo peeking out from her red cardigan, not exactly a trademark of a submissive high-strung prude.

She always wore long-sleeved shirts—even in the summer. She was always complaining about being cold.

"I was distracted by the noises," she muttered. "I wish they would finish this building expansion."

I looked at the closed-off section of the building. It didn't look like it was being worked on. The wine cellar door was closed.

"Where are they working?" I asked her as she got back up.

"The wine cellar I think," Gretchen adjusted her geek girl glasses and blinked at me. "I really don't know. Katharine says she's expanding the cellar. Can never have enough wine around this place."

I glanced up and down the hallway. No one was in sight. My eyes met back up with Gretchen's and I cocked my head to the side. I backed up from her quickly, flicked my black blazer open to expose my red Donna Karen top and my gun holster. I drew the small, yet effective pistol from its confines, and before I even had the chance to register it on Gretchen, she had tucked and rolled out of view into another classroom in a flash of dropped files.

"Hail, Hydra," I rolled my eyes.

"Are you fucking nuts?" Gretchen's voice sounded from the room. It wasn't mousy anymore. It was lower and had a twinge of a New York accent.

I chuckled. "Cut the crap, Gretchen. You practically have the word Osiris painted on your forehead."

Gretchen's surprised face peeked out from the bottom of the doorway she had rolled into and she blinked a few more times. "I uh... you're an asshole."

"Thanks. I mean, I wasn't sure until recently, but Emma had mentioned that there would be more agents hanging around. Looking back it's pretty obvious. Kat's last assistant conveniently quit two weeks before I moved back here... Judah moves you in to keep an eye on me. Nice tuck and roll by the way. "

Gretchen lifted herself off the floor, straightened out her skirt and brushed her short hair back behind her ears.

"I think I sprained something." She winced and then shrugged at me. "Playing house in this hellhole really keeps me out of shape."

Gretchen's entire demeanor changed in seconds.

I nodded. "Why the secret identity once Emma came forward?"

Gretchen rolled her eyes at the name. "Protocol. My orders were to just stay under the radar. I think Judah figured Katharine would be more relaxed around me if she thought I was just some loser assistant she could control."

"You know how to operate around this family." I glanced back down the hallway toward Katharine's office.

"How's she doing?" Gretchen asked as she kneeled down to pick up her papers for the second time. There was a hint of concern in her voice. Kat had a tendency to grow on people—even if she wasn't well liked.

I sighed. "I'm not sure. I want to say she's fine. Addi seems to think so, but I think the last few months have caught up to her. I haven't been the most understanding person in the world. Addi definitely hasn't been."

"So I hear." Gretchen chuckled. "You know, it's pretty much not my business, but I see and hear things around here. Katharine really loves you. I think that's her driving force to be a better Wingback. She may not like it, but I think the adventure aspect drives her. She loves sharing that with you and Addi."

"I'll take your word for it."

"I completely loathe her mother, but I actually like Kat a lot. I like all three of you. I don't want anything bad to happen to you. As much as I hate manners, I'm glad I'm here." She smiled and stood back up.

I turned back to her. "Thanks. I'm struggling with some morality lately. I think I needed to know there are others around."

"Just talk to each other," Gretchen said. "If there's one mistake I've made in life, it's shutting people out. I've been completely comfortable acting like someone I'm not for a year. I don't have friends or family. You're the first person I've talked to with any sort of honesty in a long time. Don't be like me."

Gretchen did look sad. I saw it before, but now I understood why. She couldn't hide her despondency. It was just easy to overlook when she was invisible. Lord knows I did my share of ignoring her.

"You know," I said, shifting awkwardly, "I'm not any good at the whole friendship stuff, but if you want to hang out with me I clean my guns on Wednesdays. I order pizza and watch really bad horror movies."

"That'd be nice," she said. "I haven't done anything like that in a long time."

I smiled. "You don't hang out with Emma?"

Gretchen looked off to the side and scrunched up her nose. "I can't stand Emma. She's so fucking cheerful all the time. It's like being around a Stepford wife."

"Yeah, it's bullshit," I said, "but living among killers, we can't judge other people's mental disorders."

Gretchen shrugged. "Give these to Katharine," she said, handing me her newly organized files, "and maybe I'll see you next Wednesday."

"I'm not really a people person," I told her.

Gretchen started to walk off the opposite way, toward the construction zone. "None of us are."

She disappeared around the corner and left me to ponder our discussion. I wanted to think Katharine was happy. Maybe she was transitioning into a more stable agent. Maybe it would take a while.

I walked down the hall to Kat's office. When I got there, I did what any adult would do and pressed my ear against the door.

She was giggling. It was that stupid-girl giggle too, the one where you're obviously flirting. *What the hell?* She had been moping around for days, and now she was all giggles.

"I would like that." Her voice was muffled.

I barged in.

Katharine's eyes were wide, and she clumsily ended a call on her cell, which fell to her glass-top desk with a crack.

"I'm not interrupting, am I?"

"No," Kat stuttered. "I was just talking to— returning phone calls."

Liar. God, Kat was such a bad liar. She was like a nervous insect fluttering around trying to form complex sentences.

"You need to learn to lie better." I cocked my head to one side. "Who is he?"

"What? On the phone? No one important."

She had sobered up. She was now just genuinely nervous. She wasn't going to tell me what she was up to and that was fine. Lord knows, I kept plenty of secrets from her.

I threw the files down. "Gretchen is an Osiris agent."

Katharine's crinkled up her nose. "Well that makes me feel better. If that waif can be an agent, I sure as shit can be."

"She was acting," I countered. "She didn't want to make you nervous. She's actually kind of a bitch."

"Swell." Katharine rolled her eyes. "I wonder how she's restrained herself from killing my mother..."

"Listen," I said, sitting down in one of the chairs that faced her desk. "What happened in Mexico..."

"I don't want to talk about it," she whispered harshly. "Just drop it, Frankie. I almost got us killed, and I was pretty much dead weight on the trip. I get it. So let's not keep bringing it up."

"I wasn't going to say dead weight," I said. "Rico had the drop on us. Knowing that, you did great."

"You're just saying that."

"I'm not," I argued. "In fact, you are doing really well. I'm the one who fucked this all up the moment I killed Tricia. We all need to work on ourselves. I see that now. You want to help me. You've always looked out for me, and that's why you're doing this. I need to respect that a lot more."

Katharine looked like she might cry, but she shook it off and exhaled deeply.

"I can only get better." She sat up straighter and turned a photo around on her desk to face me. It was all of us: a photo I had snapped a few months back.

"I got into the office this morning, and I sat here, and this photo was the only thing I could focus on. This is who I am. I'm a part of this team. I will do whatever I need to do to help keep us all safe."

Kat was so much different than I. *I wish I could feel what she did. Maybe, in time, I could.*

"We have a good thing going here. I'm not sure where we're going, but I'm glad you guys are with me."

She nodded.

I got up. "Glad we had this chat."

The phone rang.

Kat looked at it like it was a trap. Should she or shouldn't she answer it?

"Oh, for Christ's sake, just go get laid." I crossed my arms in front of me.

"I love you," she said.

I paused. "Love you, too."

She smiled and picked up the phone.

"Thank you for calling Elegance, Inc., this is Katharine," she said.

Elegantly Wasted

Chapter Twenty-Seven

I returned from shopping with my Marlene-approved vanilla, a new camera lens and a Martha Stewart book on cookies. Apparently my mother wished me to bake. *I can take a hint.* My mother knew I wasn't all that normal, and she was trying to push me toward the light.

I had just settled down at the dining room table with my current book when Addison rushed into the house, looking frazzled.

She dumped a bunch of paperwork on the table, reached into her pocket and pulled out a couple bottles of prescription medication. She shook them at me.

"Here," she said, holding out the first bottle, "start taking one of these in the morning. Every morning."

"What is it?" I took the bottle from her hands and looked at it. "Lexapro."

"It will help with your downtime between hits," she said quickly. "It's an antidepressant."

I blinked at her.

"It's not as bad as it sounds," She started to leaf through the paperwork. "It will treat all the symptoms you've been complaining about between jobs. Help you relax and stay focused."

She held out the second bottle. "This is Xanax," she said. "If you're having a bad week and you feel more stressed, take one of these, but those are strictly once in a while pills. If you have a bad spell just let me know immediately."

"Will do." I clutched the pills in my hands.

"And hide the Xanax from Kat," she said. "It's highly addictive. In fact, don't tell her I gave it to you."

Her phone gave off a cheerful chirp, and she checked her messages.

"I'll be right back," she muttered.

I looked down at the medication bottles. Inside could be salvation from the static... Katharine must have followed up on her "get me help" speech. Who knew how long it would be before another job? Judah might let things cool with us for a while.

Addi had been on antidepressants since birth. I might as well give it a try.

"That stupid bitch!"

Clearly they were working for her.

I perked my ears up as Addi shrieked from the other room. I could hear her slam the phone down in pure anger and a moment later start banging around the kitchen.

I sighed and put the meds down.

"What's wrong?" I called to her.

The banging stopped, and Addi emerged in the dining room archway. She looked like a demon had taken full possession of her body—a typical Thursday afternoon.

"I don't know why I bother with any of them." She threw her hands up. "All of them are two-faced cretins."

"Start making sense if you want me to give a shit," I muttered.

"Greta," Addi seethed. "That was her account manager. She just canceled on me and pulled her

Elegantly Wasted

funding. She talked me into depending on her, and now..."

I smirked. "Addison Fairholm, you did not just depend on a family member! That is Kat's job."

She slapped her hand to her forehead.

"It's not like I wanted to. She has so much influence and she was looking for a new project. I wanted her to stand behind a good cause and not fall for some trafficking front—not to mention give her a good side."

"Greta doesn't have a good side." I frowned. "She's all teeth. Razor-sharp, carnivorous teeth. Hell, maybe she knew exactly what Tricia was up to."

Addi's face softened a bit. "Don't say that."

Addi sank down on the couch. "I've been working so hard on this charity. I should have known better than to count on someone in the family."

"Hey now." I threw her a look.

"Other than you and Kat," she said quickly.

"Greta is the devil," I said and opened my book again, "but I'm biased."

My cell phone rang.

I grabbed it, noting that it was my mother's number.

"Hello?"

"Francesca?" My mom had a certain high-pitched shrill to her voice whenever she answered back into the phone. *Of course it's me—it's my fucking cell phone. Why yes, I'd love to go shopping with you... again... for the second fucking time today.*

"Yes, mom," I answered.

"Your grandmother is dead."

See this is one of those things I love about my psycho fuck family. They just get right to the point. No "brace yourself," no "I have bad news," just fact. I love facts.

"Dead?" I wasn't sure what else to say.

It was Addi's turn to perk up.

"Yes," she said, and I could hear a bit of instability in my mother's voice.

"Audrey and I are at the hospital now, finishing up paperwork. She was brought in around five tonight. She suffered a massive stroke. The doctor said she was gone before they took her out of her house."

"Do you need me to come down there?"

She was silent for a moment. "No, just get a hold of Katharine. Audrey says she's not answering her phone. I'll come by after I'm finished here."

"Okay, love you," I said, then hung up.

Addi and I looked at each other, but remained silent.

Slowly, we both started to smile.

"Joan's dead," I finally said.

"Dead?" Addi's face lit up.

"Yes, dead, the opposite of alive."

I could practically hear the chorus of munchkins erupt in her head. *Ding dong the witch is dead.*

Dead. Dead. Dead. My mind kept repeating the word.

I've never seen a more sparkling smile from Addi as I did in that moment. It was if I told a ten-year-old that we were going to Disneyland. She jumped up and started to turn circles around the room.

"That's totally respectful," I said, laughing.

Addi stopped. "The woman gave you a lobster bib for Christmas."

That much was true.

I was sixteen when Joan and all of her greed gave me a white gift bag full of hotel soaps collected from all over the world for Christmas. It would have been a cute gesture if the soaps hadn't been old and smelled like sulfur. I didn't even know soap went bad.

To top this grand gesture of affection off, there was a plastic lobster bib nestled sweetly in the confines of the bag.

I mean, I'm not picky—I kill people for a living—but a fucking lobster bib? Looking back, I should have burned the bib in front of her face. Part of me wanted to think she just didn't realize it had gotten mixed up with the other array of shit she was doling out. She had millions of dollars tucked away and gave her grandkids shit. *What am I supposed to do with a lobster bib, other than smother her with it?*

She was the ultimate re-gifter.

"The lobster bib wasn't even the worst thing she gave out. That gift went to Uncle Robert, and you know it." Addi had stopped dancing, but was still swaying back and forth, swinging her arms like a kid on a playground.

Katharine's father had gotten one of Uncle Anthony's old ties. That wasn't the worst part. I mean, if it was just a tie, no one would have known it was dead Uncle Anthony's. No, Joan had taken (rather stolen) one of his fancy initialed ties and tried to change the initials with white-out to look like Robert's. On top of that, she got the initials backwards.

Robert put up with a lot from the family—namely being married to Audrey. But he wasn't about to wear his dead brother-in-law's tie.

Joan was psychotic. *I wonder why I want to kill people.*

"Our grandmother is dead, and all we can talk about is her shitty gift-giving skills," I said.

"She just gave you the best birthday present ever."

"My birthday isn't for two days," I muttered.

"Close enough!"

I tapped my cell phone on the counter.

"That's sad."

"That's life," Addi said. "You're a bitch then you die."

I rolled my eyes.

"I'm going downtown," Addi said, breaking my train of thought. "I need to do some damage control and unfuck the situation that Greta has so lovingly caused."

Addi didn't give a flying fuck that Joan was dead. I didn't blame her. I didn't feel much of anything myself.

I would have welcomed it at this point. The emotions just never came. In fact, I wasn't even happy she died so close to my birthday. I viewed it as one last attempt at alienation. I sighed.

I spent the rest of the evening cleaning and playing with Bodhi.

Emma came over and dropped off a series of books she insisted I'd like to read: girl stuff, much more positive reading than The Bell Jar.

I told her about my encounter with Gretchen to which she replied, "Fuck that bitch."

Her instant drop in cheerful demeanor left me wondering what was up between them. My mind immediately started to wander through various scenarios.

"She stole your boyfriend?"

"No." Emma glared at me.

"Judah likes her better than you?" I offered.

"Shut up, Frankie! Mind your own business!"

"You're so touchy about this," I said. "I was thinking about hanging out with her Wednesday."

Emma smirked. "Oh, I'm not sure you'll be in the same state of mind come Wednesday."

I snorted. "What do you know?"

She smirked. "A lot. You're going to love your next hit."

Something in her tone made me want to hit her because she knew something that I didn't.

My phone buzzed with a text.

"Bullshit," I muttered. It was only five days past Mexico. I was hoping for another weekend off. It would be a good chance to test the magic pills.

Emma watched me with interest.

"Why would I have another hit right after such a big showdown?" I muttered.

Emma's expression didn't falter. "Loose ends, Frankie."

I fumbled with my new iPhone and squinted at the screen. The text was from a foreign number, as usual. It was definitely a hit. I clicked on the link.

The name blared back at me, and my mind went totally blank. I double-checked, triple-checked—I even shook the phone. *This is some kind of mistake.*

I held the phone up to my eye level, willing it to change.

Go ahead, Osiris, fuck my world right up. The name was quite clear:

Greta Siriso-Fairholm.

Elegantly Wasted

Chapter Twenty-Eight

I let the name sink in a moment before my brain jumped to the first wild conclusion it could find. I blocked out Emma's weird smirk and focused on Addi's recent bitch fit.

Addi and her twisted sense of humor is faking a hit.

I turned away from Emma and called her.

"Yes?" Addi sounded distracted—maybe guilty.

"What the fuck," I spat, "is your problem?"

She was quiet for a moment, and I could hear ambient city sounds behind her.

"I, uh... What?"

"I don't know how you did this, but it's not funny."

Addi was either a great actress or had no idea why I was pissed, because she sounded genuinely confused.

"Calm down and tell me what you're talking about!"

"A new job was sent to me just now. Greta Fairholm? You want her offed and so you thought to yourself, 'Hey, I'll just have the family psycho do it!' That's not how the business works."

Emma tapped her heel behind me. "Frankie, don't talk like that over a phone call."

Addi's voice was just as edgy as mine when she shot back at me. "I wouldn't forge a contract. I wouldn't make you—"

I hung up on her.

The buzz started up. I grabbed my head. This wasn't good. I tried to keep calm.

"Frankie," Emma said, putting her hand on my shoulder. "It's not Addi. Relax. Everything is going to be fine."

"Don't touch me!" I was overreacting. I knew it.

We stood there and stared at each other in silence for a moment before I turned and stormed toward the kitchen.

I grabbed my keys and flew out into the garage.

"Where are you going?" Emma called after me.

I didn't answer her. I just got in my car and revved the engine hard as the garage door took its precious time opening. Emma backed up inside to get out of the way of the exhaust.

I made it to Elegance, Inc. in record time. I unlocked the doors and let myself into Katharine's office.

She was gone for the day, but there was an envelope on her desk with my name scrawled on it.

I shivered, immediately noticing the room was cold.

Shit.

I was right back where I started. I was suddenly eighteen again—standing there, furious with my family, confused about my life and faced with a choice.

I snatched the note up and tucked it into my sweater.

Fuck this.

I wanted out of there. I ran from the building as if my life were in danger. Maybe it was, I'm not sure.

I got in my car, locked the door and turned on the ignition. Paul Simon blared out at me, and I jumped.

"God, Frankie, get a grip," I said, trying to soothe myself. I turned Paul down and retrieved the letter from my sweater pocket. I tore it open and stared at it. Same slate paper, same logo... only this one wasn't an invitation. This was instruction.

Francesca,

You have proved yourself an asset to this company, and I am presenting you with this gift—the gift of killing your Aunt Greta. This is to tie up some loose ends.

You wanted a trust factor and now is your chance to gain that trust. You want answers. I have many.

Much more will be revealed to you, but you must complete this hit. All questions will be answered.

Attend your dear grandmother's funeral. After this funeral, find a way to execute your mark. Use a gun, shoot her in the head, but first make sure she knows why she's dying. Tell her anything you want. Tell her how you feel. Trust me, she deserves it.

This is your chance. Enjoy the ride.

I'll be watching.

X.

So... the big wig had written me himself—or herself. I would have been honored if this weren't so screwed up. They knew everything about me. I wasn't surprised, but maybe I shouldn't have told Judah all of my dark secrets. *What kind of game was Osiris playing?*

I dialed Katharine's number.

"Where have you been?" I barked.

"Sorry, I took off after work to run errands and got held up by some things. Then my mom called and told me what happened to Grandma. I'm on my way home now."

"Have you talked to Addi?"

"No, she called, but I didn't pick up." She sniffed.

Jesus, was she actually crying? "I'll be back at the house soon," I said.

"Is everything okay?"

I paused. *No. It wasn't okay. Nothing was okay.* "Everything will be fine."

When I walked through the front door, Addi was right in my face. "You have a lot of nerve talking to me like that," she said.

"I'm sorry." I held up my hands in surrender. She stood there for a moment, sizing me up.

"Fine," she said, though she didn't seem fine. "I told Kat."

Katharine cleared her throat, then took a long drink from her glass of wine. "We can't fight over this... situation," she said after she lowered the glass.

"The situation being I have to kill Greta." I rolled my eyes.

"Why do you get to do it?" Addi sounded disappointed.

I held up the note. "Does this look familiar?"

Addi snatched it up and read it. "It's like the invitation to Osiris."

I nodded. "It was sitting on Katharine's desk. Someone put it there for me to find."

"Then we have a huge problem."

"That's a switch," Kat said, sarcastically.

"You have to kill her at Joan's funeral." Addi looked back up at me. "That's two days away! Greta is planning the whole thing!"

"On your birthday, I might add." Kat drank the rest of her glass and poured herself more wine.

"Greta Fairholm," I muttered.

"Who would want her dead?" Kat asked.

"Anyone who's met her." Addi rolled her eyes.

This is the last kill of your current ties.

I looked at my phone screen, willing Judah to call me. He had to know. He knew everything.

"Joan dies on November fifth, and I have to kill her daughter two days later. The royal lineage is dwindling."

Kat snickered to herself as she examined the contents of her wine glass.

"What are you snickering at?" I asked.

"You're loving this idea, aren't you?" Kat said.

"What?" I crossed my arms in front of me.

"Best birthday present ever. Killing off the worst people in the family."

"Better than a lobster bib," Addi commented. "With Joan and Greta gone, you would sever the main evil arteries of the family."

"The note said Greta is the last kill of my current ties... Tricia, Rico... how is Greta involved?"

Kat downed her second glass. "I'm guessing it's all dirty. Everything is fucked."

Tricia and Greta, funding a crime lord. It didn't make sense.

"There really is too much coincidence here," I said.

Addi's gaze drifted up to the ceiling as if it were fascinating. "Maybe it isn't. Maybe it's just Rich Ellingson trying to cover up his wife's dirty work and Greta is some unfortunate collateral damage."

"Well that's a nice and easy solution, but Frankie can't kill Greta," Kat said, slurring her words ever so slightly.

"Excuse me?" My head snapped to her.

"You can't." Kat shook her head at me. "She's family. You promised me you wouldn't hurt family."

She sounded like a pouting child—like I was breaking a promise to take her to get ice cream. I was going to shout at her to shut up, that we had a lot more to figure out than the endgame, but her phone rang.

"Hi, Mom." She had little enthusiasm in her voice. "No, I don't want to eulogize."

Pause. "No, I have nothing to say. How much have you been drinking?"

She walked out of the room to haggle with Audrey.

Addi was studying me. I hated when she did that.

"You really promised her you wouldn't hurt anyone in the family?"

"Yes," I replied.

Addi thought for a moment. "Why?"

I blinked. *What a loaded question.*

"I mean," she said, shrugging, "aside from your mom and us, who really matters in our family? Everyone has treated you like you don't belong—especially Greta. They've always made you feel outcast—Joan was downright nasty. Why care? Killing Greta should be no problem for you."

"You sound like that note," I mused.

She was right. I didn't care about Greta. I didn't care whether she lived or died, just like I didn't care about Joan—six feet under and one less bad answer. Greta has verbally assaulted me on many occasions—poked, sneered and looked down her nose at me. Greta hated me. I never really asked her why. I just assumed.

Come to think of it, I did want to kill her. It wasn't the first time either. My memory suddenly flashed back to the night I almost attacked her. How odd that it was the night I left to join Osiris... the night I got the very similar note.

Something is about to come full circle.

"I mean, her own sons disowned her," Addi said.

My brain snapped at the thought. "I need to go figure this out."

"Figure what out?"

"I just have to go check Greta's house." I grabbed a sweater.

"For what?"

"Answers." I had a feeling, and I was acting on it. "I think I have a theory."

"Wait 'til morning. It's late and she's home."

I was acting irrationally. I knew it. My mind was racing a mile a minute.

"In the meantime... let's start researching some things," Addi said. "We'll figure this out."

Katharine had started to talk in elevated tones in the other room before saying a curt goodbye and resurfacing with tears in her eyes.

"What's wrong with you?" Addi's tone wasn't the least bit sympathetic.

Kat frowned as if she couldn't find the right words. "I don't know. I guess I'm a little sad."

"Sad?" I raised an eyebrow.

"Oh, that's right." Addi gave a short laugh. "Grandma treated you better than us because you kissed her ass, so you actually feel something."

Katharine stood there, deciding whether or not to defend herself against Addi's bitch move.

"Or should I say, you're conditioned to feel bad about her death because your mother said so. You have to be the favorite so you get all the money. Hell, Audrey was so far up her ass, she hasn't seen daylight in five years."

"Addi," I started as Kat's lower lip started to tremble. It was true, but that didn't mean Addi had to attack Kat for it.

Kat whirled around and left the room quickly without a word.

"You know," I started, turning to Addi, "you do what your mother tells you to do as well."

Addi blinked. "I don't know why I just said all of that to her. I saw her crying and just…"

"This isn't about money," I said.

"Grow up, yes it is," Addi snapped back. "Greta and Tricia invested in Elegance, Inc.! You think Kat isn't thinking about that at every moment since you popped off Tricia?"

"So, Kat is terrified of losing everything, again," I said. "Go easy on her. She didn't ask for all of this."

"All of this let her know who not to trust," Addi countered.

I searched my brain for an idea. "Tomorrow I want you to call Emma Wake and have her yank the files for anything Greta has done in the past twenty years."

"If she's smart she covered her tracks." Addi rolled her eyes.

"Somehow I don't think so."

The next afternoon, I let myself into Greta's house fairly easily. She was a creature of habit, and since I was a little girl she had kept an extra key in her back garden under a cat statue. *A cat—the guardian of the underworld.*

Greta was shopping for her funeral dress. I had time.

You would have thought I wouldn't need to case a hit on my own aunt. I had known this woman all my life, but knew nothing about her. I had to poke around.

I hadn't been in Greta's house since I was a kid... since her husband's funeral reception. That seemed like an eternity ago. She was angry and mean to me that day, too.

I tossed my camera bag onto her couch and retrieved my Canon.

I wandered down the dark hall of her Scottsdale manor. It was cold, just like her. I glanced into her bedroom. The bed looked sad and solitary. The woman probably hadn't had sex since she got pregnant with the twins. I took a shot of her nightstand.

I scanned her shelves. *Ann Coulter books—Greta's spirit animal.*

There wasn't much there. She lived very minimally. I couldn't decide if that was smart or just sad. She had paperwork concerning Bloom and Wishing Well. She indeed was pulling her money from Addi's charity. From the looks of it, she was trying to salvage Bloom instead—a charity built on lies to help fund Rico's trafficking. Greta really was involved and she really didn't care about the effect on all the children Addi tried to help—she just wanted to piss off Addi. It was a personal blow that held extreme consequence for others. That was a classic Fairholm move. Joan had taught her daughter well.

Addi had a right to Greta's head, this much I knew. *So why not give Addi the job?* She was more than ready.

The answers weren't in the bedroom, so I dared to venture down to my uncle's old office.

An invisible weight pressed into my chest. My bad memories of the office returned.

The door creaked in disapproval as I opened it and peered inside. There was thickness to the room, like it didn't have much air... or my imagination was getting away from me. White sheets draped over parts of the large oak furniture. Some had managed to droop and fall. A layer of dust covered everything, and I could feel it invading my lungs. My eyes focused on the large wooden desk at which my uncle used to sit. I hid under that desk as a child when I played hide-and-go seek with Lex and Kat. Then my uncle blew his brains out.

I stepped inside before I could change my mind and walked to the long-forgotten desk. The chair where his dead body lay was thankfully long gone. I looked closer. There were fingerprints in the dust on top. Someone had been there recently. The top drawer was cracked, so I impulsively opened it.

On top, a document was staring at me. It was an old admittance form for Bellevue Mental Hospital in New York signed by Greta. A rush of fear rendered me unable to touch the document and photo attached. The paper was dated almost thirty years prior and was partially torn, hiding the last name of whoever she admitted.

"Alexandria," I read.

Never heard of her.

Anthony's name accompanied Greta's. They were listed as family.

My gaze shifted to the small snapshot of a very angry looking young woman with long dark hair... and eyes so very similar to mine.

A wave of panic washed over me, and I hurried from the room, slamming the door shut behind me.

I walked back down the hallway and leaned on the wall, trying to chase the panic away. I didn't know what to think.

My eyes focused on the door in front of me. It pulled me back into my childhood memories and made me pause... the twins' room.

Something pushed me toward the door. Instinct made me whip the camera back and draw my gun before I looked inside. I was on edge, but this house had ghosts that I couldn't protect myself from.

The twins hadn't been around since I was little. Who knew what they were up to?

If Osiris wasn't just plain fucking with me by making me kill a family member to prove my loyalty, then the twins were the only people I could think of who would order this hit.

I stepped inside the room and immediately noticed the air was as stale as Anthony's office. The shades were drawn, and the room was eerily dark.

I felt the side of the wall and switched on the light.

As I crept farther into the room, goosebumps rose on my skin. This place was exactly as the boys left it. Greta had just closed the door and shut off her emotions and, just like her husband's office, there was dust everywhere.

The room was fairly large and split up into two very different areas. Most twins had different personalities, and these two had been no exception.

Alexander and Nero.

So... who was Alexandria from thirty years ago?

I secured my weapon and began to walk around the room. I let my fingers run over the surfaces of dusty, expensive furniture and tiny, odd figurines. The bookshelves were packed with various musings. A case held mainly karate and soccer trophies. At one time this had been a semi-normal family.

I remember Anthony being a good dad. He adored his children... just not enough to stop his own depression.

You know, Addi told me after Anthony's death. *Men over forty are the highest suicide rates in the country.*

One of the walls in the room was mirrored and made the area look bigger than it was. I made my way over and stared at my reflection.

I looked tired. I hadn't been sleeping well since Mexico. *Hello, episode of insomnia.* I hadn't bothered to wear makeup in the past few days, so my dark circles stuck out pretty impressively.

I sighed.

I needed answers and there weren't any. It was just a job. I had to come to terms with it. It wasn't like I had a code against killing family. I had been ready to kill

Addi when she first discovered what I did. So, I had to break a promise to Kat—she'd get over it.

I took a deep breath, and my eyes focused behind me. It took a moment to register. I blinked and whirled around to face what had caught my eye. A newspaper clipping hung on the opposite wall on a cork board full of photos. I cocked my head to one side.

Suddenly a wave of panic rose in my stomach and it launched me toward the article. It had taken up the entire front page—the untimely death of one of the most promising litigators in Arizona.

ANTHONY SIRISO: DEAD AT 46

The boys had saved the article—not only saved, but tacked it up for everyone to see. The bold headline had been lost in the room, long boarded up by a woman consumed by her own denial. I ripped the article down, and underneath it was a photo.

My fingers tentatively grazed it, then plucked it from the wall.

I remembered the photograph in that moment. I should have remembered it years ago, but the trauma of an uncle blowing his brains out hid it in the back of my twisted mind. The photo sat behind my Uncle Anthony's desk when he was alive. I never paid it much attention, but it sure as shit made a lot more sense to me now.

"I know you," I whispered. I searched my memory: a man coming up to me at Anthony's funeral... a man smiling and giving me his condolences... a man turning to my mother and hugging her. Then, years later, that same man walked into a dark room to untie me from a chair.

Judah Fucking Cohen.

I looked around the room once more, this time with a new angle of realization. The books on the shelves were about Egyptian mythology, serial killer biographies and financial business manuals—an odd combination for some. The small figurines were now familiar, too—jackals and scarabs and little green Egyptians.

Realization is a bitch. Especially when it should have been so goddamn obvious.

I ripped the photo down and walked back over to the mirror, where I had first seen the name. The answer was so simple, and yet so unbelievable, that it hadn't once crossed my mind. I had to be right. I held the paper up to the mirror. The big bold letters told a story. Anthony's last name, spelled backwards, was Osiris.

Elegantly Wasted

Chapter Twenty-Nine

Driving always helped me relax. I drove for the rest of the day. I took I-17 up past Black Canyon City listening to music. Music made everything better. I kept muttering to myself about how stupid I was as my surroundings became more and more isolated. I reached an exit, pulled off the road and decided to get out of my car and empty my clips into the side of a mountain. I hadn't been up here since I was a kid.

Bullets hit their marks as more memories invaded my mind. Anthony used to take the boys and me up into the mountains in the old Jeep he refurbished himself. The roads were rough, and the Jeep would bump around a lot, making me laugh.

The boys always seemed to have fun too, even though Nero was more reserved and didn't like to get dirty.

It was fun and now that I look back, Anthony was a little bit on the crazy side himself. He liked guns, adventures and motorcycles—all things Greta hated.

Anthony took me on these excursions to help my mom out in the wake of her messy divorce. I remembered that now. My dad had episodes where he didn't want to see me at all. All the repressed memories were flooding back.

I lifted my gun, aimed it at a saguaro cactus and fired one more highly illegal and frowned-upon shot.

Yeah, that helped. I wasn't as angry as I should have been. It shocked me that I felt more hurt. I don't think I ever felt this hurt in an emotional sense. Even with the verbal abuse I endured from Greta, I still never gave a shit. I had been through a roller coaster over the past decade of my life, but this was a kick in the stomach. I didn't know what to do with these emotions.

Christ, why couldn't my family be normal. That was the problem with normal people—they didn't exist. But I wasn't asking for some stereotypical bullshit. Just a few less drunks and self-loathers, maybe some aunts that actually knew how to love, maybe family who didn't run away from home to form a contract killing ring, who didn't drag me into it and play puppeteer with my life.

It was too outlandish to think that Anthony was somehow alive. I saw his dead body. No, this was the work of two devious little shits who blew town after their mom cut them off. The question was how did they manage to build the company? How did they get such amazing connections, and why did they want me to kill their mother years after their father's death?

Judah. He had to be the missing link. He would have to answer my goddamn calls eventually. "Call me back," was all I could manage to say into his voicemail.

I drove back to the house, trying to convince myself that I was wrong. Maybe I was just jumping to conclusions. Maybe Osiris was run by Dr. Claw, and Greta was just an asshole who needed to be exterminated.

As much as I tried to talk myself out of a clear truth, it kept slapping me in the face. Nero and Lex Siriso had been gone from the face of the planet for about eleven years. Osiris was about that old. *How do you form a society of killers? You have money from a rich inheritance that you somehow managed to retrieve from your dead father's estate.* Judging from their rooms, they might have been planning the idea for a while.

I ignored the 101 loop, which led back to my home and an inquisitive Kat. I instead drove to central

Phoenix. I ended up in front of my mother's quaint little house on the corner of Encanto Blvd. and Fifth Ave.

I got out of the car on impulse and ran up to the door. I had a key, but I knocked instead.

When my mom answered, I fell forward and hugged her tightly. She wasn't ready for that. She stood there for a moment, wondering what to do. She was more like me than I thought.

Finally, she wrapped her arms around me in return. She hadn't held me in so long. She didn't do it much when I was a kid, during my influential years—*you know, when I needed it.*

"It's alright, Francesca." Her voice was soothing. Thankfully she just thought I was upset about Joan. That was fine. It wasn't like I was going to say that I was mainly upset at the prospect of capping her sister in the head.

She held me for a few minutes before I pulled back.

"I'm sorry," I said.

She looked at me questionably.

"I'm sorry I'm not who you wanted me to be," I finished.

"Francesca," she said, her face sympathetic.

She finally motioned me inside. "I'll get you some water."

I followed her into the kitchen and froze in the archway, unable to move.

As my mom bustled her way around the kitchen, Greta looked up at me from her spot at the table. She was on the phone and immediately looked extremely irritated with my intrusion. She quickly motioned for me to be quiet, even though I hadn't said anything yet.

I must have had a horrified look on my face, because my mom gave me a disapproving look as she handed me the water.

"Watch your mouth," Marlene whispered.

She means, don't fucking say anything that will make Greta mad. She was, after all, chief executor of the Fairholm estate. She was all-powerful!

I wanted to turn around and leave, but that would upset my mother. *Francesca and her insolence strikes again.*

Greta hung up the phone after telling someone they were incompetent and nodded to me.

When I didn't say anything, she rolled her eyes. "You have a weird child, Marlene."

"I'm not a child," I spat. *Uh-oh here we go. Stop it now, Frankie. Shut your big stupid mouth.*

"Sorry," I muttered quickly, before she had the chance to counter. "I had a long day."

"Oh, you had a long day." Greta chuckled. "Try planning your mother's funeral."

I can plan yours if you want.

"Must be difficult," I managed. *I'm so sorry for your loss.*

My mom looked grateful that I wasn't running off at the mouth. I was pretty impressed myself. I took a long drink of water.

"Francesca," Greta drawled. I hated when she said my name. She never called me Frankie—just Francesca, with her over-enunciated smoker's voice.

"Since you're here and the only grandchild I can get a hold of..." she continued.

The only one? No shit? Where are the others? Where are your dickhead sons? Christ, woman, you are worthless.

"You can help set up for the funeral service," she finished. "Perhaps help me clean up after."

Oh, hell, this woman is setting herself up.

I stared at Greta, but out of the corner of my eyes I could see my mother nodding at me with her brows in a knot. I knew that look well. It meant do what you're told or else.

I never put much stake in "or else." I didn't know what it entailed, but the old Fairholm women had a way of instilling that little bit of unknown fear in your heart if you didn't do what they said.

"Sure, what time do you want me there?"

Greta seemed almost disappointed that I didn't pitch a fit or cop an attitude.

"An hour before the service, thank you." She didn't smile. I'm not sure she could. "And most likely an hour afterwards."

I put the glass down on the counter and hugged my mom quickly.

"I need to get going," I said. "I'll see you tomorrow."

Marlene followed me back to her front door.

"Are you okay?"

I turned back toward her. "I don't care that Joan is dead." I paused and looked into her solemn brown eyes.

"I stopped caring about people in this family after Uncle Anthony died."

A bit of pain crossed my mother's face. Her brow creased again, and she crossed her arms in front of her.

She was shocked I'd even uttered his name after all these years.

"Is it really necessary to bring him up?"

"Probably not," I answered, "but I need to feel something right now and I don't. I'm sorry I could never talk to you and tell you how I really felt, but the woman who just dropped dead of a stroke has a lot to answer for. I never loved her. You cowered under her influence and subjected me to people like Greta: self-righteous assholes who think their privileged bullshit is more important than anyone or anything else."

"Greta has been through..." Marlene stopped and shook her head.

"You like defending her," I observed.

"I really don't." Marlene locked her gaze on me. "It's just... she's my sister."

In my mother's head, a family bond was important, yet the base of it was fear of losing status, money, a social life—the list went on. My mother could stand on her own two feet, but she just wouldn't and I wanted so badly to know why.

"Greta goes out of her way to hate me, Mom. Why does she hate me so much?"

My mother winced, as if her memories caused her pain.

"She..." Her voice was soft. "She doesn't hate you, Francesca. It's complicated."

That didn't sound the least bit convincing. She looked like she wanted to say more, but she didn't elaborate. There was an awkward silence.

"I'm sorry you don't feel anything toward your grandmother. I wasn't aware that... his death affected you so much. You could have told me," Marlene finally said, glancing behind her. She didn't say his name for fear of Greta overhearing. My mother had a way of talking low and cryptic when she thought Joan or Greta might hear.

"There's just so much going on in my head right now, and I can't sort any of it. I can't talk to you about any of it because I don't think you'd be honest with me."

"You can talk to me about anything," she said. "I want to know what you're thinking."

I shook my head. "No, Mom. You don't. Trust me on that one."

She pursed her lips together and let out a sharp breath.

"Fine." I tilted my head. "Who's Alexandria?"

Marlene Fairholm's expression went through a few emotions at my question. Her eyelids fluttered, and she sneered for one brief second before her lower lip began to tremble.

"How... who..." My mother blinked more as if suddenly confused.

"Why did Greta have her committed?"

Tears formed in the corners of her eyes.

Marlene Fairholm didn't answer. She just shook her head, like if I said the name again, Greta would materialize and slash her throat. No one ever mentioned an Alexandria, but something told me she had been important. Alexandria with the angry eyes.

"Who the fuck is she, Mom?" My voice rose, startling her back into the doorway.

She kept shaking her head. "Francesca," she whispered. "I can't-I can't have this conversation today."

Or ever, she meant.

"I love you," I said, holding back tears, "but this family is really fucked up."

So fucked up that I murder people and should be committed, too.

There was a stern cough, and my mother froze. Greta appeared behind her in the doorway.

"Are you upsetting my sister the day before our mother's funeral?"

"Mind your own business," I hissed. "I'm speaking to my mother. Crawl back to your cave."

Greta's face twisted into her usual gaze of contempt at my presence.

"You little… " Greta started.

"What?" I interrupted. "You know better than to butt in here. This is none of your business."

"I can make it my business," Greta spat. "This family is my business. Conserving the dignity of this family is my business and you are nothing but a stain."

My mom just stood there. *Speak up, woman—do something, say something! Slap her—slap me, for fuck's sake!*

Marlene sighed. "Please don't talk to my daughter like that."

It was a little weak, but I was intrigued.

"Excuse me, Marlene?" Greta curled up her lips into a snarl. "Are you insinuating that your daughter isn't an insolent and troubled failure?"

Marlene shoved her out the door. "Get out of my house."

Finally, I thought. Maybe my mother would kick Greta's ass on her front lawn.

"You know my kids weren't the only ones to walk out," Greta spat as she looked back to Marlene and me. I followed her with my eyes; she turned back to us. "Your kid left too."

"Mine came back, Greta," Marlene spat.

Oh snap—even a retort!

"A most unfortunate event," Greta seethed.

Marlene gave us both a sad once over before she stepped back into her house and closed the door. I didn't take my eyes off of Greta. I stared at her with my blank stare hoping to bore a hole in her chest.

Greta turned to me and scoffed. "You are wretched, and you will start respecting me, or I *will* drive you back into whatever hole you crawled out from."

I raised an eyebrow. "Or what? You'll have me committed?" *Oops, too far.*

Greta's eyes widened and her mouth dropped open.

She closed her mouth quickly and raised a hand to slap me. I braced for it, too.

Instead, her face twisted into a smile and she let out a laugh. Her hand lowered to my shoulder and clamped on, digging her talons into my skin, still laughing.

She released her grip, turned, and walked off to her car.

My confrontations with Greta always ended the same—with one or both of us flying off the handle. I remember the last time we clashed, telling her one thing very clearly.

If you ever touch me again, I'll kill you…

"I'll see you tomorrow," I whispered after her.

Elegantly Wasted

Chapter Thirty

Addi called me with news as I was driving home.

"Get this," she said excitedly into the phone. "Greta is broke!"

"I'm listening," I said.

"You know how we thought that Anthony left her everything?" Addi went on. "We assumed she was his next of kin, and she inherited everything?"

Those thoughts never crossed my mind, but I wasn't invested in any part of my family's money.

"I guess," I responded.

"Well, she didn't," Addi practically sang. "Anthony left all of his assets to his kids and... get this... a third party."

My curiosity grew.

"I can't find a name or an organization," Addi said, "and Emma is being weird about digging."

Probably because she already knows, I thought.

"Right," I said. "So, Greta has been—what— laundering money for almost two decades to keep her lifestyle going?"

"Through Joan and Bloom," Addi laughed. "With Tricia! This is so much deeper than we thought!"

The darkness surrounding the revelations hung heavy in my mind. I should have been overjoyed and supremely vindicated that Greta was just as bad as she'd always been in my head, but in reality I was terrified of digging further. Our family has never been legit...

What a mess. What an utterly irrevocable mess.

"These hits have been crafted by someone with a major vendetta," Addi started.

"It's Lex and Nero," I blurted out.

"Excuse me?" Addi asked.

"I'll be at Kat's in a minute." I hung up.

My foot pressed on the gas, and I sped back to the house.

Addi waited patiently at the dining room table, sipping a beer.

I threw down the camera bag and collapsed on the living room couch with the newspaper article in my hand.

Bodhi jumped up near me, clumsily tried to fit his one-hundred-and-seventy-pound body into the remaining portion of the couch and began to breathe heavily.

Addi sat down on the opposite couch.

Kat walked quietly into the living room and sat on the opposite end from Addi, careful not to make eye contact with her.

"I need you two to put aside whatever feelings you're having for just a sec." I leaned my head back on the couch and stared up at the ceiling.

Addi sighed. "Spill it."

I lifted my head to turn it toward them. "I'm pretty sure Lex and Nero are the heads of Osiris."

"What?" Kat snorted. "Have you gone off the deep end?"

"I'm not joking," I said. "We don't know who started the company. But it started around the time the twins blew Dodge with their inheritance. Coincidence?"

"Not enough of one to—"

I shook the article in Addi's face. "I found this in their room, along with Egyptian figures and weird serial killer books."

She took it from me and arched an eyebrow. "So?"

"What's Siriso spelled backwards?" I asked her.

Kat tilted her head to the side. "O... oh... my God."

How fucking dense am I? Focused on Egyptian mythology when it's really just a palindrome.

Addi considered this as she gazed at the newspaper and then passed it to Kat, who grabbed it with a passive-aggressive chin tilt.

"So," Addi said, her face relaxing, "this is all their doing."

"Why would they want us to kill their mother?" Kat asked.

"Yeah, this doesn't solidify their involvement." Addi waved the paper at me.

"Okay." I reached into my back pocket and pulled out the photograph. "You want more proof?"

Addi took the photo from me and studied it.

"Surely you'd recognize Uncle Anthony and..."

"Judah Cohen," Addi breathed. "Where did you get this?"

"In the twin's room," I replied. "Anthony used to have it behind his desk with all of his other photos, photos that meant something to him—family and friends. I am wracking my brain trying to remember facts from back then. There's a distant memory of mine that's fairly sure Judah Cohen was at Anthony's funeral. Then I thought back to when Kat's mom told me about some weird drug ring they all ran back in the day, and I thought maybe Judah had something to do with that too."

"So, maybe he's in charge," Kat offered.

"The thought crossed my mind," I admitted. "But no way it's just him. Maybe they all started it and the twins used him to gain my trust. You said Anthony left some of his inheritance to a third party, so, that could be Judah. Or..."

I cleared my throat. *Never mind, don't get into it.*

Kat opened her mouth to say something, but closed it and pursed her lips in thought.

Addi finished off her beer and took a deep breath.

"Okay well, let's say that Lex and Nero are in charge," Addi went on. "Why go through some elaborate plot to make their little cousin kill their own mother?"

What a great question, with a limitless amount of answers. Hell, my sociopathic side has thought up many ways to murder Greta in the past, none of which involved the rest of the family.

"Because it's the sport," I turned to her. "Those two were meticulous strategists. Not to mention they were always competing in something. This has to be a game to them."

And that pisses me off.

"So... you're going to kill her?" Kat asked. She shifted uncomfortably like she did before told me something disparaging about my altered work dress code.

"I don't know," I said. "It *is* my job. Should I do what I'm told? I'm sure they've thought this out. They'll be waiting for me to reject the hit. They might send one of the other known agents around here to kill me."

"I have to tell you both something," Kat said.

"They wouldn't," Addi said, ignoring Kat.

"How do you know? We know nothing about who they are or what they're capable of. They've successfully cornered us. Our lives are controlled by them. We're all accountable now."

"I wanted to say this earlier, but I was verbally attacked," Kat tried again.

"There has to be more to the story," Addi said. "I understand holding a grudge against your own mother, but this is ridiculous."

"Do you think they killed Joan?" I asked. "I mean... we have the drugs to do it."

"It's possible, but why?" Addi frowned.

"Frankie is inheriting everything from Joan," Kat spoke up quickly, then clamped a hand over her mouth.

That got our attention.

I looked over at her, certain I heard wrong. "What?"

Kat removed her hand and managed a meek smile.

"My mom told me last night. She was really drunk, so I wasn't sure if it was all true, but with all this insanity, it seems Greta is definitely out to get Frankie."

Kat bit her lip, realizing she just spilled one of her mother's secrets. *A big no-no.* Audrey was like the oracle of the family. She knew everything, but kept a tight lid on it. Sometimes she let information trickle down to us when she got drunk—which was often.

"Wait a minute." Addi laughed. "Frankie is the heir to the Fairholm fortune?"

"Why," I started, "in the ever-living fuck would Joan leave her estate to me?"

Kat cleared her throat. "Technically it's Hershel Fairholm's estate."

I got to my feet and started to pace.

Hershel Fairholm was long dead. He died of liver failure when I was a baby. I never gave him much thought, because no one else in the family seemed to. The only thing I really knew about it came from Addi, who said he had once built her a fort in his living room out of beer cases. It certainly never crossed my mind that he wanted me to inherit his fortune.

"Marlene was Hershel's favorite," Kat went on. "I-I think it's that simple, but…"

Kat shifted in her seat again.

"But what?" I spat.

"I don't know," Kat whined. "There's a lot of secrets in this dynasty, Frankie—including yours. I do know that Uncle Anthony was Hershel's trusted confidant and lawyer. Anthony was in charge of the estate until he died. Maybe Greta took over. I don't have answers, but maybe Greta does."

"What? You want me to grill her before I kill her?" I asked.

Addi snorted a laugh.

I stopped pacing.

"Wait," I said. "How did Joan not change her will after she inherited her husband's estate?"

"She didn't inherit it." Kat pursed her lips. "You did, but you weren't eighteen yet, and when you did turn eighteen…"

"I was gone," I breathed.

Aunt Audrey and her fucking secrets.

"The term is 'missing heir,'" Kat corrected. "I think Greta thought she was in the clear when you took off. You didn't know and she didn't have to tell you."

"But now Frankie's back so she's been silently plotting against all of us." Addi shook her head. "She knows Frankie doesn't care about money and doesn't use it to control people. Greta will lose her hold on her sisters, on your school, on you, and her strange venture into trafficking."

Somewhere in my chaotic thoughts I managed a laugh. "It's really not that strange given everyone's past."

Kat looked like she was going to throw up. "Frankie still can't kill her. I know she's an awful person, but—"

Kat's voice cracked and she leaned forward, putting her head in her hands.

Addi's hackles immediately went up as her nostrils flared. I held up a hand.

"Kat is allowed to feel," I said. "She's allowed to be upset."

"Why have we never heard about this," Addi asked Kat. We all knew the answer, but Addi probably needed to hear it out loud.

Kat raised her head. "Joan and Greta hid all the paperwork... maybe in hopes Frankie would give in to the high society grooming? My mom went along with it because..."

Kat stopped and her gaze drifted down to her hands.

Addi leaned forward and sneered. "Because why?"

"Come on Addi," I said. "You know Greta had the pull there. Audrey is just as afraid of losing status as

Bette and Marlene. She does whatever Greta tells her to do."

"And you're the same way." Addi pointed to Kat. "I'm surprised you're even telling us."

"Fuck you, Addi," Kat snapped. "I care. I love you both or I wouldn't be here. I wouldn't have given Frankie a job, I wouldn't have kept your big secret. My mom has to care on some level, too. She knew Greta's time had come and Frankie—the family Black Sheep—is now in charge."

A theoretical light suddenly snapped on inside my head. Something Emma said the night we all fell into this shit storm. Something about economizing processes and taking on new investors.

"Oh, God," I breathed. "Osiris is a family company. I wasn't plucked from obscurity. I was being groomed! They used Addi to start the process. Then things went wrong, and they had to involve Kat."

"This is..." Addi started to rub her temples. "This is stupid."

"Stupidly brilliant," I said. "If they've been running Osiris this entire time, then they've been watching all of us. They know the family secrets—they must know all of this."

"What are you going to do?" Kat asked me.

"Inherit millions, apparently." I pinched the bridge of my nose.

Kat got up quickly and sat down next to me. "We can figure this out the right way. We can prove Greta is dirty and she goes to prison."

"Then you lose your reputation and school," I replied. "I have to kill her."

Kat looked at me with pleading eyes. "Maybe that doesn't matter anymore."

For the first time in a long time, I felt like bursting into tears. Kat would really give everything up to just help me be a little more human.

"I appreciate it," I managed, "but it really does matter. I see how hard you work, Kat. I can't let them take it away."

Kat tried to smile.

Addi joined us on the couch and they hugged me. It felt good.

"I won't let them take it away," I stated.

Lex and Nero wanted to play a game of chess with my life—time to king them.

Maybe I had an advantage. I mean, just because they ran a group of contract killers doesn't mean they've ever killed anyone.

"What are you going to do?" Kat asked.

I felt a sense of anger I had never felt before. I liked it. I could definitely use it.

"I'm going to lure the dragons out of their lair, and Greta's the bait."

Elegantly Wasted

Chapter Thirty-One

"Your gun is digging into my side," Addi whispered.

I scooted over and threw her a side glance of irritation.

The funeral was taking far too long. There was only so much driveling bullshit I could take.

On the other side of me, Kat was shifting her weight, and I could feel her agitation. She was now on the sober side and could think clearly about what I was going to do.

I was watching Greta intently. I could only see a bit of her profile. Her nose protruded a little too far from her face. She was the conductor of this symphony of crap. She would stay after everyone left. I could only pray she would give me a vantage point. I never prayed, but this seemed like the place.

The priest offered up words that echoed in my head, mixing with my anxiety and determination.

"The Lord is my shepherd; I shall not want."

My eyes shifted to Joan's coffin.

"He maketh me to lie down in green pastures; he leadeth me beside the still waters."

The irritating buzz that often plagued my mind decided to subside so I could get an earful of this religious drivel. The priest delivered a sermon in vain.

"Yea, though I walk through the valley of the shadow of death, I will fear no evil; for thou art with me; thy rod and thy staff they comfort me."

Do they allow sarcasm and a gun into this valley of death, Father?

There was no God here—if there was, he would have struck me dead upon entrance to his holy fucking house.

"Surely goodness and mercy shall follow me all the days of my life; and I will dwell in the house of the Lord forever."

Yeah, you will, Father. Somehow I don't think me or the bitch in the coffin are granted such divine access. In fact, I would be willing to bet the entire audience would sooner or later be on an express elevator to hell.

Katharine's hand lightly touched mine.

"Remember your promise," she whispered.

I didn't look at her—couldn't. I went ballistic when someone broke a promise to me, and here I could do nothing but bask in my own hypocrisy. At least I was in the right building for it.

"For God so loved the world that he gave his only begotten son, that whosoever believeth in him should not perish, but have everlasting life."

Everlasting life sounded horrible. I mean I get it, God is amazing and comforting. I get why people dig him so much. But living in harmony forever sounded boring as fuck.

I guess it came down to that old saying… be a slave in heaven or a star in hell.

The priest—I realized I never caught his name—did his father-son-holy-spirit nonsense.

This is the biggest crock of shit. I had been going to this church off and on since I was a kid—I used to like church. I felt protected once… then my favorite priest hung himself before mass one Sunday afternoon and I decided I was done with the religion.

I looked to the side of the altar, toward the church's side rooms. They were my best bet for offing Greta and, ironically, where my old priest had hung himself.

The service ended and people began to filter out.

Bette was quick to get up and out. My guess was she wouldn't be attending Joan's after-party at Audrey's house, which was where everyone else was headed.

My mother passed and tried to smile at me. She was probably still thinking about our encounter yesterday. Thankfully she didn't use it as an excuse to drink. Audrey was clinging to her doormat husband... tears streaming down her heavily botoxed face.

Just like that, Joan Fairholm's book had been closed. The daughters she had mentally terrorized were now walking away.

All but one.

Greta got up and walked toward the casket. She stopped in front of the priest—Father Darling she called him—and thanked him.

She stood at the coffin while the rest of the church filtered out.

Father Darling, who looked the exact opposite of his name, ventured off in the opposite direction, much to my delight.

Greta turned suddenly and pointed at us.

We all took a startled intake of breath, and Kat clutched my hand.

"One of you help me with the flowers," she barked.

I relaxed as Greta grabbed one of the elaborate stands of flowers and carried it into the vacant side room.

Oh, how perfect. Not only did she walk where I wanted her to—she actually asked me for help. Francesca, could you be a dear and come into this side room and shoot me in the head?

"Wait for me?" I asked. "I'll be quick."

Katharine got up and silently walked away before I could say anything else.

"She'll be okay," Addi said to me with uncertainty. "We'll be outside."

I nodded to her as she got up.

Addi turned back to me in that moment, with a sad look on her face. The light from the stained-glass windows lit her face up in an angelic fashion.

"Happy Birthday, Frankie."

I managed a smile as she turned and walked out of the church.

Empty churches gave me the creeps, and I was a mentally unstable contract killer. My method and madness, my unwavering lethal sense, was now shaky.

It wasn't God I feared—it was the idea that what I was doing was eternally wrong. I didn't believe in heaven or hell—I figured my mind tortured me enough every day. But on the off-chance that there was an afterlife, I did worry that I'd be punished in it.

I walked up to Joan's coffin and placed my hands on the cold metal.

"I just wanted you to know," I whispered. "That I kill people for a living. Greta is making money off a crime lord, and her sons ordered me to put her out of her misery. They're broken because their dad died."

I felt a surge of emotion. Tears did their best to well up in my eyes, but I blinked them back with a deep breath.

"You let Greta destroy this family," I said, my voice braking. "You were a terrible person, and this is all your fault because you value money over love."

There. I felt better having delivered a more truthful sermon.

I moved past the coffin to the door Greta had gone through.

Unbuttoning my black blazer, I reached for the gun that was secured in my right side holster. I then grabbed the silencer from the other side.

As I connected the two together, I went over in my head what I would say. There was so much I could say, but nothing I really wanted to say.

My hands were shaky.

Suck it up, Frankie, No one is scared of a jittery killer.

Time to face some facts. This is me. I had to accept it. I was dangerous, and I did terrible things that might or might not put the world in a better state. I wasn't ever going to be a teacher, or a photographer—not at heart. At my core, I was a killer.

I put the gun down to my side and walked quickly into the vestibule room, shutting the door behind me. Sadly, there was no lock.

My gaze studied the room. There was an antique-looking set of chairs and matching table in the corner next to a doorway leading down. The large wooden beams above me ran the length of the ceiling, and I wondered which one Father Murphy had used to shuffle off this mortal coil. I focused on Greta. I had a clear shot, but I knew this charade would take more time.She turned to me in surprise.

"You didn't bring any of the flower stands," she noted.

I cocked my head to the side and didn't respond. I went to a different place before I killed someone, and I had never spoken to them in such an intimate way beforehand.

I raised my gun and pointed it at her, then silently gestured for her to walk down the stairs to the basement.

It took Greta a moment to assess, but she understood that I had a weapon.

"What are you doing?" Her voice cracked.

I lowered my weapon slightly, stepped toward her, and gestured to the doorway again.

"Down the stairs, go. Scream and I shoot."

My mind filled with static and my voice always sounded a lot more sinister and unstable in my head. It might have been my imagination.

She was such a skinny and frail little thing. The other three were curvier and healthier-looking. Greta looked more like Joan—short, curly hair and an unpleasant face. Her beady eyes narrowed at me, but she did as she was told.

"I hope you realize what you're doing.""

"Sadly, I do," I replied.

I found a light switch on the wall at the top of the stairs and switched it on. The lone bulb in the middle of the room cast minimal light into the area.

The basement had a familiar scent of mold and wet dirt. Old file boxes stacked up the cracking walls. Years of neglect and water damage stained the cement floor. I wondered what kind of dirty secrets I could find if I had the time.

Greta gave herself a good space between us before turning to me.

"So," she started, "tell me what this dramatic display is about."

I smiled at her. "Remember when I was about nine, and your husband shot himself?" I began. I might as well go for drama. *Go big or go home.* I spoke slow and enunciated my words—I was good at that.

She registered what I said, and her eyes narrowed even more.

"How dare you, you little… "

I raised the gun up and pointed it at her head.

Her mouth snapped shut quickly and her face switched from hate-filled to worried in a second flat.

"I'm so very tired of you referring to me as 'you little' anything, Greta," I sneered. "So please let me speak."

She didn't move.

"I didn't think much of 'why' at the time," I went on. "I figured… guy couldn't take your cold, heartless bullshit and needed a permanent out."

I took a couple steps toward her and she jumped back. There was a rush of excitement at her fear. Greta had ruled by it for so long. It was good to give some back.

"He was gone. You treated your kids like shit so they left too, so it's safe to say you completely isolated yourself from feeling much of anything. You just resurfaced when you needed to bully someone in the family."

I saw her eye twitch. I continued to monologue.

"Fast-forward to high school graduation—the same night you felt the need to open your big fat mouth and tell me how worthless you thought I was, but instead, I was recruited into a corporation of contract killers."

I leaned forward and winked at her. "They call us Strikers," I whispered.

I straightened up as she flinched at me.

"Skip forward to a few years after that, I find out that Addison is employed by the same corporation. A series of events let Katharine right into the dragon's den as well, and before you knew it, Elegance Inc. was a front for a..."

I thought a moment. "Well, I guess it's basically an assassin ring, but that's a pretty extravagant term." I giggled. "And I never questioned it. That's the insane part!"

Greta opened her mouth, but no sound came out. She was processing the information and trying to figure out if I was lying to her.

"I was so desperate to just break free and be my own person," I said and shook my head, "that I didn't question anything. Hell, I was raised to never question anything."

"You're crazy," she finally stuttered. "You're psychotic!"

"Sociopathic," I corrected. "But I'm not impressed with the hypocrisy here. You're a bad person, too."

Greta stiffened and narrowed her eyes at me. She didn't say anything. The silence was, indeed, awkward.

"Alright, I don't know how to carry this conversation, so I'll just lay it all out for you."

I moved a little around the table, making Greta back up more.

"Let's just forget for a minute that you've been keeping my inheritance from me," I started. "I honestly don't even care about that."

Greta shifted her weight from one foot to another and brought her arms up across her chest.

"My main concern is that I've been cleaning up after this big mess you're involved in," I went on. "I was tasked to kill Tricia. That was me."

I waited. Greta blinked but said nothing.

"Anything?" I gestured to her.

Greta's mouth opened and an "A-a-a-a," stutter came out, but that was it.

"I felt a little guilty at first, but then I found out you were both helping a drug lord who trafficked everything but the kitchen sink, and I felt less so."

Greta shook her head. "I don't understand. I-I don't..."

Greta was getting paler by the moment.

"What don't you understand?" I asked. "You can drop your act. I know you're broke and you've been laundering money through Bloom and probably Elegance, Incorporated into the hands of the Sinaloa."

Greta's confused face was making me a little uneasy at this point. I mentioned Tricia, and that I knew about her involvement with the Sinaloa, yet she still wasn't changing her demeanor.

Her gaze darted around the room, and I knew she was either looking for something to clobber me with or another exit. I stepped closer for good measure.

"You," Greta said, slowly, "killed Tricia? My God... that's not possible. How..."

She swallowed and took a breath. "I don't know what you're talking about or why you're fabricating these stories... but we-we can get you help, Francesca. Let me help you."

Like she helped the woman hidden away in Anthony's desk.

"Right," I said. "So, you don't know that Tricia was banging a congressman from Mexico who is running drugs, guns, and people across the border? You don't know the name Rico Escandon?"

Greta kept opening her mouth like a fish gasping for breath. She wanted to scream, but with a gun pointed at her she was being smart.

"My dear," she said, her lower lip trembling. "No. I have no idea what you're talking about."

Tap. Tap. Tap. I stared at her while I clicked the barrel of the gun on the side of my head gently. The more unstable I looked, the better at this point. The woman was infuriating. I had to assume her confusion was an act.

"It's over, Greta," I said. "Lex and Nero run a contract killing company, they know what you've been up to, and they've sent me to kill you."

Her gaze snapped to me.

That sparked a different reaction. She clenched her fists together, and her stance became more aggressive.

"It's called Osiris by the way—your dead husband's last name spelled backwards. Probably also has something to do with the Egyptian god of the dead, but whatever. Point is, this is business."

Above us, I heard the turn of a doorknob followed by the faint creak of a hinge. Greta looked up to the ceiling, took in a sharp breath and gave a short cough.

Silence.

Greta's hands released and curved into claws. She was trying to decide if she should say something.

Defend herself, keep lying, plead... I'd accept anything at this point.

Talk me out of it.

She remained silent.

"Say something," I spat.

Greta's expression relaxed and she tilted her head while looking me up and down.

"My boys want me dead," Greta said, finally finding her voice. "That much makes sense. I saw it coming, but never thought they'd send you."

This was more of the demeanor I hoped for.

"But it doesn't seem like you know the truth, which I think is rather odd—then again it's Lex and Nero and you're stupid if you think you can trust them."

The room seemed to close in around me, and my body broke out into a cold sweat.

"In fact," she said and stood up straighter, "the truth seems worse than some piss poor story about Tricia having an affair with a criminal."

"So... you didn't know Tricia was dirty?" I asked.

Greta chuckled. "We didn't talk about her... other business endeavors. Money is money. I knew she was unhappy in her marriage. Who isn't?"

"Indeed," I said. "Tell me more. Tell me the truth."

Greta sighed and glanced around the room.

She shook her head. "I don't have to tell you a goddamn thing. I know why they want me dead. So... do it."

The moment became strikingly clear. Not only was I tired of this extravagant game of chess, I realized how this truly just wasn't my job.

"You know," I lowered the gun and stepped aside. "I don't think I will. If Lex and Nero want you dead they can do it themselves."

I took a few steps back, leaving a clear path to the stairs. *This plan had to work.*

I made my choice.

Elegantly Wasted

Chapter Thirty-Two

I had faith in my actions.

Right before I entered church that day, I called Judah's emergency line.

He didn't answer, of course. What would he even say? I left him a message instead.

"I can't do it, Judah. I can't kill Greta. I'll scare the shit out of her. I'll tell her everything. I'll monologue to high hell. I'll tell her about Lex and Nero. Then I'll let her go. If this means goodbye—then... well goodbye. I'm sorry for screwing up."

I hoped that my words sent Judah into a panic. I imagined him picking up a phone and yelling at the twins that they had to intervene. I had faith that Judah honestly cared about me and didn't want me dead. *I hope...*

When I hung up, I noticed that across the street, Gretchen, dressed in ripped jeans, a loose button-down black shirt, and maroon Doc Martens, was sitting on the hood of a black limo. Even through her dark sunglasses, I could feel her watching me. Maybe my luck had run out.

The moment I lowered my gun, Greta took off toward the stairs.

My mind went back to Gretchen and how the twins probably just sent her to kill me. In those mere seconds I imagined having to kill Gretchen—someone I liked, while letting Greta—someone I extremely disliked, get away. The similarity of their names alone made me laugh out loud.

Greta got about halfway up before she stopped.

The stairwell suddenly got crowded as Addi and Kat descended, being pushed by two men.

Greta remained silent as she stumbled back down. At the bottom step, her right heel got stuck in a wood groove. She toppled over backwards, ripping the side of her stiff black sheath dress.

Addi and Kat looked distraught as they were shoved the rest of the way in. They got their footing and moved aside as two lumbering men came into the light.

It was time for Greta to really get worried. I watched her face as the recognition dawned.

The years had been kind to Lex and Nero Siriso. They looked nothing like I remembered, but then again, they were young men when I last saw them.

They were tall—topping six feet. They had a hint of Italian Guido to their looks, but were ruggedly handsome all the same. Lucky for them, they had taken most of their father's attributes. If I were to paint a photo of a stereotypical hit man—these two would be it. A little less Léon a little more Agent 47 meets the Super Mario Bros.

I picked Lex out right away; his hair was more curly Fairholm—a trait I remembered from childhood. Nero's was short and to the point with a bit of wave in front.

It surprised me that I was so eager to take in their features. It was as if my brain was searching for more answers.

They sized me up with a mixture of uncertainty and amusement.

So now what?

I took a few steps to join Kat and Addi, then holstered my gun. I glanced around the room at Nero, then Lex, then Greta.

"Seriously, guys," Katharine said, dejected, "I just bought this outfit. I don't want blood on it."

I shifted my gaze back to Nero. He smiled at me. He had some nerve.

"I knew you'd show up," I told them.

I glanced at Greta. She had managed to scoot over to the far wall and pull herself up into a sort of half-huddle. Poor Greta, who was always tall and confident with something to say, was now silent and cowering in the corner like a scolded pet. *Five to one wasn't great odds.*

"Tell me the truth," I said again, although I began to see it.

"Francesca," Lex called my name. Slowly I shifted my gaze from Greta to Lex. "Are you abandoning this contract?"

"Hey, Oedipus and Rex." I gestured to them. "Enough with the mind-fuckery. You kill your own mother. I'm not going to. Not without justifiable cause, and being a mean bitch isn't one."

"She killed our father," Nero spoke up suddenly.

It wasn't that he said it. It was how he said it. Almost as if including me in his statement.

"She shot him in the head and covered it up as a suicide."

I glanced back to Addi and Kat. Both of them shrugged helplessly.

Greta chuckled from her corner.

"You," she spat at the twins, "you were ungrateful brats. You never listened to me, you only listened to your father!"

Nice. This surely wouldn't help her cause.

"I did everything for him!" Her voice rose. "Years wasted on him and his work and tolerating people loving him more than me! I gave him my time, my mother's money to build his business while I raised two brats and what does he do? He fucks your whore of a mother!"

She raised her bony finger and pointed to me.

I blinked.

The missing piece of the puzzle that had pushed at me since yesterday finally clicked into place.

Fantastic. Way to go, Mom. No wonder Greta hated me. Her husband knocked up her sister and then her father left everything to me.

"Anthony is Frankie's father?" Addi asked.

Hearing her say it out loud was a mixture of relief and embarrassment. Part of me was grateful my mother wasn't here, while the other part needed her right then.

The memory flashed into my head again. I was eight or so: the room full of people, Anthony Siriso trying desperately to keep my dad from getting to my mother —to stop him from hurting her. Only that's not what was happening. He was fighting with Anthony. He swung, at least twice, missing both times out of pure blind rage. Judah was trying to pull him away.

The same rage I felt boil up inside me in that moment.

Apparently, that little revelation was news to everyone but the boys, because they didn't flinch.

"Wow, you really shot Anthony for having an affair with Marlene?" Kat spoke up.

"Wow," Greta mocked. "Did I really shoot a man for wasting my life and fucking my sister? Of course I did, you vapid idiot! If you had any backbone, you'd have shot your husband for disgracing this family! Go back to being eye candy and shut your mouth!"

Katharine flinched and scooted back behind Addi a little.

The dark feeling crept up my spine. I kept it so calmly at bay until that moment. Now Greta pointed fingers, calling Katharine an idiot and my mom a whore, and while I was relieved to hear her call someone else in the family names for fucking once, I knew this had to end.

"Somehow I don't think that's all you're hiding," I shook my head.

"This is unbelievable." Addi's voice cracked. "I mean we knew you were a bitch, maybe a money launderer, but we never guessed..."

"That she was a murderer?" A voice spoke up from behind us, making us all turn.

A woman appeared at the base of the stairs. She was probably around Greta's age, dressed with fabulous taste that might have screamed Fairholm—yet I knew immediately she wasn't.

It was the woman from the intake photograph— aged, but the same woman. Her petite yet curvy frame walked with intention.

Her heels clacked on the cold stone floor, and as she came into Greta's view, my aunt gave her trademark evil smile.

"Hello, Xan," she seethed through clenched teeth.

The woman—Alexandria—stopped next to me and tilted her head. "Hello, Greta."

"Who the fuck are you?" I spat out, frowning at the woman.

"Francesca," she said, smiling at Greta then turning her gaze back to me, "it's a pleasure to meet you. I'm your Aunt Alexandria. You can call me Xan."

So, this was the elusive X.

Xan looked around the room. "I suppose none of you young women have heard of me," she said.

"Aunt?" Kat looked confused.

"Anthony's younger sister." Xan laughed. "I was diagnosed with schizophrenia back when mental health was viewed as an excuse for attention. Greta didn't like my rebellious and uncouth behavior so…"

"She had you committed," I spoke up. Everyone looked at me. "I saw the file in Anthony's desk. It's why I know this is all the truth."

Xan regarded me. "You're a resourceful one. I wanted to be the one to train you, but Judah felt that we looked too much alike and you'd catch on before we could firmly assess you."

She glanced back to Greta. "We all have a flair for the dramatics."

"So, you're…" I started.

"The family's original Frankie," Greta spoke up and gave a short chuckle. "Who let you out of your cage? I would have guessed they'd keep you for eternity."

Xan smiled at Greta, looking her up and down.

"Lex and Nero," Xan replied. "They knew you only put me there to dispose of me. I didn't fit into your perfect idea of the elitist white bitch family."

Xan turned to me and looked at me as if she were watching a memory. Her cold, gray eyes were unforgiving. She brushed a stay strand of dark brown hair from her face.

"Once upon a time, I was Anthony Siriso's mentally unstable older sister who was never invited over for family dinners," Xan said with a sardonic smirk. "One day, I got angry with someone and killed them—they deserved it.

I blinked at her. "You're a killer?"

She shrugged. "A rather poor one, at that, but my brother covered it up nicely. That gave him the big idea —we could do it for a living. It was a rather outlandish thought back then, but so many of Anthony's 'brotherhood' were immediately onboard."

When Xan said brotherhood, she held up her fingers to make quotations.

"But then Greta snooped around and found out that I was a murderer. She wasn't impressed. She threatened all kinds of fun things if Anthony didn't agree to commit me. So, they had me locked away at a state hospital while she sat pretty on her throne of hypocrisy. I guess the joke was really on her, because Anthony cheated on her ass and had a love child who turned out almost exactly like me."

"You are just loving this." Greta rolled her eyes. "You horrible disgrace of a human."

"I hope she made your life miserable," Xan snapped. Her graceful body took a defensive stance.

"Trust me, she has," Greta retorted.

Jesus, twats, I'm right here.

Nero turned to me. "There's your justification. Finish the job."

"Hold on." I held up a hand. "How is any of this my issue? Sounds like the three of you have more reasons to kill the bitch."

"Every one of us has reasons," Xan said. "But trust me when I say that you're the one best suited to take her out."

"Really?" Greta spat. "You're all manipulating her to do your dirty work? Even I'm not that callous."

She turned her furious gaze to Nero and Lex. "You should have protected her, like your stupid father would have wanted. Instead you abandoned her. Don't pretend you're any different than I!"

Nero turned his face to me, and I locked eyes with him—the cold eyes of a killer.

Lex cleared his throat from somewhere behind me and sighed—a long heavy sigh.

The realization hung much heavier. These two were my brothers.

My heart dropped into my stomach. A thousand different emotions came flooding in, as if some dam in my chest had been broken. Greta was right. Where the fuck were they? Sending me obscure letters, and Judah Cohen to emotionally abuse me in a dark basement while molding me into a trained killer didn't fucking count. All of the Gretas in the world didn't forgive the fact that Lex and Nero knew this whole time and didn't reach out until this moment.

"I don't get it," I said, trying desperately to keep my voice from shaking. "I understand why you hate me. I understand why you said the horrible things you did. It just doesn't make sense keeping it all a secret. It's almost like you were protecting me."

Greta's shoulders lowered and she relaxed a little.

"Maybe I had hopes you'd turn out okay," she said. "Someone who looked up to me and respected me—but no, you turned out just like them."

Greta looked away from me. "I'm not sorry, if that's what you want to hear. I'd do it again, too."

I felt Katharine move toward me and place her hand on my shoulder. I started breathing harder, fighting furiously to keep an impending breakdown at bay.

"I used his manic depression as an excuse to fake his suicide. No one would question it. The entire Siriso family had a history of mental disorders." Greta got this far-off look in her eye, transfixed on the memory. "He had been so happy since he started his affair. Marlene was, too. The insipid slut would have done anything for Anthony."

Greta turned her attention to Xan and sneered. "Isn't that right, Xanny?"

The room fell into a defending silence.

"You really don't regret any of it?" I asked.

A chill rushed down my spine as she leaned in closer to me, the same wicked smile stuck on her dry lips. "Not one bit," she hissed. "And I should have killed you, too."

My eyes widened. It felt like she has just plunged a knife into my chest. A sad realization hit me in that moment. Greta wanted to be killed. She was egging on every single person in this room.

I wanted to kill her. I wanted her to shut up. Nero was right, I had my justification.

"Just get it over with," Greta seethed.

There was still that nagging sense of doubt. If Lex and Nero had mommy issues, they should deal with it themselves. If Alexandria wanted revenge, she'd have to take it herself. I had a promise to keep.

"Sorry." I shook my head. "I'm not like you. I don't want to hurt people just because I hurt. It doesn't make sense anymore."

All of us stood in the basement of a Catholic church, waiting for something to happen.

Dear Greta Fairholm. Her life hangs in the balance. Maybe mine does, too.

The gun was on the table. There was an unsettling silence. Nobody moved.

"Ah, hell," Katharine sounded off next to me.

In one swift movement, she reached down, picked up my gun, and aimed it at Greta's head as Greta's shocked expression focused on the gun. Katharine Fairholm pulled the trigger.

There was a quiet pop, Greta's head snapped back, and blood and brain matter painted the wall behind her.

The other four of us jumped in surprise.

My aunt's body teetered for a moment before slumping forward in an awkward heap.

Kat sneered down at her body. "And I am *not* vapid!"

Without missing a beat, Katharine straightened up, turned to me and shrugged.

She handed me back my gun, which I took with my face still frozen in shock.

Kat smiled at me. She was as calm as I had ever seen her.

"I didn't promise shit."

"Well done, Katharine Fairholm." Lex was clearly impressed. "I didn't think you had it in you. Looks like I lost a bet."

The boys grinned at each other, and Lex handed his brother a hundred-dollar bill.

"Looks like I'm the better judge of character." Nero laughed.

His voice snapped me out of my disbelief, and I fixed my gaze on him. I drew back and punched him hard. It felt like I broke my hand in the process.

The room came alive in that instant. Addi reached to pull me back as Lex stepped in to stop his brother from retaliating.

Xan moved in between us and held up a stern hand. "Enough."

"I deserved that." Nero was practically smiling.

"You fucking fuck," I hissed from behind Addi, pain starting to register in my hand. "Why not kill your own mother years ago? Why put the burden on us? Why not tell me any of this?"

"Why Francesca Fairholm," Nero said, rubbing his cheek. "You deserved that promotion!"

"Promote this." I flipped him off with my good hand. "Someone better start explaining this cluster fuck of a situation before I shoot everyone—including the priest outside. Why did you start Osiris?"

"It really was our father's idea," Lex spoke up. "Our dad had a lot of connections that still benefit us today, Judah Cohen being the biggest one. He was our father's best friend and the brainchild behind most of Osiris' tactics. He was an army general specializing in chemical warfare."

"Guess where Set came from?" Nero smirked.

Xan wiped at a small speck of blood on her cream and black designer dress. "It wasn't exactly an easy start. Judah has his own demons, but he's given us quite an array of talented killers."

"We hire the best possible mental cases," Lex added. "But something was missing. As time went on we realized we had the perfect team within our grasp if we could maneuver it right—Addi the Stopper, Kat the Wingback and Frankie the Striker. Pair that up with the perfect family front..."

I rolled my eyes.

Lex pulled out a cell phone and began to text someone.

Nero's eyes were studying me. He looked a bit angry, yet amused at the same time. He would have a bruise where I slugged him. Good. Choke on it, bro.

"I really don't understand all the mystery," Kat complained.

Nero nodded and let out a long sigh. "It all was a little theatrical."

"A little?" Addi criticized.

Lex groaned. "You try dealing with people like Richard Ellingson fearing for his reputation and see if you need a grand distraction. It ain't fun."

"Isn't," Xan corrected harshly. "Isn't fun."

Kat looked over at Xan with more admiration. *She probably already placed the woman into a teaching position at Elegance, Inc.*

Nero chuckled and turned to me. "In your early years, I could tell you'd make a good killer. You were the stereotypical weird kid, and you had a mean streak. You really did mirror Xan, which should be taken as a compliment. You were the perfect choice for our head Striker. You grew into a beautifully trained weapon."

More memories flashed into my mind—*Billie Holiday and a lot of cold water.*

Xan patted me awkwardly on the shoulder. "I'm proud of all of you. Anthony wanted this to be a family-run corporation, and now it can be."

Right, because a family of sociopathic contract killers isn't creepy at all.

I turned to Xan and got my first good look at her. It was a bit unsettling, looking at what would probably be me in thirty years. Her greying hair was pulled back in the same fashionable ponytail I always kept. She wore a golden letter X around her neck.

"It's nice to meet you, Alexandria." I held out my hand.

She smiled back at me and shook my hand. "Likewise, Francesca."

She glanced down at Greta's crumpled body. "I'm sorry you never really got to know your father. He truly loved you."

"I—" Suddenly a wave of dizziness hit me. I felt my legs lose strength and my balance failed.

Kat's arms were around me in an instant and I leaned into her for support.

"Why?" I asked. "Why didn't anyone tell me at least that much? It's so unfair."

"Life isn't always fair," Nero said.

"The Sweeper is on his way." Lex closed his phone.

Nero nodded to Lex and then looked down at me. "I'd like you to stay here and wait for the Sweeper. Give him a rundown of what happened."

No, I'm fine, really.

He looked at Kat and Addi. "You two get to Joan's reception."

Xan beckoned to the boys, and they moved to leave.

"Wait." I was exasperated. "You said you'd give me answers. You can't just come in here and jog my fucked-up memory and then vanish again."

"We can't linger here," Nero replied. "We'll be in touch. I promise."

Nero turned back to me as he reached the staircase. "By the way," he said, staring me down. "Don't ever hit me again."

They disappeared as quickly as they had entered.

"Well, wasn't this situation totally predictable," Addi muttered.

Kat let go of me, walked over and kicked Greta with her Manolo Blahniks.

She looked over at me and curved her lips into a devious smile.

"Cute," I said.

"Some people deserve to die," she responded. "Literally none of what went on in the past is your fault. She couldn't forgive her husband for cheating on her, and I couldn't forgive her for blaming you for it. No reason her death needed to be strictly on your hands."

"Let's go," Addi said. "I hope that Sweeper has a brilliant idea up their sleeve. It's going to be hard to keep a straight face when everyone starts asking where Greta is."

"Oh, do try, dear cousins," I waved after them.

Kat followed Addi out of the basement, and I was alone with dead Aunt Greta.

I dismantled my gun and tucked it away into my holster. After a moment I surveyed the damage.There was a lot of blood. Not only was it beginning to harden on the walls, but it was pooling and spreading under Greta's head. Thank goodness the floor already looked like a crime scene.

I let out a long whoosh of air. Katharine had killed Greta for me. Somehow that meant a lot. She defended me. She avenged my father's death.

My father. The term would take some time to get used to even though on some level I always knew.

I wasn't sure how long I stared at the lifeless corpse before a hand rested gently on my shoulder.

I knew who it would be before I even looked up.

Chapter Thirty-Three

Spark Dawson had amazing eyes. That's one of many things that popped into my head in that moment. *Dead aunt, dead dad, lying mother, lying dickhead bosses, Catholic Church, Heckler & Koch USP Match .45, Vans with red shoe laces, beautiful blue eyes... I'm going to need my whole bottle of Xanax and a vodka chaser to deal with this sort of mind-fuckery.*

Logically, I should have hit him, but my hand had hit its face-punch quota and was beginning to throb. I could have yelled at him, too, anything but what actually happened. I started crying.

Since I'd learned to fake most of my emotional responses, I was surprised that I couldn't stop this one.

No, no, no don't cry. Don't cry, you dumb bitch!

Spark dropped a duffle bag to the ground, pulled me to my feet and hugged me. *Too many hugs recently—I better not be turning over a new leaf.*

The hug was pure relief. I cried into his chest as he stroked my hair. I'm not sure how long we stood there like complete jackasses, but it was a while. I inhaled and took in his familiar scent: coconut and cigar smoke.

He finally pulled back and tilted my chin up to look at him. "You did good, kid."

I wasn't sure if he meant that day or since he left me on my own.

"Thanks." I smiled.

"Takes guts to do what you did," he said. His voice was encouraging. "More than most killers have. You'd be surprised at how cowardly a lot of us are."

"Did you know about all this from the beginning?"

"Yeah." He hugged me again. "One of my first conversations with Nero went something like… 'so how about you help me train my half-sister to be an elite killing machine? My dad is her biological father, but she has no idea—think of all the daddy issues you'll have to diffuse. Sounds rad.'"

He let me go and smiled at me.

"Very funny," I said, wiping my eyes. "I appreciate you adding to those daddy issues, you asshole."

We were back at it, just like old times. Something felt a little different though.

"I'm sorry," he responded. "Can't say I didn't enjoy every minute of it though."

"You're disgusting. You actually disgust me."

He responded by kissing me—which threw me off. I shoved him back, instinctively.

"Sorry," he said, "I've wanted to do that for a while now. Sometimes the life of a contract killer ain't very fair."

I brought my hand up to my lip, trying to wipe away the kiss.

"Isn't," I muttered.

He smiled. "Look, I *am* really sorry. I don't have a lot of tact when it comes to you."

"No shit." I rolled my eyes. "You're a Sweeper now?"

"I'm a few things," he grabbed his duffel bag and placed it on a table. "Nero finally pulled the stick out of his ass and let me see you. That guy has serious control issues. I hope you're not like that."

Control issues? My family? Please…

"There is so much information running through my head," I said as I shifted my weight. "I don't understand why you'd want to be my trainer."

It was silly; I felt silly. Now that I had more time to think about the situation, my body was screaming at me for pushing him away when he kissed me.

"Judah suggested it."He brushed his shaggy hair back with his hand.

"I have a lot of capital in the company thanks to him."*Maybe Spark and I do have a lot in common.*

"Nero *did* tell me about his plans for you and the rest of the family. I liked the idea. I knew it would be a bitch and a half, but I wanted to be the one that taught you everything you know."

"Almost everything," I said.

"Right." He rolled his eyes. "Judah and his kill a drug dealer in an alley training program really works wonders."

"He's a lot nicer than you." I smirked at him.

"Agreed." Spark nodded. "I asked to sweep today's mission so I could see you. It was a lot cleaner than the Escandon adventure."

"Speaking of which," I said, frowning, "fuck you for sending Yeh to babysit me."

"I knew you'd like that." He winked. "Nero already had Yeh doing errands for him—I figured why not use him to protect you. That way you'd be forced to trust someone who you knew didn't have your interest at heart."

"More lessons," I muttered.

"There are always lessons," he responded.

"You really wanted to see me?" I tried not to sound too hopeful.

"Yes." He looked down at Greta. "I missed you."

The empty hole in my chest fluttered a little bit.

"And Nero wouldn't let you before now?"

"Technically, Xan wouldn't. Nero just sticks to her suggestions. They have some grand plan up their sleeves—always have. Plus, I don't question her anymore. She's a genius, but she's bat-shit crazy. So is Nero. He's way more deadly than Lex. Lex is more of a softie. He's got my back. I guess he's more like Katharine in that respect. He doesn't kill people—he just builds things. Guns, mostly."

I must have looked as sick as I felt, because he nudged me a little. "See? Here I've been dealing with your family the whole time and I still like you. That should tell you something."

I wrapped my arms around my chest. I wanted his words to be comforting, but they weren't. I still felt like a puppet—Nero's cute little puppet on a cracked glass floor. *Kill my mom, and I'll give you the world.*

"I punched him," I said.

"You punched Nero?" Spark seemed impressed. "And he didn't kill you?"

"He deserved it," I spat. "Everyone with their abandonment, lies and deceptions. I'm sick of it."

"Hey," Spark said and brushed my arm, "it's alright. I'm not going anywhere. I shouldn't have in the first place. I'm sorry if I hurt you."

I let out a strangled laugh. "You're apologizing while you clean up my aunt? How romantic."

"I mean it," he said. "Nero's moving the whole company here if you didn't catch on. Now that Greta is dead, that ends a big chapter in their lives. They can resurface now."

I didn't like the sound of that. *What did that mean for me?*

Nero said something about a family-run business, but I didn't think he was serious. *How would that even work?*

"I need to get this done," Spark said.

"You need help?" Fuck I didn't know if there was politeness involved in a sweep.

"Nah." Spark shook his head. "Uly and Gretchen are outside. We'll wheel her out in your grandma's coffin."

Despite the horrible thought, I laughed. It echoed into the basement and I clamped my mouth shut.

"Can I see you later?" Spark smiled. "I'd like to catch up."

I considered it. "I'll be around. Come find me."

"I look forward to it, Francesca."

I left him there. I left Greta and all of her bad memories. It was time to move on. I made my way up the stairs. I forced myself to walk to the front of the lavish church, past my grandmother's coffin, past all of the lies and deceit.

The heels of my Louboutin's echoed into the vast chapel as I made my way to the entrance of the church. Xan's words repeated in my head as I touched the heavy wooden doors.

I'm sorry you never really got to know your father. He truly loved you.

I pushed open the doors, engulfing myself in sunlight. I left the church. I didn't look back.

Elegantly Wasted

Chapter Thirty-Four

Monday morning in the Fairholm household seemed pretty normal. I had my favorite fuzzy blue bathrobe on, and I opened my Diet Coke and my bottle of Lexapro.

Katharine was at the table, reading over some paperwork and eating a grapefruit.

Addi had yet to show up.

"I took you off the schedule this week." Kat looked up at me. "Enjoy your vacation."

While part of me wouldn't have minded the activity, I still had a lot to digest. Teaching annoying housewives to sit properly in a skirt would not help my emotional state anyway.

"I have a few meetings today." She looked over at me. "You don't need me for anything, do you?"

I shook my head. I had been rather withdrawn since the funeral. Kat didn't pry. She knew I would come around and talk eventually.

Nero hadn't reached out yet.

Addi let herself in the house and sauntered into the dining room. She smiled and threw down today's paper.

"Read it and weep, bitches."

My mom had called early Sunday morning with terrible news.

"There's been an accident," she said. "Greta's dead."

How horrible. How tragic.

I swallowed my anti-depressant as I looked down at the headline.

SCOTTSDALE HOUSE FIRE KILLS ONE

Kat grabbed the paper and made a little noise of excitement.

"Police responded to a nine-one-one call around midnight, November eighth... a gas main ruptured... explosions, explosions..." Kat giggled. "Greta should have had her ancient gas lines checked more often."

Greta had been incinerated and the rest of the house burned before the fire department could get it under control. Everything was gone: The twins' room, Anthony's office... all burned to the ground—lost forever.

Spark was good with fire. At first I thought his handle was from that sexy glint in his eye. *Nope. Just hand the man a match and stand the fuck back.*

"I'm going to frame this," Kat said.

"Not the best idea," I responded.

"But I did this," she pouted. "It's my first kill."

"And we're really very proud of you." I snatched the paper from her. "But keep it all in here." I patted my heart.

"Or on some blood slides stored behind the air conditioner." Addi smiled.

I looked around the table at my cousins. They were chatting excitedly, and I couldn't help but feel a little at ease with everything. Maybe I wasn't the lone weirdo in this family anymore. Most of the people closest to me knew who I really was and, in fact, loved me for who I was. Maybe one day I'd tell my mother...

Nero finally called later that day and told me it was best if I didn't let the rest of the family know that I now knew who my real father was or that Xan was in town.

Trust me, Nero had said. Too many complicated memories.

"What they don't know won't hurt them," he said. "If your mom ever wants to tell you, that's different."

Like that would happen.

The normal day dragged on. Katharine left to "console her grieving mother." Addi took a nap. I did laundry and took Bodhi to the park where I only got two saddle comments.

Around five o'clock, my mother called.

"Guess who just dropped by for a visit?" She asked.

I probably don't want to know.

"Greta's boys, Lex and Nero," she said.

I sat up straight in a panic. "What?"

"Do you even remember them?"

I took a deep breath. Nero said to trust him. It made sense they'd come around—they said as much. I just didn't think it would be this soon nor did I think they'd do family rounds.

"Yes, I remember them. I'm remembering a lot more from my childhood, lately."

"They've been in Europe this entire time." My mom didn't get the hint. "They have done very well for themselves."

"Yeah? Well, why would they come see you?"

"Actually, they were looking for you."

Excuse me? They know where to find me. Then I remembered it was all a show.

"We will need to go see the family lawyer but..." she hesitated. "Apparently, they've uncovered some documents at what's left of their mothers. The Fairholm estate goes to you."

I didn't say anything. I knew, and I also didn't know how to sound surprised.

"That's..." I paused for effect, "a plot twist."

My mother chuckled. "Lex and Nero are here to give you their blessings and make sure everything is situated in a timely manner."

"Why is everything being left to me?" I asked, trying to keep my tone inquisitive.

"Well," she started, "I suppose no one thought about it because Greta just ran things and that was that. Joan certainly wouldn't have said anything to you, or me, or even Bette. Now they're dead before any wills could even be read. Lex and Nero got into town and opened Greta's safety deposit box, where she was hiding your grandfather's will. He never left anything to Joan. He left it all to you."

"Wow," I said. It was mostly genuine. Hearing my mother say it did hold some surprise.

"I didn't even know Grandpa. Why would he leave everything to me?"

"He left some money for me and Bette as well. My father was strange. He had... favorites," Marlene said. "I can't believe Greta was hiding it. It never would have been found had she not been killed. I'm so sorry — so sorry she was terrible to you. I understand more now."

You have no idea.

"Karma is a bitch," I muttered. It was hard for me not to snap at my mother. I always followed through with the sarcastic comments, yet her life depended on me keeping quiet.

Oh, now you get it? You mean you didn't understand that she hated me because she saw your lies and unfaithfulness and didn't know who to blame.

I was certain she could never handle the truth. Neither could Daniel—a master at denial.

Parents, man...

"Anyway, any time you're ready to deal with this is good. They aren't having a funeral. I can understand why—I mean they didn't even really like their mother... and well..."

"No one liked her?" I finished for her.

"It's horrible to say, I know." Marlene tsk'ed. "First Joan and then poor Greta... there's not much of anything to bury."

Hey, Mom, don't sweat the small stuff. The cousins and I avenged your lover—my father—by incinerating your sister... by the way, I kill people for a living.

I laughed inwardly to myself. Aunt Greta was erased from existence. Just like that. Killed by her own family who couldn't quite grasp any boundaries.

"This is kind of a lot to take in," I said. That was the truth.

"I know," Marlene went on. "I know you've been in a funk lately, and I'm not trying to add to it. They just want you to be looked out for."

Do they?

"That's nice of them," I said. "Give them my address and phone number."

"Already did. Nero said he'd be in touch."

Yeah, that seems to be his motto.

"Thanks. I'll call you later," I said.

"I love you, Francesca," she responded.

"I love you too, Mom."

You lying harpy with a hairdo full of secrets.

As I hung up, my phone buzzed with a text.

"Elegance, Inc."

I sighed. I was going to need a vacation away from my vacation.

Elegantly Wasted

Chapter Thirty-Five

The last two weeks of my life were terrifying. I'll admit it.

As a bad-ass trained killer, I was only allowed to let that sink in every once in a while, on some random off day. That was today.

Driving to Elegance, Inc., as the text so lovingly commanded, the past handful of weeks began to catch up to me. I could feel my hands get clammy and a pending anxiety attack creep up.

As I turned onto Thunderbird Road, I sat on the verge of an anxiety attack.

Shit, I almost botched a high-profile hit of a prominent congressman's dirty ass wife, almost died, almost got my cousins killed, killed a drug lord, almost got my cousins killed again... almost, almost, almost. What would I have done if Rico had killed Katharine? What would I have told her mother? Audrey—that snotty, shallow twat—loves one person on this planet and that is her daughter. I almost took that away.

On top of these thoughts, I was still pissed I had to be saved by Kung Fu Hustle. And let's not even forget that my MIA family members have been mind-fucking me since I joined Osiris.

I watched my own aunt get blown away by the less-than-capable, death-o-phobic Katharine. She didn't even bat an eyelash about what she had done.

I had lost a father and gained two brothers. Yeah, I was definitely having one of those days.

I managed to not crash before I pulled into the parking lot.

I parked, turned off the engine and tried to control my breathing. My heart was about to explode out of my chest.

I gripped the steering wheel and willed myself to calm down. *I was in control. I was alive. That's all that mattered.*

Once my heart beat normally again, I got out of my car.

I frowned up at the building.

The hand crafted, cursive, white neon Elegance, Inc. sign lit up as the sun set behind Kat's temple to gentility. It cast a long, cold shadow, and I shivered.

I let myself into the dark reception area. The high ceilings and practically glass areas made me uneasy.

I glanced at the large metal stairway to my right, leading up to classrooms. I flipped a switch and a few of the high-placed lights came on.

I walked farther into the building and passed the dark rooms on the main level. My curiosity was honed in toward the back of the building. The basement door was still blocked off, all signs warning it was still "Under Construction."

It was time for me to trespass.

Driven by the lasting adrenalin the panic attack gave me, I reached up, ripped the tape down and kicked open the door. There should have been stairs that led down, but it was like someone had erased them. Now there just stood a very small room with another door on the opposite wall. This door meant business. It was metal, it looked heavy and there was a lighted plate next to it on the wall that looked like it belonged in a science fiction novel.

I reached out to touch it.

"Evening," voices said in unison behind me.

I sighed and turned to face Lex and Nero Siriso.

"Hello," I responded, dryly.

"You took your time getting here," Nero said critically.

"You took your time telling me you were my brother," I snapped.

Really this guy was on my last nerve. I was having a hard time remembering he was my boss, because the smart-mouthed ass-hat in me wanted to just disrespect him.

Lex smiled at me as if he liked that I challenged Nero.

"What are you doing?" he asked.

Not "how are you doing," "what are you doing."

They dressed in dark suits that matched their hair. They were hard to focus on in the poor light—probably on purpose.

"I'm pretty sure I'm about to venture into Narnia," I frowned at them.

Lex smiled a crooked smile at his brother then back to me.

"You place your fingers on the plate," he pointed. "Your fingerprints are programmed in already."

I turned back to the door. "That easy? What if someone cuts off my hand?"

I stuck my palm on the pad and it made a series of beeping sounds. Then a contraption lowered from above me, opened and flashed my surprised face a series of times.

It retracted quickly as I stood there dazed.*What the fuck just happened?*

"Welcome, Francesca Fairholm," a soft feminine voice sounded from the walls. After a series of clicks, the heavy door began to slide open.

"It also takes a bone structure and retina scan," Lex said. "We aren't complete morons when it comes to security."

I saw Nero clench his jaw, but I turned my attention to the entrance.

On the other side of the door, a set of metal stairs led down, instead of the old stone. *So they were still there—trickery, trickery.*

They led me in, and the door closed behind us with a loud clang.

We descended into the dark. It got lighter and warmer the further we went, and when we reached the bottom, my eyes went wide. Nero, Lex and I stood in a small, private receiving room lined with glass windows looking into what was now the bomb-shelter basement.

The area was not only being reconstructed, it was now enormous. The far walls looked like they had been blasted into the bedrock. I had to squint to make out that they were covered in caution tape. The remaining walls had been smoothed out and soundproofed. *That explained the earthquakes over the past months.*

Spread out to my left, a few fluorescent lights let me see into a high-tech computer area.

This was getting a little too True Lies for me.

"I take it Katharine's wine-tasting classes are discontinued."

"New base of operations," Nero said. "We're not as gothic old school as Adficio. Italy is a little too medieval. I want to centralize the company and have a good front. Katharine accepted the idea that we use Elegance, Inc."

"You're really moving back here?" I made a face. I wasn't thrilled at the prospect of them being close by.

"I can tell you don't like us." Nero smiled.

"What's to like?" I shrugged.

"Yes, we're moving back," Lex intervened. "Once you sign all the legal paperwork concerning your inheritance, you'll be a partner. And head Striker."

"Oh, you *do* have an ulterior motive with my money." I smirked. I enjoyed saying 'my money' to them.

"Of course," Nero said. "I'm not hiding that from you. It's not like you haven't given everything up for this company anyway. You love what you do. Ensuring its future shouldn't even be something you'd have to consider."

"Look," I started, turning to look at him, "it's not about the money. Take it. I relish the fact that the fortune goes to such a worthwhile cause. My problem is that for years I've put my ass on the line for you. I've gotten beaten, shot, used and fucked with, and I've had to babysit Kat. Then I find out that you and Lex have been at the helm this entire time in a grand scheme orchestrated by a secret aunt, Judah, and your father—oh, my father—and I'm just supposed to smile and wave?"

Lex glanced at his brother before backing away and letting himself through the glass door into the lab-like headquarters.

"Francesca," Nero's brow creased as he searched for words. "You mean a lot to us—to me."

I wasn't expecting that. I looked back out the window at Lex as he approached a gangly young man sitting at a computer.

"I really do mean what I say. I've had specific plans for you," he went on. "You're not the most graceful agent I have, but you certainly have the most potential."

"Thanks, I think," I muttered. It was frustrating talking to him. I had never wanted to beat the ever-living shit out of someone and hug them at the same time.

"I remember when my dad told me you were his daughter," he said, staring through the glass windows. "I wasn't surprised. You were a young kid by then and showing more Siriso genes than anything else. Defiant, stubborn, cruel... you're more a Siriso than a Fairholm, believe it or not. I welcomed the thought. I was so busy thinking about this company coming together that I didn't notice my mother going off the deep end."

"How did she even find out about Anthony and Marlene?"

Nero sighed. "My father loved your mother. He wanted to be with her. They knew you were theirs, and they weren't happy with their spouses. Obviously... the next step was divorcing, but that can be tedious— especially when money is involved and they find out about infidelity."

"I just had no idea." My voice cracked. I was trying hard not to cry, but the thought of my poor mother losing out on the love of her life because of her bitch sister was really getting to me.

"I had no idea my mother felt that way about him. If I'd known..."

"Nothing would have changed," Nero said quickly. "Daniel found them together, and that started a downward spiral of events, which ended in our dad's murder. It's a sad story. But it's important to remember we're still here, and if Anthony Siriso could see us, he would be extremely proud."

Nero didn't want to hash out the details.

"Did your mom's death bring you the closure you were looking for?" I asked.

"I thought it would," he sighed, playing with a golden pinky ring I recognized as Anthony's on his finger. "But I didn't feel anything when she died."

I looked over at him. We were similar creatures. *Maybe we could get along.*

"Well," I said, shrugging, "it brought some great closure for me, if that matters."

Nero laughed. He was much less intimidating when he laughed.

"Here," he said reaching into his jacket pocket. "Happy belated birthday."

He handed me a jewelry box.

I gave him a quizzical look as I opened it and pulled out a silver necklace strung with a circular charm. "Beatrice" was engraved into it.

Ugh. The dreaded middle name.

"Do you know why you're named after a Shakespeare character?"

"Do you know why you're named after a psychotic Roman Emperor who burned Christians alive to simply light his dining hall?"

Nero threw me a distasteful look.

"My mother named me Beatrice, after her favorite character in Much Ado About Nothing."

"Anthony and Marlene's first date was to go see the play *Much Ado About Nothing*—filling in for Daniel as usual." Nero smiled. "The two of them chose that name for you when you were born."

I smiled at the charm. "I think I like that version of the story."

"One day you can ask your mother more."

He took the necklace from me and fastened it around my neck.

I turned to him and nodded. "By the way, don't ever fucking call me Beatrice."

"Shall we?" He walked over to the glass door and opened it for me.

I nodded and stepped through into my new world. I scanned the area. It was impressive, and I was trying not to give Nero the satisfaction of my awe. He had turned the entire basement area into a top-secret installation.

"So," I said, starting down the next set of stairs, "you're just going to blast out more rooms down here and we're all going to be one big happy family?"

Holy shit, I actually have a real family.

"Look... I need to know you're on my side," Nero responded. "A lot comes with your new responsibilities. I want you to curb your sarcasm for a while."

I scrunched my face. "I'll see what I can do. But you can't expect me to just tone down my best trait."

There was a commotion from the upstairs doorway, and Judah Cohen emerged from the stairway and pushed through the doors.

I couldn't stop the stupid smile from forming on my face as he looked at me.

I hadn't seen him in a good while, and he looked older and tired. I hoped that wasn't entirely my fault.

"There she is." He opened his arms. "The long-lost Siriso daughter."

"Yeah, I don't think I'm ready to acquire that name just yet." I put my hands on my hips.

He wrapped his arm around my shoulders. "I see your cynicism hasn't been damaged in all of this."

I dropped my arms and shoved him slightly with my hips. "Whatever."

"I'm sorry things got so out of hand. We debated seriously about just telling you everything from the beginning, but thought that you needed a break from your DNA... mold you into a proficient killer without any distractions."

"Solid strat." I rolled my eyes, hoping Nero's embargo on sarcasm hadn't taken effect yet. "What now?"

They both stared at me like I was supposed to know everything that was going on. *Leave it to men to think women can read minds.*

"What?" I said.

"You've been through a lot in the past week," Nero stated.

"Thanks, Captain Obvious," I pushed.

He gave me a stern look. *Nope, embargo in full effect.* "I mean, I want you to know that I'm aware of what you've been through—not just in these past weeks, but over the years. I've read Judah's notes; I've chosen your missions; I've been the one to make the calls on Yeh and Spark; and I have had a hard time just letting you run on your own. I apologize."

He was sorry. He was sorry for being a totally untrustworthy asshole.

"I think what Nero is getting at," Judah started, "is that we're all proud of you. You've grown up fast and even taught your two older cousins how to function in this business. I'm genuinely impressed."

"But I'm screwed up," I blurted out. "Every mission seems to fail."

"Those missions were a big deal," Judah spoke up. "We think you have been an effective problem solver, a crack shot, and you don't hesitate."

Well that's comforting. There had to be more to their madness.

"So now what? We operate out of the dungeon here and I keep my day job?"

"You are going to be training our new recruits," Nero picked up a pile of folders from a nearby desk and thrust them into my hands. "We need at least two to four additions to the Osiris family in the coming year. One of our top partners is working hard to restructure our business model and training program. You're going to be working with them and Yeh to give us a shorter training timeline."

"Are you serious?" I frowned.

"You trained Addi in no time and even taught Kat how to overcome her fears."

"No, I know. I mean about working with Yeh."

"I am." Nero walked over to one of the computer banks. "I decided to hire him full time, and he has certainly proved himself, putting up with your bullshit."

"Hire him, sure," I stuttered. "But making him work with me?"

"You have a problem with that?" A side door opened, and Yeh walked through. "I mean surely after I have saved your life, we can at least be civil."

I looked him up and down. He was wearing sunglasses. *At night. Indoors. Underground. What a doucher.*

"Is the subtle track lighting hurting your eyes or is this a cosmetic choice?" I asked.

"Men like Yeh are a dying breed," Judah spoke up. He knew a fight brewing when he saw one. He was also king of deflecting my behavior. "He's very lethal, and his knowledge and techniques are priceless in our industry. We need him to teach his skills to the younger generation."

I saw Yeh's forehead wrinkle a bit.

"Which means you will also be learning from him," Nero added.

That's it, I found it—I'm in hell.

"Any other 'fuck yous' you would like to bestow upon me before I go drown my sorrows in some Ben & Jerry's?"

"We're not finished." Nero walked back over to me. "Xan is waiting for us in the conference room. We have some people we'd like you to meet."

Wondering what the fuck else I was supposed to deal with next, I cautiously followed him through the door Yeh was holding open.

Yeh took off his sunglasses as I passed him and entered the large room.

I was greeted by another surprise—a room full of people.

Some I knew: Uly, Spark, Emma, Gretchen and my cousins—who all apparently knew more than me at this point.

There were a lot of new faces.

"I want to introduce you to the rest of Osiris," Nero said from behind me. "It's about time you all met."

Nero entered the room and turned back toward me. He smiled—this time it was genuine. I trusted him. I had no reason to, but I did. I would now meet the rest of the company for the first time since joining Osiris. *He was right, it was about fucking time.*

The strangers slowly stopped talking and turned to look at me. The quiet din in the room faded.

Some nodded and smiled. In their eyes, I saw the same look that would often stare back at me in the mirror.

Our eyes weren't dead. They were just a little darkened. We held secrets. We did dirty deeds.

It was a motley crew to say the least. *Other killers, just like me. More people to be myself around. I could get used to this. This was who I was.*

I was a contract killer... and this was my family.

I took a confident step into the room. The door closed behind me. Far above my head were the streets of Phoenix—beyond that a vast world of corruption and lies. Somewhere, someone would need to be killed.

I hoped it was soon.

Special Thanks:

To Jeff, Amanda, Amie, Angela and my husband, John. You pushed me, pulled me, laughed with me and believed in me... and read about eighteen variations of this book.

Thanks Mom, for teaching me proper grammar and giving me manners... but mostly for being a saucy minx.

Thanks to my supportive friends—especially Michelle and Karen for moral support, and Erin for all her beautiful typography.

Thank you to Lindsay for avidly beta reading new versions.

And a very heartfelt thanks to the rest of my family and friends—all sides of them... you're all inspiring in more positive ways than you know, and I love you dearly.

Grandma... thanks for the fucking lobster bib.